Who's Afraid of Virginia's Woof?

Susan C. Daffron

An Alpine Grove Romantic Comedy

Book 13

Published by Magic Fur Press
An imprint of Logical Expressions, Inc.
P.O. Box 383
Ponderay, ID 83852

Who's Afraid of Virginia's Woof?

ISBN: 978-1-61038-071-3 (paperback)
         978-1-61038-072-0 (EPUB)

Like all of my books, *Who's Afraid of Virginia's Woof?* is
dedicated to
my husband James Byrd,
my best friend and biggest supporter.
Thanks for everything!

<u>Books by Susan C. Daffron</u>
The Alpine Grove Romantic Comedies

Chez Stinky

Fuzzy Logic

The Art of Wag

Snow Furries

Bark to the Future

Howl at the Loon

The Good, the Bad, and the Pugly

The Treasure of the Hairy Cadre

The Luck of the Paw

Daydream Retriever

The Hound of Music

The Last Train to Barksville

Who's Afraid of Virginia's Woof?

The Jennings & O'Shea Mysteries

Sensing Trouble

Sensing Secrets

Sensing Truth

Chapter 1

Scare Wear

"I don't know about this one." Tori Merrill ran her palms along the shocking pink fabric, attempting to smooth it out over her stomach. "We're not in Florida, you know."

"Oh, come on. You don't like anything, and we're not getting anywhere. Scare Wear is the only costume shop for a hundred miles. You have to pick something." Hope Hildebrand waved her arms in exasperation. "The one you're wearing isn't so bad. I think flamingos are cute."

"I refuse to be seen in public resembling a demented fuchsia macaroon. It's not going to happen. Next."

Hope walked to the costume rack, grabbed a hanger, and held up a black-and-white garment. "How about this one? I've seen lots of cows around here. Is this better?"

"How about we move on from the animal theme? It's bad enough I have to dress up. I draw the line at looking like a zoo or farm animal."

Hope turned to the rack and slapped through the hangers. "Fine. But we need something that disguises who you are. That's part of the deal. And you already vetoed the fairy princess and Catwoman."

"I'll be handing out candy to little kids in a barn. It's going to be cold, and the event is PG-13. Half-naked princess is not the image I want to present. This is 1997. You'd think costume designers could come up with classier ideas for women's costumes. I don't want to look like I'm soliciting business for the oldest profession."

"I didn't argue, did I?" Hope held up a skimpy sequined cheerleader outfit, frowned, and returned it to the rack. "Marketing 101 is about knowing your audience. Are you sure the cow won't work? Kids like animals."

Tori removed the awful flamingo getup and yanked her turtleneck over her head. This process was taking forever. "Hurry up and find something. I'm getting cold."

Hope held up a white jumpsuit. "This one would be warm."

"Elvis? I think not." Tori rubbed her upper arms, trying to restore her circulation. This room was arctic. "This store specializes in Halloween costumes. How can there *not* be a demure princess outfit? What about Snow White? Doesn't anyone watch Disney movies anymore? *Cinderella*? Or the *Wizard of Oz*? How about Glinda the Good Witch? Or what about Dorothy?"

"They still have a lot of zombie outfits."

"Yuck." Tori dropped her arms and walked to the costume rack. "Those are gory and disgusting."

"I'm sorry, but we're late to the game here. All the good costumes are taken."

"That's obvious. What's this one supposed to be?"

"Maybe Elvira?"

"Okay, we've hit rock bottom now." Tori held up a dress. "Is this supposed to be a Santa elf?"

"Nope. That won't work. Wrong holiday." Hope pointed at a pink dress. "It's kind of awful, but not completely tacky or indecent."

"The bubblegum color is nausea-inducing, but at least it would be warm enough, I suppose."

"Can you face being Little Bo Peep for three weekends in a row?"

Tori fingered the fabric. "It's not like I have a lot of choice. And, look, it comes with a stuffed sheep on a leash, which meets your farm-animal criteria."

"That's true." Hope clutched her dress to her chest. "I'm so glad I found Little Red Riding Hood before you did. Red is looking better all the time."

"Sure, rub it in." Tori knew that no matter what Hope wore she'd look amazing. She had the type of willowy figure that could make a potato sack look glamorous. She wasn't classically beautiful, but something about her thick russet hair and wide-set blue eyes gave her a mysterious allure that men couldn't resist. Although Tori tried not to be jealous of her friend, she wasn't always successful.

Hope picked up her ruby-red costume. "I wish Morgan were around to play the Big Bad Wolf. That would have been a lot of fun."

"When does he come back from London?"

"Next month." Hope held up the long red cloak. "He'll be sorry he missed seeing me in this. I was going to tell him I'd wear the cape and nothing else for him, but he won't be back before Halloween. His loss."

"No doubt." Tori gathered the expanse of pink Bo Peep fabric, petticoats, and ruffles into her arms. "Let's get out of here."

Tori gave Hope a goodbye hug and got into her car. She was dubious about her role in this bizarre Halloween fest, but Hope was convinced it was a good idea.

Hope was not only her friend but also her business partner. Tori had reluctantly agreed that the only way to know if the new line of candy she was developing would be appealing to kids was to test it on them.

The Haunted Barn was a local event that was held at a farm north of Gleasonville near the turnoff to the ski resort. Over the years, the fund-raiser had raised hundreds of thousands of dollars for charity. It was billed as a Field of Screams with the Haunted Barn, the Harvest of Terror, and the A-maizing Corn Maze. The Halloween activities sprawled across many acres of the old Jensen farm and employed countless volunteer actors. Dubbed the Scream Team, many locals looked forward all year to donning ghoulish garb and scaring the stuffing out of little kids.

Posters were hanging on bulletin boards all over the region, proclaiming that monsters would mash, werewolves would howl, vampires would bite, and everyone was going to live it up like zombies on acid. But Tori was less than enthusiastic. Although it was essentially a giant Halloween party on steroids and it was for a good cause, Tori wasn't a big fan of the holiday in general. She hated being startled, scared, or otherwise dislodged from her regular routine.

Tori never, *ever* watched scary movies. Or not willingly anyway. When Hope had coerced her into watching *The Omen*, Tori had closed her eyes and covered her ears. But the sensory deprivation hadn't been enough to block it out completely. Afterward, she ran to the bathroom and threw up. When Tori was a kid, she had been persuaded to watch *Psycho* because it was a classic movie she absolutely must see. Afterward, her mother couldn't understand why Tori refused to take a shower for the next three days.

Halloween was all about candy, but Tori was horrified by that aspect of the holiday as well. Hope always said Tori was just being a food snob, but honestly, what rocket scientist thought that feeding kids confections like wax lips was a good idea? Or wax anything? No one ever said, "Hey candles might be tasty." Yuck. Then there was all the candy no kid ever wanted like Bit-O-Honey, which was basically wrapped concrete and nuts. Or the horrible chewing gums, some of which were inexplicably trying to emulate carcinogens. Candy cigarettes? Bubble gum cigars? Ugh. And the rest of the gums simply tasted like old chalk. Outside of Halloween, did people willingly chew Dubble Bubble? It was revolting. Next on the list of undesirable candies were Smarties, Necco wafers, and candy corn. But the list went on and on.

On her way home, Tori stopped by what she thought of as the generic grocery store. They were having a big produce sale, and she wanted to try a few mushroom gravy experiments. If she grabbed a loaf of their day-old ciabatta bread, she could turn it into a quickie stuffing. Thanksgiving was only a few weeks away after all, and she wanted to refine her gravy recipe.

Tori loved grocery stores the way other women loved high-end clothing boutiques. She could spend hours wandering the aisles, studying her grocery list, and pondering all the creative meals she could make. But she curtailed her dawdling because her dog Ginny was expecting her dinner soon. Tori was well aware that Ginny didn't like to be kept waiting and had a number of objectionable ways to express her displeasure.

The mushrooms weren't up to Tori's standards, so she stopped at the super-expensive grocery store for some creminis that were in better shape. At least they didn't look like they'd been run over by a shopping cart. Of course, they also cost six times as much as the ones at the cheap grocery store. But it would be worth it.

Tori unlocked the door to her apartment and was greeted by ferocious barking, whining, and howling. "It's just me, Ginny. Settle down."

With a final grumpy growl, Ginny stomped over to her dog bed and sat down with a thump, glaring at Tori. She raised a paw and offered an imperious wave.

The small dog had a black and brown coat and huge pointy ears. She was a mix of a variety of different breeds that would undoubtedly be difficult to replicate. Tori's best guess was that Ginny might have a little German shepherd, corgi, Pomeranian, or maybe dachshund in her heritage. And maybe some other incredibly stubborn breed with a reputation for being imperious and a bit snotty.

Tori laid the garment bag that contained the ugly costume on a chair and bent to ruffle the dog's ears as she walked into the kitchen. "I know. I'm late. Let me get this stuff put away, your highness."

Ginny followed Tori into the gleaming white kitchen and supervised the food-unpacking process closely. Tori pulled a bottle of wine from the stainless-steel refrigerator and grabbed a glass from the cabinet.

She poured the wine and carried it over to her favorite easy chair. Ginny jumped up into her lap and Tori stroked the dog's long silky brown fur. It was time for a difficult conversation. "So, tonight we need to discuss your upcoming trip to doggie camp. I have a feeling you're not going to be excited about this idea, but I have no choice. Look at the bright side. At least you don't have to dress up like a shepherdess. Maybe that would work if you were a border collie, but you're definitely not."

Ginny appeared to be utterly unmoved by Tori's emphatic entreaties for good behavior. The unfortunate truth was that over the next few weeks, they both were going be spending quite a bit of time outside of their comfort zones.

Tori fed Ginny and then started on her mushroom gravy. She methodically scrubbed the fungi and began slicing. After having been a chef for so many years, Tori was justifiably proud of her knife-wielding skills and made short work of the pile of mushrooms. Ginny returned to her supervisory duties, watching intently to make sure nothing hit the floor without her noticing.

When Tori looked back on her family life, two things were constants: dogs and food. That meant she'd spent a lot of time shooing dogs from kitchens. And Ginny was no exception. She knew exactly what the "get out of the kitchen" and "go to your bed" commands meant, but didn't necessarily choose to follow the directives.

Even though Ginny might not be the most obedient dog, Tori loved her with all her heart and told her regularly that she was like a snowflake—one of a kind and special in her own way. Ginny had a habit of raising her paw as if she were a conductor directing an orchestra or a queen waving to her subjects. It was funny because at the animal shelter, they said that the dog had been named Victoria or Vicky after the long-serving British monarch.

Tori couldn't handle having a dog with the same name as hers, so she changed it to Ginny. Virginia was a strong classic name and Ginny and Vicki sounded reasonably similar. Because Ginny wasn't particularly interested in following instructions, her name didn't matter much. She happily ignored whatever name was given to her.

Tori threw the mushrooms into the pan with diced onion and began stirring quickly. She glanced down at Ginny, who had her nose raised toward the ceiling to better enjoy the redolent scents of cooking wafting through the immaculate kitchen. "Hey, you're supposed to be over there. You know the rule. Out of the kitchen."

Ginny wagged her tail a couple of times, but didn't move. Tori waved her spatula at the dog. "Ginny, no. Go on. Out of the kitchen. *Now.*"

With a small snort of disgust, Ginny stood and stomped over to the cabinet that demarcated being outside of the kitchen area, versus inside. She lay down with her snout between her paws, looking forlorn.

After pureeing the sautéed onion-mushroom mixture and returning it to the saucepan, Tori adjusted the spices in the gravy. Maybe a little cumin? She'd always been fascinated by the science of cooking. A tiny pinch of spice could take a dish from simply flavorful to exceptional.

In culinary school, she'd gotten into a heated (so to speak) discussion with a classmate about the differences between caramelization and the Maillard reaction. Shannon had insisted that they were the same, but Tori correctly asserted that the two processes were completely different. Although both involve heating food and browning, everybody knew that the Maillard reaction involves amino acids and caramelization involves sugars.

At the time, Shannon had called her opinionated and annoying, but Tori couldn't help it if she was correct. She'd found that in many situations, there was a right way and a wrong way to do something. It wasn't her fault if she happened to know the right way. Over the years, she'd learned that it often was better to keep her thoughts to herself to retain the peace. But it didn't make her any less right.

The fact that she happened to be extremely talented in the world of food wasn't her fault either. Everyone she'd ever met had benefited from her skills. Let's face it, the friend who loves to cook is the friend you want to hang out with a lot. And in the intense environment of a restaurant kitchen, you learned to take action. Being bossy and remaining in control was part of the job. You needed to have nerves of steel to watch people slice their fingers, bandage them up, and move on to the next task.

Working in a busy restaurant kitchen was like nothing else. The speed and movement was an adrenaline rush, and you needed to focus so intensely that it was almost intoxicating. You didn't have time to be polite or pussyfoot around.

Tori missed many aspects of being a chef. The prestige, the tight-knit group of people who became your work family, and the thrill of watching everything come together perfectly to create a memorable meal. But the pay, insane hours, and non-stop stress took their toll and Tori didn't regret leaving that world. She'd needed to reclaim her life.

Many people couldn't understand how she could give up her elite position and return to her hometown. Starting a gourmet chocolate boutique might have seemed like a step down after her career as a chef, but working 80 hours a week, including nights, weekends, and every single holiday wasn't sustainable. She'd worked breakfast, lunch, dinner, and catered VIP parties. Sometimes she'd get home at one in the morning and then have to wake up at four for a private breakfast party. It had been fiercely intense, but no one could work twenty hours a day forever. In her heart, Tori had known she was on the road to burnout, but the day she'd collapsed onto the floor from exhaustion was a wake up call. Getting lectures from paramedics and doctors hadn't been a good way to end the day, but they were right. It was time to move on.

Even though she'd fallen out of love with restaurant work, she never fell out of love with food and cooking. She was happiest when she was in a kitchen devising a new recipe or learning a new technique. Food was her passion and she couldn't imagine ever doing anything else.

After Tori finished improving the ciabatta-bread stuffing, she set up a small plate of stuffing, drizzled the gravy over it, and carried it to the easy chair. She took a sip of wine and took a few moments to savor her creation. Not bad.

Ginny hopped onto the ottoman and stared at her until Tori relented and handed her a piece of the seasoned bread. The dog gulped it down and resumed staring. Tori smiled. "You didn't even taste that, did you?"

Unmoved by the criticism about her lack of decorum and refined palate, Ginny continued to watch intently. Tori gave her another piece. "I like it, but it's not quite there yet. I think it needs a smidge more pepper."

People always asked Tori what the worst food was that she'd ever eaten. She usually responded with a noncommittal response because it was undoubtedly something her mom had created when Tori was growing up. Tori loved her mother, but the woman was not a cook. Mom used to get distracted while cooking, so veggies often ended up the consistency of glue. Sometimes even frozen dinners didn't work out. Destroying a prefab meal took some special anti-culinary skills.

After Tori learned to read, she'd studied the extensive collection of cookbooks that people had given her mother, probably in hope that they might help her improve her culinary abilities. The cookbooks made food sound so delicious, it was no wonder Tori started offering to cook dinners almost as soon as she was tall enough to reach the stove.

Tori handed Ginny another piece of bread with a smile. "Please consider chewing it this time."

The dog gulped down the bread and Tori chuckled. An ex-boyfriend, Don, had proclaimed that Tori was so uptight and such a workaholic that she couldn't do normal things like have a dog or a cat. She'd dumped him long ago, but the conversation had grated at her for years after he'd exited the scene. It was satisfying that she'd proved him wrong in the end.

To be fair, even her parents were a little surprised when Tori had adopted Ginny. But everything had worked out well. Yes Tori was tidy and created lists for everything, but that simply meant she was organized. Don had claimed that in addition to her never being home, she'd freak out about all the dog hair. But he was wrong yet again. The fur level was perfectly fine. Yes, Ginny had a lovely coat, but she had a standing date with the groomer every two weeks. In between visits, the dog seemed to work really hard not to shed too much.

Tori had never for a second regretted adopting Ginny. In return for giving the dog a home, Tori received unconditional love and a brave defender who would bark at potential marauders. For such a small dog, Ginny had a menacing voice. Some might call the sound that came from her grating or ear-splitting, but Tori tried not to dwell on it too much. Mostly she focused on keeping Ginny happy. Doing so helped keep the dog quiet, which was good for neighbor relations.

Tori gazed out the window, noting the lengthening shadows. It was odd sitting around like this, knowing that tomorrow morning she wouldn't be getting up at five, racing to the store, and unlocking the front door of Victoria's Confections. Her little shop was closed for good, and rather than lamenting what had been, she needed to focus on what was next.

Tori drained the rest of her wine, got up, and walked to the kitchen, followed closely by Ginny. After washing the dishes, Tori put everything away and picked up the little dog, carrying her to the bedroom.

She snuggled Ginny to her chest. "Tomorrow is the big day. I promise you're going to *love* doggie camp. You'll see. It will be great."

Ginny squirmed slightly in her arms, and Tori could tell the dog wasn't buying it. Oh well, what could you do? Tori's latest career change was going to require a lot of adjustments. Ginny was going to have to cooperate whether she liked it or not.

∼

The next morning, Tori looked at her list of things to do and sighed. She began packing Ginny's favorite toys into a duffle bag as the dog looked on from the safety of her dog bed. Tori tried to act nonchalant, but she felt really, really guilty. Did working mothers feel bad when they dropped their children off at day care?

Ginny was already sulking because she didn't get any breakfast. The kennel was north of Alpine Grove and it was a long drive for the dog to endure. She wasn't necessarily prone to carsickness, but Tori wasn't taking any chances.

Tori clipped on the leash, grabbed the duffel, and locked the door behind them. She said in an overly cheerful voice, "Okay! Next stop, doggie camp."

Ginny rode in a dog bed in the back seat, but turned around a few times and faced the back seat rather than forward. Tori glanced over her shoulder. Ginny was a spoiled brat and wasn't shy about letting her feelings be known. At least she had no pent-up emotions or hangups. At any given time, it was easy to tell what Ginny's opinion was about whatever was happening. And right now, she was annoyed.

The boarding kennel was farther out in the trees than Tori had realized. Although it was a beautiful drive, it seemed like it took forever to wind through the rural roads. By the time she finally found the driveway with the sign for the Wag On Inn, she had been half convinced she'd missed the place. The gravel drive snaked through a copse of massive trees. Although it certainly was stunning back here, it was a good thing the owner had given her such detailed directions.

Tori pulled into the parking area in front of the kennels and got out. A short woman opened the door of the kennel and smiled. "Hi, you must be Tori. You're right on time."

Tori thrust out her hand. "Hi Kat. Thanks again for taking Ginny on short notice. Everything is a little chaotic right now, and Ginny is sulking."

Kat leaned over and peered in the window. Ginny was sitting up, and if a dog could frown, she was doing it. "She does look a little annoyed, doesn't she?"

"Normally, I take her everywhere. Closing my store has completely disrupted her routine, and now this. I'm afraid she's going to be a bit cranky about being here."

"It's okay. We'll adapt. I'll take her for a long walk, and that will help. Exercise is good for stress." Kat gestured toward the car. "Do you want to take her out so we can get acquainted?"

"Of course!" Tori hurried to the car and fumbled with the door. "I'm sorry."

She put Ginny on the ground and Kat crouched in front of the dog and took the leash. She pulled something out of her coat pocket. "How do you feel about treats?"

Ginny sniffed disdainfully, paused, then slurped the item out of Kat's palm. The woman stood up and faced Tori. "I think we'll be fine. Dogs that like food tend to enjoy their stay here. They figure out pretty quickly that almost every person they meet has pockets full of treats."

Tori chuckled, "Ginny definitely likes food. As much and as often as she can get it."

"After you leave, I'll get her settled and then take her for a long walk to tire her out. Exercise is good for stress management in dogs as well as people. When she's sleeping, she's not thinking about being grumpy."

Tori crouched and cuddled a somewhat recalcitrant Ginny into her arms, whispering a few more entreaties that the dog behave herself. She stood up and swept the dog hair from her slacks. "I'm afraid she's not a big fan of being outside."

"Don't worry, we'll figure it out. Good luck with the Haunted Barn. It's supposed to be a lot of fun."

Tori tried to muster up a smile. "Yes, I've heard quite a bit about it now." And everything she'd heard made it sound absolutely dreadful in a corny, overly costumed way.

"From the look on your face, I get the impression you're not excited about attending?"

"Halloween is my least favorite holiday." Tori shook her head sadly. "And the whole thing was all so last-minute that the costume I have is just awful. I'm going to look like someone threw a bottle of Pepto Bismol on me."

Kat put her hand over her mouth to somewhat unsuccessfully stifle a laugh. "Um, okay. I can't think of anything quite that pink off-hand. What are you wearing?"

"I'm wearing a dress with a giant hoop skirt because I'm supposed to be Little Bo Peep. It's so humiliating. You can imagine how bad the other options were if that was the best costume I could come up with." Tori waved her hand toward the towering cedars. "You're so lucky you can stay here far away from all the fake ghouls and goblins. With such a long driveway, you probably don't even get trick-or-treaters."

"We never have since I've lived here. But maybe we'll get some intrepid little kid who is training for a marathon or something." Kat pointed toward the house. "Every year, I make sure our pantry has three bags of fun-size candy, just in case. I figure it's best to be prepared."

"I haven't eaten candy bars in years. Being involved with food for so long, I'm a bit picky. Then when I opened my gourmet chocolate shop, my palate became even more refined in terms of candy." Tori mentally cringed because what she was saying sounded so elitist. But it was true. The idea of eating a Milky Way or a package of Milk Duds made her mildly queasy.

Kat wrapped Ginny's leash around her hand. "I'm disappointed that I never got to visit your store. I'm sure I would have loved it."

"I was sorry to close, but there was no way I could grow it. The market is just too small. I couldn't get to the point where I could afford to hire an employee and working all day every day was exhausting."

"I'm familiar with that situation. The day I hired my dog walker Mia was probably one of the best days of my life. Certainly my business life."

"So you know *exactly* what I mean!" Tori smiled with relief. Most people thought she was nuts to give up such an ostensibly successful business. "When my friend Holly and I discussed changing the business model, it seemed like the right thing to do. I confess that I do miss my little shop though. Some of my regular customers were crushed."

"Maybe they'll stop by the Haunted Barn to get some of their favorite treats."

"They'll be disappointed if they do. I'm working on developing a new product line designed to appeal to children that can be mass produced. That means no more perfectly enrobed truffles with delicate hand-crafted leaves."

"Most kids probably wouldn't care about that, I suppose."

"Kids are a primary consumer of chocolate, so it's a market we can't overlook."

Kat crouched next to Ginny and stroked the fur between her ears. "It sounds like your mom is about to find out how refined the palate of the average eight-year-old actually is."

"While dressed as Little Bo Peep." Tori sighed. "Every weekend for an entire month. I'll be so happy when Halloween is over."

Kat stood up again. "Well, only twenty-eight days to go. In the meantime, Ginny and I will see you on Sunday."

After Tori left, Kat put Ginny into a kennel and got the dog set up with water and food bowls. When she exited the kennel to refill the water for the other dogs, Ginny launched into a tirade of the most awful high-pitched barks Kat had ever heard. She'd been exposed to a lot of different canine noises, but Ginny's bout of personal hysterics was a new realm of auditory agony.

The dogs in the other kennels started howling, barking, and joining the general mayhem. Kat rushed back to Ginny's kennel to make sure the dog wasn't dying. At the sight of her caretaker, Ginny abruptly stopped the awful noise, sat, and stared.

Kat leaned down. "Are you okay?" Ginny continued to offer a fixed stare, apparently unmoved by the question.

"You're stressing everybody out." Kat glanced at the clock on the wall and opened the kennel. "I think you need a special walk. An extra-long one. My article is going to have to wait."

Kat put the leash back on Ginny, took her outside, and headed for one of the dog-walking trails that snaked through the forested property. Unlike most dogs, Ginny didn't seem particularly enthusiastic or interested in the trail, which had been marked by the hundreds of dogs that had passed through before her. Her short legs slowed and then finally she sat down.

Kat stopped and looked down at the dog. "No, I don't think so. Nice try, but you need exercise, and I need you to settle down." She tugged gently on the leash, "Let's go."

Ginny didn't move. Kat picked her up, placed her on all four paws again, and moved forward. Ginny had no choice but to follow. Kat picked up her pace so the dog wouldn't have a chance to stall out again. "Sorry, but I'm on to you. I was warned about your aversion to the great outdoors. The more times you stop, the longer this walk is going to take."

Kat had encountered dogs that preferred being in charge before. Usually they were small and incredibly spoiled. Ginny fit the profile, and now having met Tori, it was clear she definitely did not have the upper hand—or paw—in the relationship with her dog.

Although Kat was used to being the director of the canine show at her kennel, she wasn't sure what to do about the agonizing barking. Sure, all dogs barked, but this was different. The other dogs sharing living space were going to be more than a little put out by their new roommate. It was possible Ginny would tire herself out, but if the noise was excruciating for a human, Kat couldn't imagine what it must be like for a dog.

After motoring the recalcitrant dog through all the trails in the forest, Kat returned to the kennel and put Ginny back into her assigned space. "It's time for your afternoon nap. Please behave yourself."

Ginny sat on the blanket Tori had brought for her dog bed, surrounded by her pile of toys, glaring at Kat. Relieved that the dog seemed to be quiet for the moment, Kat slipped out the kennel door. All the dogs would need their afternoon walk in a couple of hours, so she'd be back soon enough.

She was halfway up the driveway making her way toward the house when the noise resumed. With a sigh, she turned around. This was going to be a problem. Kat's dog walker Mia had taken the day off for a three-day weekend with her boyfriend, so Kat was on her own.

She opened the door to the kennel building and the other dogs settled down. After handing a treat to all the quiet boarders who were politely sitting in front of their doors, she opened Ginny's gate, clipped on a leash, and took her back outside. "Okay, we're going to try something else."

Ginny refused to move from her sitting position, and Kat lifted her up, putting her four paws on the floor. "Let's go."

Hustling out the door, she ran the dog up the driveway and behind the house. At the back door, she picked the dog up like a sack of potatoes, tucked her under her arm, and went inside.

Ginny stiffened in surprise at the collection of curious dogs that greeted her. Kat waved the dogs back, walked a few steps down the hallway and stepped over the baby gate that was blocking the door to her husband Joel's office.

Ginny ran up to him and he swirled around in his office chair. He looked down at the dog, then at Kat. "Why have you put a small dog in my office?"

Kat smiled weakly. "Isn't she cute? Her name is Ginny. She looks like a miniature version of Lady."

"She does." Joel reached down and let the dog sniff his hand. "But why is this mini-dog in my office?"

"We have a problem."

"I have to work."

"I know. But I have to run to town. I need you to babysit her."

"I thought we agreed that babysitting boarding dogs is your responsibility."

"I know you don't agree with the idea that certain dogs need special-dog time inside, but this one is going to cause problems for everyone else if I leave her outside."

"We built the kennels so we wouldn't have to have other people's dogs in our house anymore."

"I know. But she…"

"We keep having this conversation." Ginny put her paws on his knees and Joel picked the dog up, so she could settle into his lap. "Every dog can't be special dog."

"But look, she loves you already."

He stroked the fur between the dog's ears. "I'm a sucker."

"No, she needs you. The other dogs need you too. She has this bark that is like fingernails on a chalkboard. I can't express how incredibly awful it is. Please let her stay in here. It's only for a couple of hours."

Joel continued petting the dog. "I'm having enough trouble concentrating on this project as it is."

"You do seem sort of depressed about it." Kat walked to his chair, leaned over, and put her arms around his neck. She kissed his ear. "Are you okay?"

"I don't know. It's just work. I'm tired of it."

"Tired of what? We agreed you don't have to fly off and train geeks anymore if you don't want to."

"I know. And that's good because I don't want to. It was draining, and all I wanted to do was come home."

Kat kissed his ear again. "And here you are. I have to say that I was happy about your decision. So what's bothering you?"

"I'm wondering if it's time to find something else to do."

Kat stood up straight. "You mean something other than programming? Are you kidding? But you're so good at it."

"I'm not sure. Maybe it's because of this project." He ruffled Ginny's ears. "What's her name again?"

"Ginny. Her owner is Tori Merrill, and I found out that Tori wasn't kidding when she said this dog hates the outdoors. What dog doesn't like going for walks?"

Joel chuckled, "Why go for a walk when you can sit in someone's lap and get affection?"

"Apparently I'm not the only one who fell in love with you at first sight." Kat gave him a kiss. "Thanks for doing this. I hope you feel better. Maybe we can talk about it more when I get back."

"My legs might have fallen asleep by then, so it's your fault if I can't walk by the time you return."

She waved as she stepped over the baby gate. "Understood."

Chapter 2

The Haunted Barn

During her drive south Tori tried not to think about how Ginny was likely to behave at the kennel. It would be a real problem if Kat didn't let Ginny come back for the upcoming weekends that were scheduled this month. Tori said a silent plea for the canine gods to smile upon her spoiled little dog and her caretakers.

The folks who organized the Haunted Barn event every year had signs up all along the highway. Any drivers passing through the area would have to be completely oblivious to everything around them to miss the turn. Thirty-five signs later, Tori turned down the gravel road that led to the Jensen's farm. When it wasn't commandeered for Halloween festivities, the Jensen family grew corn, potatoes, asparagus, strawberries, beans, and various other crops on their 2,000 acres.

More signs indicated where vendors and staff should park, and Tori quickly found a spot and unloaded her supplies. Hope was bringing the displays and was probably already there. Tori was supposed to have met her half an hour ago, but driving down from the kennel took longer than she'd expected.

She found vendor area number 53 in the barn where Hope was watching a teenager set up straw bales to demarcate their assigned space. A fake skeleton coated with stringy spider webbing dangled from one of the rafters above. Tori mentally cringed, not only at the ick factor, but at the corny factor. Having a hanging plastic corpse next to their display was so tacky.

Although being surrounded by straw bales wasn't ideal, Tori had brought a bunch of old sheets to drape over them. At least they hadn't ended up stuck in one of the old horse stalls. That would have to be worse.

Pots had been set up to hold tree branches that had plastic spiders hanging from them with fishing line. Webbing was everywhere. Somebody must have purchased all the cheesecloth in the greater Cedar County vicinity because it was being used for countless ghosts and macabre curtains. More cheesecloth had been dyed green to create fake moss, and a reddish version simulated old decaying tablecloths. Tori couldn't understand why they didn't just spring for real tablecloths, but she didn't have time to think about it.

Hope helped her unpack. "You didn't get any of the scary decorations we talked about."

"I didn't have time to stop by Kmart on my way back from the kennel. I was already late, and I knew you'd be getting anxious."

"This is too fru-fru." Hope held up the end of the tablecloth with her fingertips as if the ruffles had a hideous communicable disease.

"It was all I had. I think my mother gave it to me for Christmas a long time ago. Everything else I own says Victoria's Confections all over it."

"Oh well, I guess it matches your dress." Hope draped the cloth over their long folding table. "You need to go change."

"I know. I'm almost done. We've still got lots of time. What's your hurry? They don't open this place until it gets dark."

"I know. I'm just excited. This is going to be fun."

As the sun sank lower in the sky, Tori busied herself setting up the candy displays and setting out the flyers they'd had made up with information about the new line of candy. This idea needed to work and work well, or they were in trouble.

While she and Hope were working, the organizers of the event were testing lights and adding more displays designed to frighten visitors. Various costumed people appeared on the scene and were walking around checking things out or standing in groups laughing with one another.

The inside of the barn turned into old home week for all the zombies and ghouls, which Tori found a little disconcerting. Bloodied faces weren't usually smiling and laughing, but the members of the "scream team" seemed to enjoy chatting about their past experiences. A huge man with flaming red hair and a chain saw was having an animated conversation with a gruesome scarecrow and an undead clown about his best techniques for making little kids run screaming for the hills. He seemed to be omitting the obvious though. Tori figured the huge orange chain saw was the primary reason those poor little kids felt the need to flee. When he'd fired it up and revved it to demonstrate, Tori had almost had a heart attack.

Hope agreed to watch what they were now referring to as their Candy Land Stand while Tori went to find a place to change. The Jensens had brought in a herd of bright blue portable toilets, but there was no way she could maneuver the gigantic hooped petticoats onto herself in that space, so she wandered around the barn with her long hooked staff and her garment bag, trying to find a discreet place to put on her costume. The sun was setting and more spooky lights were being turned on, so it was getting difficult to see.

Startled by something on her neck, she frantically whapped at what turned out to be more of the fake spider webbing. She'd launched the associated plastic spider into a dark corner, but there was no way she was going to retrieve it. He would have to stay there.

The darkening shadows and strange lighting was giving her the creeps. When a zombie dressed in striped jailbird garb leaped out from behind a post, she shrieked and slapped him on the arm. "Don't do that! I'm working here too. Do you know if there's a closet where I can change?"

He shook his head. "Dunno. I did my makeup and got dressed at home. You'd better hurry up. The other areas are rolling and they're about to open the barn doors."

Tori glanced around her. "What about over there? Could you hold up the sheet covering the ghost? That way it can be like a screen."

"Um, I don't think I should do that. We're not supposed to mess with the decorations."

"It will take five minutes." She shoved him toward the ghost and held up the sheet. "Like this. It will only take me a second to get dressed."

He gave an indifferent shrug and held up the sheet between his arms. "I feel stupid doing this."

"Oh *please*. You're dressed as a zombie criminal and you're worried about feeling stupid?"

"Hey, my costume is cool." He turned to peek over his shoulder at Tori. "What the heck are you supposed to be?"

Tori pushed the sheet aside. "Could you zip up the back?"

He complied and plucked at the pink poufy fabric at her shoulder. "Are you a wedding cake? Or okay, I get it. You're a donut!"

"My costume has nothing to do with food. I'm a shepherdess." Tori put on her pink mask and waved her fake sheep at him. "Didn't you ever hear the nursery rhyme?"

"About donuts?"

"*No.* Little Bo Peep. She lost her sheep." At his blank stare, Tori gave an exaggerated sigh. "Oh, come on. Everyone knows it. Mother Goose?"

"There's a goose? What happened to the sheep?"

"Never mind. Thank you for your help."

"No problem. See ya around" He waved and strode off, probably to find another dark corner to hide in.

The sun had disappeared and fog was rolling in. Tori waved her hand in an effort to see better. Fog? Was it about to rain? But they were inside. Had they seriously put a fog machine in here?

She tried to figure out where she was in relation to the Candy Land Stand, but the red and black lights combined with the fog made it difficult to figure out where she was. The lights began flashing and Tori pressed her hand to her chest. Her heart rate was actually keeping time with the strobing of the lights. Ugh.

A shriek came from the front of the enormous barn and Tori turned, evaluating her position. Oops. She was walking in the wrong direction. Readjusting her garment bag on her arm, she set off toward the front of the building. She stumbled on something lying on the dusty floor, looked down and yelped at the dead body below her. With her heart leaping around in her chest like a toad on amphetamines, she vaulted to one side, flipping the garment bag into the air as she smashed into a stall door and crash-landed in a heap on the ground.

When she opened her eyes, a masked man was kneeling next to her, holding her staff in his hand and looking down into her face. In the dim light, it was difficult to tell what he looked like, but he was wearing breeches, a leather tunic, and a cape with a green hood. She flailed her hand, and he took it, helping her sit up.

"Greetings m'lady. You seem to have taken a bit of a tumble."

"I tripped on a dead guy."

Tori flattened her hoop skirt, which had flipped up like an umbrella and examined the man more closely while her heart settled back down to a more normal rhythm. He was wearing a mask, but he had dark, mysterious eyes. Or maybe the mysteriousness was from the lighting. His hair was dark and tousled, probably from the hood. She smacked her skirt again. The complicated petticoat practically had a mind of its own. "What happened to the guy on the floor? He isn't actually dead is he?"

"Merely an illusion m'lady. He's not dead. Or more precisely, he was never bloomin' alive, so he cannot be dead." The man pushed the hood off his head and pursed his lips, looking thoughtful for a moment. "Unless perhaps you delve deeper into his heritage and consider his days as a bleedin' tree."

Tori looked over at the perhaps not-so-dead guy. As it turned out, he was constructed from wood. The two-by-four legs were a bit of a giveaway. "I don't suppose you've seen a woman dressed as Little Red Riding Hood at a booth with lots of candy, have you? I'm a little turned around, and I'm supposed to be there giving away samples."

"Why yes, I have. That fair maiden is over yonder past the Crypt of Demons."

"Great."

"Shall I escort you there?" He took her hand again and helped her stand up. "It's a fair distance, and we must traverse several treacherous domains."

Tori glanced around for nearby treachery as she stifled a giggle. In addition to being cute, this guy had a fabulous accent. "That would be lovely, kind sir."

Like the rest of the farm, areas of the barn were designated "scare zones." Tori was distressed to discover that Robin Hood wasn't kidding when he mentioned the Crypt of Demons. Scare actors were everywhere, doing their best impression of the Zombie Apocalypse. Another area called the Demented Circus had a number of dead clowns dangling from the rafters, along with real clowns lying in wait to frighten people walking past their circus-related props.

Worrying about people leaping out at her at every turn was almost as bad as the actual experience, and Tori was still clutching Robin Hood's hand. She was being such a baby about all these cheesy scare tactics, but she couldn't quite force herself to let go either.

At her flinch, he gave her hand a gentle squeeze of reassurance. "That clown won't hurt you, m'lady. He's but an actor."

"I know that. This is all so silly, but I don't like surprises."

"'Tis all in the name of fun."

"But it's *not* fun." Tori let go of his hand to point at a skeleton. "How is being frightened by plastic bones supposed to be fun?"

"Make-believe is fun. 'Tis all about the adventure. Let us venture into the Crypt."

Tori slowed her pace. Crypt? No thanks. She'd had enough dead guys for one night. "I don't think I'll enjoy it. In fact, I'm pretty sure I won't."

"Well then, let's stop and examine the wares over here."

"You mean the competition. They're selling candy."

"Perhaps that is more accurate, but I suspect they won't conclude that someone wearing that much pink is a threat to their very livelihood."

Tori giggled as she snatched a piece of candy from the table and resumed walking. "You're right. I don't think Little Bo Peep is particularly threatening."

"Quite so, m'lady." He took her hand again and brought it to his lips. "Tell me about yourself. When you aren't proffering candy to children in this ghostly establishment, what do you do?"

"Make more candy."

"What do you do outside of your work?"

Tori paused at the question. People always wanted to know about hobbies, but she didn't have any. "I spend most of my time working. I was a chef then I opened a gourmet truffle store. But it closed because I'm partnering on a new wholesale candy business."

"I see. Tell me about your family. What are your parents like?"

"Pretty normal, I guess. These days, my father works for the county. My mom was a teacher, but she retired and has vowed never to set foot inside another classroom."

Robin Hood smiled. "I'm guessing she is not attending this event."

"Nope. She said the only thing she misses about teaching elementary school is the finger painting, so she's taking art classes."

"What about you?"

"Me?"

"What do you yearn to do?"

"Right now, I'd like to have a successful business that doesn't require working a hundred hours a week."

"That sounds a bit melancholy."

Tori turned to face him. Who was this guy? "You're awfully nosy, aren't you?"

He picked up a hard candy from the table and set it back down. "Just making conversation as we stroll by the mutant jesters rolling about the macabre carnival, m'lady."

The candy competition wasn't competitive and Tori resumed walking. "I'm not complaining. Work transitions are difficult. But I have a nice apartment, and my friend Hope lives nearby. So does my family. And I have a dog. She's a great dog too. I love her."

"Dogs are the best bloomin' company anyone could ask for, in my estimation. You're not wedded or betrothed?"

She raised her eyebrows in feigned shock. "Now you're *really* getting nosy."

"I'm a naturally curious individual. We all assume that the woman who lived in a shoe with the many children had a male of the species to help create so many progeny. But Little Bo Peep remains a mystery. I presume those bouncy blonde curls would attract more than just sheep."

Tori reached up to touch her hair. Blonde? "I'm afraid you'll be disappointed to find out that these curls are fake. They're attached to the bonnet."

He inclined his head slightly. "I stand corrected."

"But to answer your unbelievably nosy question, no Ms. Peep is unattached, thank you very much. I've been busy, and I guess I just never met anyone…you know, the right person."

"I see."

Tori was quite sure he didn't. How could he know the epic failures in her love life? She grabbed a candy from a table as they walked by. "I'm a difficult person to get to know. People say I'm no fun."

"Perhaps those people are wrong."

As she walked up to her own display, Hope handed a candy sample to a little goblin who ran off with his prize. With a swish of her red cape, Hope gestured toward the table. "Where have you been? I'm missing out on everything. I want to go see the corn maze and all the rides they set up outside."

Tori stopped to rearrange a few items that were out of place on the table display and walked behind it to stand next to Hope. She made a shooing gesture with her hands. "Go. I've seen enough zombies for the both of us."

"Who was that guy holding your hand? That was fast. I'm impressed."

"Where did he go?" Tori looked around, but Robin Hood had disappeared. "I don't know who he is. I tripped and he helped me up. I think he's from England."

"Aww, that's sweet. And British accents are hot. Maybe I can catch him."

"You're married."

"I know, but Robin Hood was cute. There's no harm in looking."

A cloud of artificial fog wafted toward them and Tori cleared her throat. "Don't get lost. The visibility isn't good out there."

"Hand out samples." Hope wrapped her cloak around her. "I'm going to explore. I'll give Robin your regards."

Tori smiled at a kid dressed as Casper the Friendly Ghost and handed him a few pieces of candy. "Please let me know what you think."

"Thanks, lady. Bye." Casper floated off into the mist and leaped into the air shrieking happily when a demented clown lurched out from the gloom.

Giving out candy seemed like a good idea, but getting any decent feedback from kids was looking unlikely. Tori had warned Hope this might happen, but Hope assured her that she would ask kids lots of questions while she was at the event. Tori didn't have a lot of experience with children, so she couldn't argue. Hope was convinced that kids were going to share deep insights on the nuances of their candy preferences.

Tori wasn't sure the candy she'd created would appeal to kids. After doing lots of market research, Hope concluded that all popular products for kids emulate something else. The idea was to take two popular items and combine them. For example, Butterfinger BBs were designed to resemble something you put in a gun. Shark Bites were fruit-flavored candies shaped like sharks. Then there was candy shaped like Disney cartoon characters and musicians and cereal designed to emulate Pop Tarts or French toast. The array of weird food in colorful packaging designed to appeal to children was at once mind-boggling and disturbing.

After a lot of brainstorming, they'd decided to combine the concept of animal crackers with chocolate. Tori designed molds that looked like lions, tigers, bears, dogs, cats, chickens, cows, and other animals. To make the animals different, she added coloring to the white chocolate coating. The chocolate center was flavored to further distinguish the animals.

Although the candy actually tasted acceptable to her, eating a blueberry cow or a minty green chicken offended Tori's sense of aesthetics. But Hope was convinced kids would love their new Choco-critters.

Tori knew the chocolates were made well with quality ingredients, but she couldn't stop worrying about the fact that quality probably didn't matter much to the average ten-year-old. When you were selling chocolate to adults, you could focus on the superior flavor. An adult could appreciate the difference between a fine truffle and a cheap Hershey bar.

She excelled at making gourmet chocolates, but to kids, chocolate was just chocolate. It was something they'd grown up with, whether as a treat for holidays, birthday cakes, or homemade chocolate chip cookies. To a kid, chocolate was good stuff, but it didn't have a lot of novelty. It was everywhere. Kids already knew and loved M&Ms, Hershey's

Kisses, and every other huge name-brand chocolate because Mom could grab it from any grocery store anywhere.

Tori wasn't sure how she was supposed to convince kids that this chocolate was better. She knew nothing about marketing to children and it nagged at her. Marketing to adults felt like a conversation, but marketing to kids felt manipulative and vaguely unethical. Every time Tori thought maybe she simply wasn't cut out for this type of business, Hope convinced her that she was over-thinking it.

Maybe she was. It certainly wouldn't be the first time. Over-thinking was practically a way of life for her. On the other hand, maybe the entire business venture was simply an incredibly bad idea.

∽

The next morning, Tori got up bright and early to go over her lists. The Haunted Barn hadn't ended until ten, and she'd driven home, stripped off her costume, and fallen into bed completely exhausted. She was accustomed to standing for hours in the store, but dealing with all the fake fog, scare actors, strangled screams, noise, and general mayhem had wiped her out. Even worse, she would have to do it all over again that night. This time she would put her costume on at home. Driving might prove challenging, but if she removed the six-hoop petticoat, it wouldn't be too bad. And there'd be no more wandering around trying to find a place to change amid a bunch of costumed weirdos.

As she packed the chocolates into containers, she considered her upcoming evening at the barn. If she were being honest, she secretly wanted to see Robin Hood again. Yes, he'd been terribly nosy, but he also was easy to talk to and funny in a droll, terribly British way. She had no idea if he was working at the event and would return that night, or if he was just a one-time visitor getting into the Halloween spirit. She'd spent a lot of time answering his questions but had learned absolutely nothing about him.

All too soon, it was time to load up the candy, get dressed, and head out to the Jensen's farm for day two at the Haunted Barn. Knowing what to expect helped considerably, and she met Hope at the table without incident. After helping set up the display, Hope announced that today she needed to explore the corn maze because everyone said it was "*so ah-maizing.*" Tori made an extraordinary effort not to roll her eyes.

A couple of hours later, Tori was tired of talking to children and wondering if Hope had gotten permanently lost in the corn field. Finally, Hope returned to the table with Robin Hood in tow. She reached for a Choco-critter and handed it to him. "You have to let us know what you think."

He held up the pink pig, attempting to examine it in the dim light. "What is it?"

"Chocolate. Actually, that one has strawberry flavoring too." Hope waved her hands. "Go on. Try it. I know you'll love it."

He unwrapped the foil and popped it into his mouth. "Interesting. I guess it's good."

A kid dressed as Spiderman walked by and grabbed a fistful of chocolates, looked at them, and tossed them back into the basket. "These are stupid. Where's the cool candy?"

Hope said in a syrupy sweet voice, "What kind of candy is that?"

"The guy over there has stuff that looks like bloody eyeballs."

Tori repressed a sigh as Spiderman ran off to find his eyeballs. This was not going well. On a more positive note, now that she wasn't focused on avoiding scare actors, Tori hadn't been wrong the night before. Robin Hood was a handsome fellow. She still couldn't tell exactly what color his eyes were because of the lighting and the mask, but his hair was brown and he had a pair of fine-looking muscular legs under those tights.

Hope held up the basket. "Try another one. We have a lot of different flavors."

He took a mint chicken. "I love these."

"What happened to your accent?" Tori asked. "I thought for sure it was real."

He took another piece of candy. "These are addictive. I'll probably make myself sick."

"When it comes to sweets, Tori is absolutely brilliant." Hope walked around the table. "Didn't she tell you she's a chef?"

"I don't announce it to the world," Tori said, although she was pretty sure she'd mentioned it to Robin Hood yesterday when she was relating half her life story to the guy. "I don't work in a restaurant anymore."

"But she loves to cook," Hope added, handing him a card. "You should come for dinner on Sunday. We'll be done with this for the weekend, and we can tell you more about our business. You and Tori can get to know each other better too."

Tori raised her eyebrows in alarm and shot Hope a significant what-are-you-doing glare. "I'm sure you're busy."

He glanced down at the card. "Nope. I'm not doing anything tomorrow."

"Then it's settled," Hope said. "Tori said you had fun chatting yesterday. This will be great."

Tori gave him a weak smile. This wasn't the first time Hope had volunteered her to cook like this, but at least she liked Robin Hood. He also was cute, although she did miss the British accent. It had sounded so real too. "I don't even know your name."

"Phillip Holbrook, but you can call me Chip."

Tori put out her hand and shook his. "Nice to meet you, Chip."

Hope gave Tori a smug smile as she handed another chocolate to Chip. "Be sure to tell your friends about Choco-critters."

"Especially any friends you have under the age of twelve," Tori added.

"Will do. See you around."

The two women watched in silence as he strode off into the foggy gloom. Tori turned to Hope. "What did you do that for?"

"You're obsessing too much about the business. Now you have something to think about other than chocolate."

"Gee, thanks. Thanks a lot."

The rest of the evening was uneventful, and after hours of peddling candy, Tori went home, crashed hard, and slept in late the next morning. She had a whole week to restock the chocolate larder before next weekend's Haunted Barn festivities, so she intended to enjoy her morning.

When Tori was anxious she had a tendency to organize. Okay, who was she kidding? It wasn't only when she was anxious. Putting everything in its place was the cure any time she was sad, angry, bored, or lonely. Whenever life felt out of control, organization made her feel safe, like nothing bad could happen.

Tidying up never failed to restore balance to her universe. She moved from room to room, encountering new items that were out of place or that needed a bit of sprucing up. Because clutter never stopped accumulating, sprucing up her environment was the gift that kept on giving. One of the worst things about giving up a regular income was saying goodbye to her cleaning service.

After the therapeutic festival of order, everything was exactly where it was supposed to be and sparkling. Feeling much more at peace with her surroundings, Tori wrote a new to-do list and got ready to pick up Ginny from the boarding kennel.

The trip north past the ski resort and through Alpine Grove gave Tori lots of time to think. Probably too much time. She made a mental inventory of the food to add to her written list of items to pick up at the grocery store on her way back home.

After she parked at the kennel, she grabbed a pencil from the glove compartment to scribble everything down before it vanished from her mind. How could Hope volunteer her to cook for some random guy she didn't even know? And if Hope somehow "forgot" to show up for this dinner, Tori was absolutely going to kill her.

When she looked up from her notes, Kat was stepping through the kennel door with Ginny. She closed the door behind her and waved in greeting.

Tori leaped from her car and ran to Ginny, who joyfully wiggled her entire body at the sight of her owner. Kat said, "Aww, she's thrilled to see her mom. I love a happy reunion."

Tori picked up Ginny and snuggled her close. "I missed her so much. I hope she behaved."

"She was upset at first, but it turns out she adores my husband. So she spent lots of time with him in his office. It was very cute."

Tori looked into Ginny's face. "I'm glad you found a friend because you're coming back here before you know it."

"How was the Haunted Barn?"

"Worse than I expected. I've never heard so many people scream in my life."

Kat laughed. "I guess all that haunting works pretty well."

"They have scare actors everywhere. I know people go there to be frightened, but hours and hours of it is tiring. And when it's not you being scared, it's difficult not to laugh at people's reactions. People freak out with horrified expressions on their faces. Some of them fall over backward, trying to get away. Men push their dates in front of them, and kids trample each other. It's by turns weird, funny, disturbing, and exhausting."

"I don't even like scary movies, so I'm feeling okay about skipping it." Kat pointed at Ginny. "Because of the dogs I don't go out much, but in this case maybe that's not such a bad thing."

"I should get going. A nice man dressed as Robin Hood helped me up when I tripped over, um, a decoration, I guess you'd say. And now I have to make dinner for him and my friend Hope tonight."

"It's not every day you get to have dinner with Robin Hood," Kat said with a grin. "Have fun."

"I don't know if fun is the word I'd use, but Ginny and I will see you on Friday."

"We'll be here."

~

Kat walked into the doorway of Joel's office and tapped on the doorjamb. "Your little furry shadow went home, but she'll be back on Friday."

"I don't normally like little dogs much, but Ginny is a nice dog."

Kat walked to his chair and put her hands on his shoulders, rubbing his neck with her thumbs. "I don't understand why you spent all weekend working."

"Because I had to. I'm so behind on this project, I'm not sure I'll ever get caught up."

"That's not like you. I'm the procrastinator. You're the guy who plans everything down to the last detail."

"I can't get into this project." He spread his fingers above the keyboard and looked down at his hands. "I'm starting to wonder if I should quit."

"You can always find another project. It seems like you know every techie human being in the Western hemisphere."

"I mean quit programming."

Kat leaned around his neck to examine his expression. He seemed serious about this. "But you've been a software engineer since, well, your entire career. You went to school for it."

"I know."

"I wasn't surprised you didn't like doing the geek training thing because of all the travel, but this is different." Kat moved to stand in front of him and leaned against the desk. "What do you want to do instead? More construction?"

"I'm not sure. I could work construction in the summer I guess. But winter is coming, so there's none of that type of work for a while anyway."

Kat reached to take his hand. "If you think of something, you'll let me know, right?"

The phone rang and he let go of her hand and reached to answer it. Kat walked back into her office. One of the constants in her life was that Joel was a software engineer. He was good at it, and for someone with such an analytical mind, it seemed like the perfect occupation. But what happened when the nerd didn't want to engage in nerdy activity anymore?

Developing software also paid well. Certainly a lot better than construction. Kat pressed her palm to her abdomen to quell a stabbing pain. Sure, she was a worrier, but there was no reason to give herself an ulcer over this situation. Joel would find something else to do. No one would ever accuse him of being lazy. And while he figured out what he wanted, they had her writing income, the kennel income, and savings. She had nothing to worry about, so her insides needed to calm down.

The hot twisting stab left her breathless and a little dizzy, so she sprawled out on the twin bed in her office trying to get comfortable, but the pain in her abdomen wouldn't go away. It was the wrong time of the month for cramps unless Mother Nature was playing some type of rude joke. Once a month was plenty. She'd had bad cramps before, but this was ridiculous. The woes of being a girl.

Curling up into a ball on the bed made her feel a little better, and she closed her eyes, trying to will the pain to stop, but it refused. Her dog Linus poked his nose at her leg and she mumbled, "Go lie down, Big Guy. I need to rest for a while."

At the sound of Joel walking into her office, she opened her eyes again. He sat on the bed next to her. "Are you okay?"

"Who called?"

"Someone about a project."

"You're overbooked already, aren't you?"

"That's what I told them, but it sounds sort of interesting." He moved his shoulder in a quasi-shrug. "It's forensic accounting."

"I don't know what that is, but if it sounds interesting to you, that's encouraging."

"More interesting than what I'm doing now. It's basically finding money that has disappeared."

"You'd probably be good at that, given how cheap you are and how much you love spreadsheets. You could solve a money mystery."

He leaned closer to her face. "Are you sure you're okay? You're awfully pale."

Kat tried to move, cringed, and reached to grip his hand. "Maybe not. I think something's wrong with me. It's like the worst cramps ever. Worse than the worst cramps ever."

Joel shook his hand free and touched her stomach. "Where?"

"Over here. Could I have appendicitis or something? I don't know what that's like, but this is agonizing."

He took her hands. "Okay, we need to go. Can you sit up?"

Kat moaned and tried not to cry at the shrieking pain in her abdomen. "No. Whatever this is, it's getting worse."

Joel scooped her up into his arms, shooed Linus out of the way, grabbed his keys, and carried her out the back door. Kat squeezed her eyes shut and clutched his flannel shirt.

He gently placed her into the truck and leaned down to kiss her forehead. "We're going to the emergency room. Everything will be fine."

Kat offered a slight nod of agreement, but she wasn't so sure. Nothing should hurt this bad. It was like someone had put a vise around her torso and was squeezing as hard as possible, then letting up slightly. When the wave of pain receded, she could move, but when the vise tightened again, all she could do was hold still until it passed. Simply breathing was too much movement. The drive to town was excruciating with every bump causing a new jolt of serious hurt.

Joel spent most of the time holding her hand, except when he needed to shift gears. Kat could tell by the sound of the engine that he was drastically exceeding the speed limit on the dirt roads and possibly taxing the mechanical capabilities of the aged truck.

By the time they reached the small hospital in Alpine Grove, Kat had her lips clamped together because she couldn't take a single breath without screaming. Joel parked, gathered her from the truck, and carried her inside. Kat opened her eyes as he flagged down a nurse. Because Kat had her ear to his chest, the sound echoed as he said, "This is my wife and something's wrong. She's in extreme pain. I've never seen her like this. We think it might be appendicitis. You need to do something."

The nurse put her palm on Kat's arm. "On a scale of one to ten, what's the pain like, honey?"

Kat mumbled, "Forty-two."

The nurse said evenly, "Please set her down over there. I need you to fill out these forms."

Kat's face twisted as Joel set her in a chair. She opened an eye at the sensation of him giving her a kiss. He whispered, "I'll be right back. Hang in there. You're going to be fine."

She watched him stride over to the nurse's station and could only hear the low undertone of what she thought of as Joel's angry voice. When he was upset, rather than yelling and ranting like she did, his voice took on an unnatural calm. It was a useful skill because people tended to find it extremely unnerving.

The nurse said, "We have lots of patients to get to and it's probably a kidney stone."

Whatever Joel said in response caused her to say, "Sir, I'm going to need you to step away from the desk."

Kat opened her eyes again as Joel whirled around and stalked off through a set of double doors that led to another area. Noise and shouting arose from the back room, and he returned with a man and a woman wearing lab coats.

The woman crouched down in front of Kat and took her wrist. "Please move your hand from your tummy, so I can take a look."

Kat took a sharp breath and made a valiant effort not to scream when the woman pushed on her stomach. The doctor pulled Kat's shirt back down and let go of her wrist. "I think you're bleeding internally. You probably need surgery, but I need to do a more thorough exam. Is that okay?"

Kat glanced up at Joel, who moved to crouch in front of her, taking her hand. "You'll be fine. You *have* to be fine."

"I'm sure they do this type of thing all the time." Kat mumbled. She turned her head to the doctor. "You do, right?"

"Of course." The woman patted her hand and stood up, waving to an orderly. "Okay people, let's get her prepped."

People gathered around and Kat let go of Joel's hand and whispered, "I love you."

"I love you back."

~

When Kat opened her eyes, she was in a brightly lit room. Where was she? Where was Joel? She struggled to move, but stopped at the resulting weird ache and shudder of nausea. Ugh. What had happened? Did she forget to walk the dogs? Did they need to be fed? It was Mia's day off. Who was taking care of them? And why did she feel like she wanted to throw up?

At a touch on her hand, she turned and found Joel leaning over her. He smiled. "I'm so happy to see you."

"I feel like crap and my throat hurts."

He gave her hand a reassuring squeeze. "They said you might be disoriented."

"Did they take out my appendix?"

"No." He shook his head slowly. "Everyone says you'll be fine."

She squinted at him. The resignation in his deep green eyes was odd. Was it her imagination, or was he omitting something important? Her head was foggy, and it was as if she was speaking to him from far away. "What did they do? What happened?"

He sat in the chair next to the bed and wrapped both his hands around hers and leaned close to her face. "You were bleeding internally. They thought it might be a ruptured ovary or an ectopic pregnancy."

"That's not possible. I'm positive I wasn't pregnant."

"No, you weren't. It wasn't either of those things."

"What's wrong with me?"

"I guess it's kind of rare, but they said the pain was from a ruptured fibroid tumor. Apparently bleeding is unusual, but they gave you transfusions and did surgery, so you should be fine."

"Do I have *cancer*?" Words like radiation, chemo, and baldness flickered through her mind like a bad silent movie.

"Fibroids are almost always benign, and they took it out. But the way it was attached...I don't know. There were a lot of long words and I wasn't concentrating very well. Torsion I think. And pedunculated. Sorry. I don't know what that means."

"Me neither."

"They said there was a lot of damage and maybe if we lived closer to a big hospital with specialists, but we don't...I don't know. I'm sorry...I just...I'm so sorry."

She squeezed his hand. "Why are you sorry? Before I got all the drugs, they said the fact that you hauled me down here so fast might have saved my life."

"Kat, they had to do a hysterectomy." He leaned to give her a kiss. "I'm so sorry."

The shock of the words hit Kat like a pile of bricks dumped on her chest. She had no idea what to say to Joel. Although she hadn't been ready to have kids, now the decision was out of her hands. And her husband's. It wasn't fair. "I, um, are you okay about this?"

"All I care about is you." He ran his hand across her forehead, pushing a tendril of hair aside. "It's going to take you a while to recuperate, but everyone says you'll be fine."

"How long have we been here? Are the dogs all right? Mia has the day off."

"I left Mia a message and talked to Maria, who went on a mission to track her down. Everything's fine at home. Mia is taking care of the kennel today." He smiled and glanced toward the door. "And Maria *really* wants to see you."

"She's here?"

"She's been driving me nuts for hours. Are you up for seeing her?"

Kat nodded. "I love you."

"I know. And I love you back. Let me know if you need anything. I'll be right out there." He kissed her hand and got up. "I'll retrieve Maria before a long-suffering nurse tries to inject her with an unscheduled sedative."

Kat giggled and winced. Ouch. No laughing. "Good plan."

Joel left and seconds later Maria charged into the room. "Girlfriend, you scared the bejesus outta me!"

Kat lifted her head to gaze at her. "What are you wearing?"

Maria looked down at her outfit, which included grey sweatpants, a pink tutu, a magenta spandex top, a lime green fake fur stole, a red stiletto on her left foot, and a wooden clog on her right. "When the engineer called me, I was trying on new outfits and I got caught in mid-change."

"That's quite a fashion statement."

"I thought you were going to die, and I ran out of my apartment without thinking." Maria collapsed in the chair and kicked off the clog, which landed with a thump. "I was terrified, and I swear every last brain cell fell out my ears, girlfriend."

"It wasn't too pleasant for me either." Kat moved to try to sit up and reconsidered. Yeesh. "So I guess you know what happened?"

"It sounds like you're missing some lady parts now." Maria looked down at her ruby-red fingernails, then back at Kat. "I always figured you'd be a great mom someday. I mean, for sure, way better than me. Heck, at least you found a decent guy to be the dad, which is more than I can say."

"Part of me feels like crying. The other part is too drugged up and numb to feel anything. Even though Joel and I were leaning toward not having children, it feels wrong to have the choice taken away."

Maria gestured toward the windows. "Well, you've already got a house full of animals. If you want, you could adopt a few small humans too."

"I know. Maybe. Who knows? Right now, I'm too confused and sad to think about it. And sick. I don't want to barf, but I might."

"Try and gimme a little warning first, girlfriend."

"I think the drugs are wearing off. Everything hurts." Kat slumped down. "I'm just so tired."

"No matter how you slice it, you've had a massively bad day." Maria patted the bed. "The doctors say you're going to be okay though. You are, right?"

"I think so. You should go home and change your clothes."

Maria bent to pick up her clog and put it back on. "What was I thinking buying shoes made of wood?"

"As I recall, you were going for an earthy, hippie look." Kat closed her eyes. "I dunno. It was a long time ago."

Maria put her hand on Kat's. "I'm thinking the engineer is getting antsy out there, so you get some rest. I'll check on you tomorrow."

Kat mumbled goodbye and let herself float away. When she opened her eyes again, Joel was sitting in the chair with his head lying on the bed, his arm stretched out so he could hold her hand. When she moved her hand, he jerked awake, and sat upright. "Are you okay?"

"I'm sleepy. Aren't you?" Kat glanced around the darkened room. "What time is it? Shouldn't you go home?"

"Mia is at the house." He pointed at the IV in her arm. "I can't leave you while you're attached to all these things."

"I think there might be fewer of them."

"Maybe, but I need to listen to the monitors."

"You were asleep, not listening. And nurses will yell at you if they find you in here."

"If something happened, I'd wake up. They already yelled at me, but they gave up and went away."

"You can be unbelievably stubborn." Kat squeezed his hand. "But I'm glad you're here."

"You're going to be fine."

"I think you've said the word *fine* more times today than you have in the entire time I've known you."

He reached out to stroke her hair. "Maybe I'm trying to convince myself. I was really scared."

"I have to say you're good in a crisis. I guess I already knew that, but thanks for bringing me here." Kat let her cheek rest on his palm, enjoying the warmth. "And you can stop worrying because I'm going to be all kinds of *fine*."

"But not for a while. You had major surgery, and you can't go up stairs or lift anything for a while. That also means no dogs yanking on you."

"For how long?"

"Four to six weeks."

She tried to sit up, which failed, so she readjusted herself, letting him pull his hand away. "That's nuts. Mia has been planning that trip to Paraguay to visit her father for months. When I get home, I need to call around to find another dog walker *stat*."

"No one will want to work temporarily. I've been thinking, and I'm going to quit the programming job I hate and take over running the kennel."

Kat took his hand in a death grip. "You can't do that. The deal was that you didn't have to help with operating the kennel."

"Yes, I can, and I want to."

"I guess you go on afternoon dog walks with me, so that won't be different. I can still answer the phone and deal with booking reservations."

"Walking alone in the forest will give me lots of time to think, which might be good."

Kat clasped both of her hands around his and looked into his eyes. "Are you upset that we won't have kids?"

"I don't know."

"Me neither. I feel sad, partly because I know you'd be such a great father. But maybe the people who desperately want kids should be the ones to have them."

"If we end up wanting to raise a child, we could adopt."

"That's what Maria said." Suddenly exhausted, Kat let go of his hands and closed her eyes. Major life decisions were going to have to wait. "I'm so tired."

"Me too." He leaned over to give her a kiss. "Go to sleep. Everything will be fine."

"Yes. Fine."

Chapter 3

Chocolate & Meltdowns

A t Tori's apartment, dinner with Robin Hood was not going well. When Chip arrived, he'd brought in so much mud on his boots that Tori almost had an anxiety attack. Hope grabbed her arm to keep her from lunging for a mop.

Things went downhill from there. Although he'd seemed witty and charming the first night they'd met, it was like the spark had been extinguished from the guy. Maybe Tori had been so nervous about the first night of the Haunted Barn and the embarrassment of falling and exposing herself to half the attendees of the event that adrenaline had caused her to consider him amusing. In the glare of daylight, he certainly wasn't.

Hope didn't seem to notice any difference and kept the conversation going by pressing Chip for more information about his family and their business. The day before at the barn when Chip had provided his real name, Hope quickly latched onto the fact that Robin Hood was the heir apparent to the Holbrook toy company.

The Holbrook family fronted the expenses for the Haunted Barn because the proceeds went to the Holbrook Family Foundation, which was a charity focused on children's health and literacy. Hope was convinced that there was marketing synergy between toys and candy and had spent much of the evening subtly hinting at investment or joint marketing concepts.

Tori ignored the marketing machinations and moved into power hostess mode, continuing to feed Chip more food. Fortunately, he liked to eat. She tried not to notice that he was spilling crumbs everywhere. She'd made prime rib, lemon-garlic roasted chicken, and eggplant parmesan, in case he was a vegetarian. He ate everything with so much gusto, it was startling. Did he never eat? How did he not weigh four thousand pounds? Tori could only dream of a metabolism that would let her swine out on four entrees.

Ginny spent the meal pouting in the bedroom, but at least she was being quiet. The small dog was not a fan of changes in her routine. The aromatic food scents must have eventually gotten to her, and she casually strolled out into the dining area and parked herself between Chip and Tori.

He pointed down at the dog. "Hey, I didn't know you had a dog. Everything's so shiny and sparkly in here, and there's not a speck of dog hair anywhere. I never would have known."

Hope waved her fork toward Tori. "Some people think organizing closets is fun. I'm not one of them, but as you can probably tell Tori is a meticulous housekeeper."

Tori smiled weakly. *Meticulous housekeeper* was the term Hope used in front of other people instead of calling Tori a compulsive, Type-A neat freak like she did when they were alone. "I told you about my dog last night. You said that dogs are the best bloomin' company anyone could ask for. I thought that was sweet."

Chip stopped chewing. "Yeah, dogs can be pretty cool."

He clearly had no idea what she was talking about, and Tori came to an obvious conclusion. Chip was not the person she had talked to on Friday night. "Hope, could you come with me to the kitchen for a moment? I'd like your help with the dessert."

Hope raised her eyebrows, but excused herself and followed Tori. "What's your problem?" she whispered.

Tori hissed, "You brought the wrong Robin Hood to dinner."

"Don't be ridiculous. We both saw him at the barn. And in case you haven't figured it out, he's *loaded.* Can you say potential investor?"

"I can, but I won't. I'm serious. He's not the same person. Or if he is the same person, he's either incredibly stupid or has some type of short-term memory problem."

Hope waved her off and started back toward the dining area. "You're over-thinking this."

Tori picked up the chocolate torte she'd made and carried it to the table. "I hope you left room for dessert."

Chip reached for his fork. "You bet. That looks great."

Tori sliced the torte, and they began eating. After taking one bite, Hope set down her fork and said, "I can't believe how late it is. This evening has flown, but I need to run because Morgan is going to call tonight."

As she stood up, Tori jumped up and said, "Let me get your coat." She grabbed Hope's arm and dragged her to the bedroom. "What are you doing?"

"I've got to go. Phone sex awaits."

Tori increased her vise-like grip on Hope's forearm. "You *can't* leave me with this guy."

"Try to get him to invest. He's not responding to my ideas, but I think he has the hots for you."

"Yuck. No."

"He's nice. And you said he was cute. Give him a chance. I'll call you tomorrow."

"I told you, this is *not* the guy I said was cute."

Hope grabbed her coat, shrugged it on, and returned to the dining room where Chip was standing with his hands in his pockets, looking bewildered.

Hope shook his hand. "It's been such a pleasure to meet you and I'm sorry to run out like this. Please finish your dessert. Tori makes a fantastic espresso."

"I like espresso," he said.

At the door, Tori hissed a few bad words to Hope and returned to the kitchen to make the espresso. She brought the cups to the table and set one in front of Chip.

He took a sip. "Hope was right. You're an amazing cook. I can't remember the last time I had a meal this good."

"There are a lot of leftovers, if you'd like to take some home with you."

"I won't turn that down." He took another sip. "So, sorry if all that talk about my business was boring. She kept asking."

"It was interesting. I loved going sledding every winter and I never would have guessed that I'd meet the owner of the company that made my Avalanche Snow Coaster. I even liked the commercials with Harvey the Penguin."

Chip laughed. "I'm kind of tired of that stupid bird, but thanks for saying so."

"I thought he was cute."

"That's the idea. And technically, I don't own the company. My father does. I'm in marketing, so you'd think I could get rid of Harvey, but I can't. According to market research, kids still love him."

"He's cute."

"My ex-girlfriend thought he was obnoxious."

Tori wasn't sure what to say about the girlfriend, so she made a feeble attempt at humor. "Well, maybe that's why she's the ex."

His shoulders slumped. "We were supposed to get married, but I couldn't make myself go through with it."

"Oh...ah...I'm sorry. I didn't mean to bring up an unpleasant subject."

He took another sip of coffee. "I'm surprised you didn't read about it somewhere. You might be the last person left who doesn't think I'm a heel. She pretty much made sure the whole world knew what a jerk I was."

"Of course I don't think that." Tori cringed inwardly. She'd totally stepped in it and it wasn't coming off her shoe. Yikes. "And I have no room to talk. Because I've always worked such long hours, I don't have the greatest luck with relationships."

"At least yours didn't end up in the tabloids."

"Well no. I'm sorry to hear that."

A pall fell over the conversation as Tori desperately tried to think of something to say. She had a vague memory of reading something in a magazine at the doctor's office about a rich playboy type who gave his fiancée a six-carat ring and then ditched her four days before the wedding. The jilted lover responded by calling up every media outlet in the known universe with her tell-all story.

Chip seemed equally uncomfortable. He gestured toward the door and said, "I should…" as he whacked the espresso cup so hard that it shot off the table and onto the floor. He leaped from his chair, knocking it over onto Ginny, who barked twice in startled outrage and hurtled herself toward the bedroom.

Tori got up. "Don't worry. I'll clean it up."

"I should get going. Thanks for dinner." He paused. "I'll, um, give you a call sometime this week okay?"

"I'll get your coat." Tori hustled off into the bedroom, whispered an apology to Ginny, and returned. "Have a safe trip home."

Once the door was mercifully closed, Tori grabbed a mop and dealt with the mess on the floor.

Perhaps she'd reorganize her sweater drawer in the morning. Erasing the memory of this messy evening from her mind would require a lot of serious sorting and systematizing.

~

The next morning after putting away mountains of dishes from dinner and re-mopping the floor, Tori was able to get down to the business of making more candy. In addition to creating the chocolates, she also had to wrap each piece in confectioner's foil. The foil colors matched the colors of the flavoring, so mint pieces were green and strawberry ones were pink.

Once the business moved into production, the manufacturing would be automated, but in the short-term while they were testing recipes, the process was Tori's problem. Every once in a while Hope would help, but she often ripped or crumpled the foil, so Tori tended to discourage her assistance. It was faster and simpler to do it herself.

Tori had a system for candy production that involved multiple steps related to creation and packaging. Because she had done it so many times, she was able to more or less operate on autopilot.

Even though she knew the process intimately, the science of chocolate remained fascinating. To coax the most flavor from chocolate, you have to temper it. The fat in the cacao bean, called cocoa butter, is made of glycerides of fatty acids called beta crystals that solidify at different temperatures. When you melt chocolate, the fatty acid crystals separate. The tempering process gently encourages the fatty acid crystals to return to a stable form.

If you mess up tempering, the chocolate seizes and you end up with a grainy, lumpy mess. But if you temper chocolate correctly, the result is shiny, beautiful chocolate that makes a satisfying snap when you break it and isn't tacky to the touch.

Tori had tried many times to explain to Hope how sensitive chocolate was. If you were paying attention, you'd probably run across chocolate failures sooner or later. Almost everyone has opened a bag of chocolate chips and discovered they had a grayish cast. Although the chips are safe to eat, it means the chocolate has *bloomed*. When chocolate is exposed to moisture or heat, it causes the sugar or fat to fall out of suspension and recrystallize on the surface of the chocolate.

Assuming it's kept at proper temperatures, chocolate that has been tempered properly won't bloom. Tori knew that the cocoa butter in chocolate has the potential to crystallize in six different ways and only with precise temperature control could she achieve chocolate with the right mouth feel and stability.

Although there were a couple of ways she could temper her chocolate, Tori preferred the "seeding" approach, which meant she had to stir solid chocolate into melted chocolate to inoculate the crystals. The formed crystals of the solid chocolate worked to "seed" the melted chocolate.

Tori was a kitchen appliance geek, and she'd actually named her chocolate-making tools because she spent so much time with them during the exacting process.

She pulled Donna the double boiler out of the cabinet and got down to the task of melting the chocolate. Stirring was also critical to keeping the beta crystals in suspension, and Millie the mixer got quite a workout, along with Stella the plastic spatula.

She grabbed Temperance the thermometer from a drawer. Temperance was arguably the most important tool in the entire process. Once the chocolate mixture was at the perfect temperature, Tori poured it into the molds. When the chocolate was tempered correctly, it set within three to five minutes. Because the tempered chocolate set so quickly, she placed the bowl over 90-degree water, making sure that no water could get into the chocolate and cause it to seize.

Ginny sat in her favorite spot in the doorway, watching as Tori went through the familiar motions in the kitchen. The first time Tori had worked with chocolate was when she was a kid and Mom had messed up an order at the store.

When she was young, her parents had operated a small community market that was a neighborhood fixture. Every once in a while, Mom would bring home food that was about to expire or that had been damaged in some way. Because

Mom worked long hours, she never had much time to cook, so Tori took on the task of figuring out how to use up extra food.

It took creativity to find recipes for fourteen heads of lettuce or sixteen pounds of cauliflower that hadn't sold, but she had. Fortunately, they'd had a big chest freezer, so she could store the resulting vats of soup and sauces.

The chocolate situation arose when Mom discovered a box of candy bars hiding behind three cases of canned tomatoes. The chocolate was too old to be sold, and when it arrived at the house, Tori figured she could use the chocolate for fondue if she melted it. Unfortunately, way back then she didn't know about the magic of tempering. Although the fondue itself was fine, the leftovers were definitely not. When the chocolate re-solidified, it transformed into a bizarre mass of glop. Tori wanted to understand what had gone wrong and enlisted the help of a librarian at the school library to help her figure out what had happened.

The never-ending challenge of using up large quantities of weird food led Tori to learn about food science and cooking. Mom was a horrendous cook, and because she was at the store all day, she never had enough time to make dinner. Tori had been eight years old when her mother taught her an important lesson. When you boil eggs and all the water evaporates, they explode.

Mom hadn't been paying attention to the eggs and the explosion that resulted had sounded like a gunshot. It was so loud Tori thought they were being attacked. She dropped to the floor and hid under the table. Mom ran into the kitchen, turned off the stove, and crouched down to explain to Tori what had happened. They spent the rest of the evening scraping splattered egg from the ceiling, floor, cabinets, and stove.

Tori's father had encouraged Tori's interest in cooking because he was tired of kitchen disasters and inedible dinners. One time Mom had read a biscuit recipe wrong and instead of adding vegetable shortening, lard, *or* butter, she added all three ingredients. The biscuits had turned out so slimy it was like consuming a block of Crisco.

Before Tori took over the family cooking duties, the smoke alarms got a serious work out. Mom routinely put garlic bread into the oven under the broiler and forgot about it. During one memorable holiday party, there had been twenty-five people in the house when the living room filled with smoke from the kitchen. It was a miracle Mom never burned the house down.

Sure, Tori might be a little anal-retentive about cleanliness and cooking precision, but who could blame her? She'd seen first-hand what happened when you didn't pay attention in the kitchen.

Ginny was startled from her slumber by the sound of the phone ringing. Because Tori was in the middle of pouring chocolate into molds, she opted to let the machine pick it up.

After the beep, Hope's voice asked, "So what happened last night? I can't believe you haven't called me. Oh wait, maybe that's because he's still there. Hi Chip! Are you two in love?"

Tori yelled "No!" at the machine, which didn't respond to her outburst. Ginny was less sanguine. Apparently disgusted by Tori's negativity, she stood up, turned around, and stalked off toward the bedroom.

~

On Tuesday morning, Tori measured exactly two teaspoons of heavy cream into her coffee mug because one teaspoon wasn't enough and a full tablespoon was too much. She was about to pour her coffee and go over her lists when the phone rang. Ginny ran into the room and sat in front of her, looking expectant because it was dangerously close to breakfast time.

After answering the phone, Tori set down the coffeepot and sank into a chair, dismayed at the news that Ginny's groomer, Maureen, had the flu. She wished Maureen a speedy recovery, hung up the phone, and looked down at the dog, who wagged her tail.

"I'm sorry to tell you that we have a problem." Tori returned to her coffee and poured it into the mug, stirring it methodically. "You're shedding, and Maureen is officially out of commission."

Although Ginny appeared unconcerned, Tori was extremely concerned. Tori had not mastered the art of grooming Ginny. The small dog was remarkably slippery, yet inexplicably, Maureen reported that Ginny was "just the sweetest thing" from the moment she put her on the grooming table. Perhaps it was because the dog was aware that unlike Maureen, Tori was a wimp. If Tori even thought about grabbing a brush, Ginny disappeared under the bed. It was quite a magical trick. If Tori managed to sneak up on the dog with any type of grooming implement and was able to catch her, Ginny slithered from her grasp like a greased snake.

After pondering her options, Tori picked up the phone and called the kennel in Alpine Grove. She was pretty sure

Kat had mentioned they had a groomer there. Maybe she could squeeze Ginny in.

At the mumbled greeting, Tori asked, "Hello? Is this Kat?"

"Yes, I'm one but there are five others too. Murphee is here next to me, but I don't know where Tripod and Dolly Mae are. You'd think after all we did for Tripod, he'd be a little more grateful for a roof over his head, ya know? I mean, he had to be cut out of a wall."

Tori made a frownie face at Ginny. Was this actually Kat? "I'm sorry, but do you mean a cat?"

"Yeah, it's a long story, but it has a happy ending."

There was a silent pause and Tori wondered if they'd been disconnected. "Hello?"

A deep and rather wonderful male voice came on the line. He sounded like a radio DJ and Tori mouthed, "Oooh, nice..." at Ginny, who wagged a few times in response.

He said, "Kat's a little under the weather right now. May I help you?"

"Oh, I'm sorry. I hope she feels better. And I'm sorry about the cat in the wall too. Anyway, my name is Tori Merrill. My dog, Ginny, stayed there last weekend and I'll be bringing her back on Friday. I think Kat said that you do grooming there, and I'm wondering if I could arrange to have Ginny groomed."

"I remember Ginny. Our groomer is about to leave on a trip, but I can check her schedule. Hold on for a second. I'll be right back."

Tori picked up Ginny, snuggled the dog into her lap, and pulled at a tuft. "Look at this. Fur is falling off you. I hate to say it, but you're a mess. I can't have you shedding all over my candy."

The man returned to the line. "Could you bring Ginny early on Friday instead of in the afternoon? Our groomer is pretty booked up, but she said she could squeeze in Ginny sometime during the day."

"That would be wonderful. Thank you. I hope Kat is okay. She sounded, um, a little different."

"We haven't quite worked out the timing of her medicines yet, but she'll be fine."

"Well, tell her to get well soon."

"I will. We'll see you Friday."

Tori hung up the phone and looked at her list. Mom's birthday was coming up. While she was in Alpine Grove, maybe she could get her something from the cute gift store on the main street. Ginny jumped out of her lap and Tori laughed. "Okay, okay, Ms. Task Master. I know. Enough procrastinating. Time to get back to the coal mines. Chocolate awaits."

By Thursday, Tori never wanted to see chocolate again, which for a chocolatier was saying something. More accurately, she was tired of slaving over the stove, stirring, wrapping, and processing thousands of pieces of chocolate that an obnoxious kid was likely to dismiss as not cool enough to consume. Or that he might even throw into the garbage. The idea of her hand-crafted creations ending up in a Dumpster somewhere made her melancholy.

In all the discussions with Hope and Morgan about the new business, it had never occurred to Tori that kids wouldn't like her chocolates. Without exception, everyone adored every edible she'd ever created. As a chef in restaurants, she'd received awards and rave reviews. And people who came into her gourmet chocolate shop had universally praised everything she created. It was demoralizing to suddenly face an unappreciative audience.

After spending way too much time plagued with self-doubt, Tori called Hope. Her friend had years of experience of talking Tori down from anxiety-ridden precipices when her thoughts got twisted into knots.

Hope was typically blunt. "You're over-thinking this like you always do. A kid says your chocolate isn't cool and now you're having a meltdown. Oops. Sorry. Poor choice of words."

"I'm serious. We're about to invest a ton of money on an assumption that may be completely and totally wrong."

"It's not wrong. Kids like chocolate."

Tori yanked on the phone cord to emphasize her point. "But they don't care about *quality*. They eat cereal that's essentially brightly colored sugar because of the packaging, not because it tastes good. And then there's Stanley Raymond from third grade. Remember him?"

"Stinky Stanley?"

"Yes, exactly! Do you recall how he got that nickname?"

Hope paused. "Not really."

"It was because his mom made him salami sandwiches every day. I don't know what that salami was made from, but after lunch, he had the worst halitosis ever. He stopped eating those nasty sandwiches, but the name stuck to the poor guy at least through junior high school. It wasn't his fault. And like you, almost no one remembered why he'd been stinky in the first place."

"So what?"

"Kids decide something, tell their friends, and it becomes their truth forever after. Last weekend, a few kids grabbed candy and put it back because they said some other kid told them it wasn't cool. The word is that revolting eyeball candy is cool, but Choco-critters are not."

"So what? It's a few random kids at a haunted house. Different kids will be there next time. We don't know anything yet. We have three more weekends to go."

"Don't remind me." Tori tried not to sigh too loudly into Hope's ear. "I've got lots of chocolate ready to give away. You need to give parents the surveys and talk to every little kid you can find."

"I'm looking forward to tomorrow. It's going to be so much fun."

Tori wasn't so sure but made an effort to curb her pessimism. "Okay, but if we get more negative feedback, I'm going to start looking for different recipes. Maybe kids hate chocolate animals for some reason and we need to do something else."

"Fair enough, Ms. Peep."

"Just so you know, I'll be in Alpine Grove earlier in the day, but I'll stop by here on my way south. Leave me a message if you need me to pick up anything."

"I will. See you tomorrow night!"

Tori hung up the phone. Hope wasn't wrong that Tori tended to over analyze, well, pretty much everything. But what if her intuition was trying to tell her something? If she invested all her money into this business venture and it failed, she would have to return to restaurant work. And after her flambé-level burnout, she wasn't excited about that idea at all.

~

Bright and early Friday morning, Tori loaded Ginny into the car for the journey out to the kennel. By the time this month was over, she'd probably feel like she'd driven a rut in the roads between Gleasonville and Alpine Grove. It was a long drive, but Ginny had made it abundantly clear that she didn't appreciate being left alone.

Ginny had also been vetoed by several pet sitters and was not well loved at the boarding kennel south of town either. At least Kat seemed to put up with Ginny. And this time the little dog would be returned to Tori all clean and brushed out.

When Tori arrived at the kennel, no one seemed to be around, so she pressed the buzzer on the building to alert people to her presence. A tall man opened the front door of the log house and strolled down the long driveway.

Tori crouched next to Ginny, "Hey, I bet that's the guy with the great voice." The dog tugged at the leash, clearly excited at his approach.

Tori giggled, "Well, this is a switch. I guess Kat did say you liked her husband. So do you have the hots for this guy?"

Ginny jumped and pranced around in a circle and the man picked her up. "Hi Ginny." He smiled and put out his hand. "I'm Joel. You must be Tori."

"It's nice to meet you. I can't believe how much my dog likes you. She's usually stand-offish with people other than me and a couple close friends."

He stroked the fur between Ginny's ears. "Last week, we spent some time discussing a frustrating project. She was sympathetic."

"Are you working on something new for the kennel?"

"No, it's a programming project. I'm a software engineer."

"Kat said she was a freelance writer. You two sure are busy." Tori smiled weakly. "I'm not good with computers. My accountant didn't like the fact that all my store receipts were paper. He was always telling me to get a computer."

"Sometimes paper is better. This project was doomed because the process they wanted to automate didn't work the old way with paper and twenty-five carbon copies either."

"I guess that was the frustrating part?"

"Extremely. I fired the client this week."

Tori laughed. "Well, that's a good thing about being self-employed, isn't it? You can say goodbye to the customers you don't like."

"True. I also have more to do around here until Kat is back on her feet, so it was for the best."

"Is she okay?"

"She'll be fine in a few weeks."

Given his expression, he clearly wasn't interested in going into details, and Tori took the hint. "I have to stop by the gift store, so I should be going. Thanks again for agreeing to groom her. She's really shedding."

Joel picked a tuft of fur off his flannel shirt where Ginny had leaned on him. "So it seems."

"Please give Kat my best wishes. I hope she feels better."

"Thanks. We'll see you Sunday."

Tori returned to the car and watched as he carried Ginny back to the house. It seemed that Ginny got special treatment. No wonder the spoiled little dog liked it here.

In Alpine Grove, Tori couldn't find a parking space on the main street, so she parked one street over in a residential area with lots of cute bungalows shaded by huge maples that were putting on their annual show of fall color. She strolled over to the gift store enjoying the crisp morning air. It was so pretty here, it almost didn't look real.

A woman with light-blonde frosted hair was sitting on a bench outside the gift store. Her legs were stretched out in front of her, her hands were folded on her stomach, and her eyes were closed. Was she meditating? Tori looked up and down the street. People were standing in front of shops chatting. Was the gift store not open yet? Maybe this woman was taking a nap while she waited for it to open.

As Tori got closer, the woman sat up and stretched her arms above her head. She beamed at Tori. "Isn't it gorgeous? I had to enjoy a moment in the sun after all the rain. Vitamin D is soon to be in short supply around here."

It was lovely outside, but Tori hadn't paid much attention to the weather because she'd been spending all day every day in the kitchen cooking. Seeing someone enjoying the moment so thoroughly made her smile. "Yes, it's lovely. Is the store open yet?"

"It is! Welcome to Bea Haven Gifts. I'm Bea Sullivan. Come inside. Are you looking for anything in particular?"

Tori followed her and the bells on the door jingled merrily, announcing her presence. "I need to find something for my mother's birthday."

"What's she like?"

"Mom? I don't know. She's my mother."

"What does she do for a living? Hobbies? Favorite color?"

"She was a teacher, but she retired. Before that, she and my dad owned a community grocery."

"Oh, so she's a fellow retailer. Where?"

"In Gleasonville. Do you remember Merrill's?"

Bea clapped her hands together. "Of course I do! I used to drive down and stock up on dry goods. What did she teach?"

"She taught at an elementary school, mostly kindergarten and first grade." Tori glanced at a display filled with sparkly stained-glass pieces hanging near the windows. "Those are pretty."

"Aren't they gorgeous? A local artist named Lorraine has been selling them here for years. She brought in more the other day because we sold out over the summer."

"I don't know if my mom would like it, but I do." Tori put her hand under a blue and white star and glanced at the windows. "The ones hanging over there are pretty too. You have a gorgeous window display. It really reflects the personality of the store."

"Spoken like someone who knows the importance of branding. Are you involved in retail too?"

"I was. I had a gourmet chocolate shop."

"Do you mean Victoria's Confections?" Bea pressed her hand to her chest. "I was despondent when my husband told me it closed. Every time he went to Gleasonville for meetings, I insisted he bring back a big box of truffles. I'm a chocoholic of the highest order, and they were utter bliss."

Tori laughed at her passion. "That's wonderful to hear. I'm glad you enjoyed them."

"At the risk of prying, why did you close? My husband said there were always customers there."

"I needed a change. Working all day every day was exhausting and I couldn't get ahead enough to hire anyone to help. My lease was up and they were renegotiating the rent. I talked to a friend, and she came up with a business idea that would allow me to change my business model. It seemed like the right time, so I agreed to partner with her and her husband."

"Although I remain devastated that you closed your shop, that sounds like an exciting new venture."

Tori took a purple and red stained glass flower from the display and held it up to the light. "Having partners is more difficult than I thought it might be."

"Have you settled on this stained glass piece? Or do you want to look around some more?"

Tori had barely glanced at the store. "I like this one, but I probably should keep looking. I forgot how much stuff you have here."

"I probably order too much. But I love it, and I can't help myself." Bea grinned as she reached for the stained glass. "I'll put this next to the register for you, just in case."

Tori followed her to the cash register and looked down at the display case. "Ordering has got to be easier than making your own inventory. And yet I miss my store so much more than I thought I would. I'm afraid I've made an awful mistake."

Bea put her palm on Tori's arm. "I'm sure everything will work out. Sometimes it's time for a change. The whole reason this store exists is because I had to leave something I loved. But it led to something new that I love too."

Tori wanted to give her a hug. "I think that's the nicest thing anyone has said to me in a year."

"If that's true, I think you were right and you've been working too hard."

~

Kat started awake at the sound of the front door closing. How could she possibly be sleeping again? It was like she had narcolepsy. Sleeping all the time certainly wasn't doing much for her writing. Although she'd received a grudging "health extension" on the latest article she was supposed to be writing, the piece was going nowhere fast.

Ginny ran into the living room and put her paws up on the sofa. Kat ruffled her ears. "I know you want up, but you're a chubby little thing and I'm not allowed to lift you."

Joel walked to the sofa and lifted Ginny up next to Kat. "Your new best friend has arrived. Mia will be in later to collect her for grooming."

"Mia is going to have a long last day."

"I know. And she told me not to put Ginny into a cage in the kennel under any circumstance. I guess her barking is bad."

Kat nodded emphatically. "You have no idea. I can't believe such awful woofy screechy sounds can come out of such a small body. It's horrible. I always wondered what a banshee is and why they scream. Now I know what they sound like."

"I think technically banshees are mythical. But apparently Mia feels the same way. I thought she might blow a gasket."

"I think she's worried about seeing her father too. They have a complicated relationship."

Joel walked to the dining room table and picked up a stack of letters. "Speaking of which, here's the mail. You were asleep when I brought it inside. I think you got a Halloween card from your mother."

"Mom does like greeting cards." Kat glanced at it and set it aside. "For her, cards are a better option than speaking to me in person."

"Better for you too." Joel sat on the couch, moving Ginny and Kat's afghan aside. "Tori is wound a little tight, isn't she?"

"She's starting a new business and I think she's working a lot. She reminds me a little of Becca when I first met her."

"At least we're not having a blizzard."

"Well not yet anyway. Maybe Tori will meet a sexy forester." Kat grinned. "Although to hear Tori tell it, all she's meeting at the Haunted Barn are obnoxious nine-year-olds and zombies. She did say she had dinner with Robin Hood though."

"Well, he lives in a forest, so that's close. I have dogs to walk, so I need to tear Linus away from you."

The huge hairy dog at Kat's feet looked up at the sound of his name. Kat stroked his head. "Sorry, Big Guy. You have to go walk Tessa."

Linus was so large and well-behaved that on walks, he was tasked with being the "boat anchor" for Tessa, the golden retriever. He was leashed to the overly exuberant dog to keep her from disappearing into the forest. Linus patiently kept the rambunctious animal in line, which was good because Tessa had the attention span of a gnat.

Joel stood up and Linus rose to his feet. After enjoying a deep stretch, the large dog ambled toward the front door. Joel leaned over and gave Kat a kiss. "The good news is that Linus is tiring out Tessa even more than usual because he wants to get back here so much. He's really making her run."

"Adjusting to my incapacitation is hard on everybody."

"We're coping. Your job is to heal. See you later."

Joel and Linus left the house, and Ginny snuggled up closer to Kat, who tucked the edge of the afghan around the dog's feet. "You really *are* spoiled, aren't you?"

Ginny wagged a few times before settling into serious napping. Kat returned to her novel, which wasn't particularly interesting. Joel had brought her computer upstairs and she should go over to the dining room table and work, but she couldn't face it. The yellow legal pad next to her was for jotting down ideas, but at this point, it only sported a doodle that looked like a squiggly vine crawling up the side of a duck-billed platypus.

Kat was tired of being tired. The last time she'd felt incapable of moving like this was during her freshman year of college when what she'd thought was the flu turned out to be a raging case of mononucleosis. Sleeping through orientation and classes wasn't the best way to meet new people. After making no friends, getting mediocre grades, and having a number of viciously memorable arguments with her parents, she'd dropped out. Now she was trapped upstairs in her own home because there was only one bathroom, and it was on this floor. Although she'd never dreamed it could happen, she actually missed her messy office downstairs.

At least she had Ginny to keep her company, particularly when Linus was out on the walks being Tessa's boat anchor. She leaned back on the pillow and closed her eyes. Being tired all the time was tedious.

At the sound of the door opening and the thundering of paws, she lifted her head. How long had she been asleep? Linus poked her with his big muzzle and she squeaked in pain. "Easy with the nose, Big Guy."

Joel sat on the edge of the sofa next to Kat and ruffled Ginny's ears. "Try to look casual. I'm here to take your shedding cohort to her grooming session."

Kat smiled. "Too bad. She used to like you."

"She still likes me. Did you open the mail? If you're done with it, I can take it downstairs."

Kat grabbed the pile and ripped open the orange envelope from her mother. "Happy Halloween. Do you have any plans for little trick-or-treaters soon?"

Joel raised a single eyebrow. "Does that mean what I think it means?"

"The last time I talked to her she started hinting at grandchildren."

"I thought she was still hinting at divorce. She hates me."

Kat shook her head. "I think she's worried my sister is going to date married men forever, so you're looking better all the time."

"You're going to have to tell her what happened."

"No way."

"Why not? She's your mother."

"My mother does not use words like *uterus*."

"How about *hysterectomy*?"

"Nope." Kat waved her hands over her midsection. "This is not an area of the female body she's willing to discuss. And if I mention the good news like 'Hey, I got to keep my ovaries, so no early menopause' she'll tell me not to be crude."

"You're exaggerating."

"Or worse, she'll say that God is punishing us for not getting married at her church. As if God somehow told my uterus to self-destruct."

Joel frowned and took the rest of the mail from her. He riffled the envelopes. "Bill, bill, bill, another card. Halloween must be big this year."

"It's from Sara and Zack." Kat took it from him and opened it. She scanned the announcement and a new ache settled in her gut. "They're having a baby. Sara must be thrilled. She's wanted kids forever."

Joel leaned to put his arm around her. "Are you okay?"

"I will be, but I think I need to feel sorry for myself for a while." Kat rested her cheek on his chest. "Thanks for doing so much work around here. I feel completely useless."

"I'm so relieved to have dumped that programming project, I don't mind."

"How's the new accounting thing?"

"Interesting. It's nice that they don't care when I work. I can disappear all day and send them emails at ten at night and no one cares. It was nice of Becca to recommend me."

"Well, she thinks you walk on water since you set up her new appraisal program."

"That was no big deal."

"It doesn't hurt that you're also the hero with the house that kept her from freezing to death."

He laughed. "I suppose so. The guy who hired me is looking for a cabin and talked to Becca. I guess he met Larry too."

"Larry. Yet another person who has another computer you fixed. You're like the geek magician fixing computers wherever you go."

"Not quite."

"But you do have many skills. Even dead accounting."

"*Forensic* accounting."

Kat waved dismissively. "Yeah, whatever. It's all a bunch of numbers and spreadsheets to me."

Chapter 4

Zorro & Black Sheep

After spending the afternoon packing her candy into boxes, Tori loaded the boxes into her car for the journey to the Haunted Barn. Hope was bringing the display items, so they could set up again for their second weekend of fun with zombies.

While Tori was packing, storm clouds rolled in and the glorious sunny weather of the morning became a distant memory. Fat water droplets splashed on Tori's windshield as she drove southward. The sky was a uniform gray, hovering like a huge blanket over the highway.

The driving rain had turned the field being used as a parking area into a slurpy mud bog and Tori ground the car into a spot as close to the barn as possible.

She stepped out of the car and her boot squelched into the mud. Yuck. Because of the weather, she wasn't wearing her costume, so she would have to find a place to change again. But first she had to make several trips through the rain with her banker's boxes and her costume.

As if the rain knew she had to make multiple trips, it increased in intensity on each journey she made back and forth to the car. By the time all the candy was safely inside, Tori was drenched. And naturally Hope hadn't arrived with the display stuff yet, so all Tori could do is sit on her cold metal folding chair staring at her blank table and shivering.

A masked man with a long flowing black cape walked up to her. "You look cold. May I offer you my cloak?" Tori looked up in surprise. He had a rich Spanish accent that was like a cross between Antonio Banderas and Desi Arnaz. Given that those two actors were from different parts of the world, clearly Zorro was faking it. But it was nonetheless still kind of sexy.

She unwrapped her arms from her midsection and stood up. "That's kind of you, but I need to change into my costume. Could you help me?"

He raised his eyebrows and shook his head slightly.

"Don't look at me like that. Last weekend, I had the same problem. There's no place to change here. A zombie held up a sheet for me to change behind. Could you hold up your cape?"

"Sí."

Tori grabbed her garment bag and released the obnoxious hoop petticoats from their confinement. "This will only take a minute. Turn around and hold the cape out. Spread it out as wide as you can."

Zorro followed the instructions and gallantly refrained from peeking when Tori stripped off her soaked clothes. Goosebumps arose the moment the cold, damp air slapped her bare skin. She dragged the annoying pink dress on, jerked the sleeves up over her shoulders, and breathed a sigh of relief. The dress might be ugly, but at least it was warm and dry. She tapped Zorro's shoulder. "Okay, I'm done."

He turned around and smiled. "I'm pleased to see you aren't shivering anymore."

"Thank you for your help. My partner is supposed to be here helping me set up." Tori looked at her watch. "I have no idea where she is. She has all the decorations and displays for holding the chocolates. It's getting dark and the kids are going to be swarming in here soon. If she ditches me tonight, I'm going to kill her."

"Is there something I can do to help?" he asked with a slight bow and flourish of his cape.

Tori glanced at him. Why was she dumping her problems on this guy? "I'm sorry to vent. Unless you want to foist candy on kids, there's not much you can do."

"I don't mind handing it out. Candy is a large part of the lure of Halloween."

"If you don't mind, that would be great." Tori gestured toward a box. "Feel free to grab a box and help yourself. We're also trying to get feedback from the kids to find out if they like them."

Zorro took the lid off a box and pulled out one of the plastic containers stacked within. "They are colorful animals, sí?"

"Sí. Our working name is Choco-critters. Reviews are mixed."

He sat in a folding chair and unwrapped a pink chicken. "Mmm, berry."

A wail came from the direction of the barn entrance and a small child raced past the table, screaming at the top of his lungs.

Tori made a wry face. "Guess it's time to get started. I've noticed this event seems to involve a lot of crying."

"There is an age limit for the Haunted Barn, and no one under eight years old is supposed to be allowed inside, but every year, it seems you get a few tiny whiners."

"I think there are more than a few this year." Tori opened three more plastic containers, which looked lonely and pathetic on the beat-up old folding table.

A kid dressed as a pirate walked up to them and pointed at the chocolates. "What are these supposed to be?"

"Chocolate animals," Zorro replied as he handed the pirate a piece wrapped in bright green foil. "Try one and tell us what you think."

"Is it a Snickers?"

"No," Tori said. "It doesn't have peanuts or caramel. It's chocolate with flavorings."

"Forget that. I want a Snickers." He tossed the candy at Zorro, who snatched it from the air before it landed on the floor. "I'm outta here."

Zorro looked at Tori. "I see what you mean about the reviews."

"This is a tough crowd."

Hope rushed up to the table carrying huge tote bags filled with decorations. "I'm so sorry I'm late. There was an accident on the highway and traffic had to be diverted down a dirt road that went off into the middle of nowhere. It took forever."

Tori took the bags and started moving the candy containers off the table so they could set up the displays. "Fortunately, Zorro was here to help me."

Hope looked up from her bag. "Who is Zorro?"

Tori looked around. "The guy dressed as Zorro. He was helping me hand out candy."

"Is this like the imaginary Robin Hood that you said wasn't Chip?"

"He *wasn't* Chip!" Tori took the tablecloth and flapped it over the folding table, letting it flutter down to cover the battered old particle board.

Hope slapped cute baskets and Halloween decorations onto the table. "You just didn't like him."

"No, I didn't. And you knew that, but ditched me anyway."

Hope and Tori assembled the display in awkward, irritated silence. By the time they were finished, Tori had fumed long enough to be utterly disgusted with her friend. "You ditched me for hours in the corn maze last time, so it's my turn to explore. You stay here and find out if kids hate this stuff, okay?"

Hope scowled, shoved her red cloak aside, and sat in one of the chairs. "Fine."

Tori stalked off. She was tired of Hope's excuses and attitude toward her. Sure, they'd been friends since elementary school, but lately Hope was treating her like the hired help. Although Hope and Morgan were investing money in the business, Tori was doing a lot of work too. She was supposed to be a partner, and it wasn't fair to treat her like a peon.

She took a few deep breaths, trying to calm down. Talking to Zorro had been a lot more pleasant than her dealings with Hope lately. Maybe she could find him again. She didn't even get a chance to thank him for helping her give out candy.

Twilight had given way to night, and as all the weird lighting came on and the fake fog rolled in, Tori discovered that finding a guy dressed entirely in black was a little more challenging than she'd anticipated. And once again she was getting turned around. The barn was gigantic and more kids were flowing in, screaming every time a scare actor made a move. The noise was giving Tori a headache, so she turned around and headed for the door to get some air.

The rain had let up, so she walked outside and followed signs toward the corn maze. Although the ground was still squishy, the air was fresh and clean-smelling. The clouds were moving quickly and when the moon came out from behind a cloud, it illuminated the people walking around the area. In the distance, the silhouette of Zorro talking to Robin Hood caught Tori's eye.

Robin gave Zorro a scornful wave of his hand and stomped away from the conversation. Zorro took off his huge black hat and ran his fingers through his dark hair.

As Tori approached, he put his hat back on and smiled at her. She returned the smile, glad to have found a friendly face amid the monster-infused mayhem. "You disappeared before I could thank you for your help."

"I didn't do anything more than hand out candy." He placed his hand on his chest. "It was my pleasure to assist a senorita in need."

"Was that Chip you were talking to?"

"Wood, corn, poker, or cow?"

Tori laughed. "Cow?"

"Don't you know what a cow chip is?" He gestured toward the vast fields. "Dried cow excrement."

"I don't think he'd appreciate being described that way."

"He never does."

Tori sat on a bale of hay. "So how do you know Chip?"

"I've known him my entire life."

"Are you friends?"

Zorro dropped the Spanish accent and said in a wry tone. "Not exactly. He's my brother."

"I could tell that accent was fake."

"Yeah, I know. It's not one of my better efforts. The British one was better."

Tori pointed at him. "Ah-ha! *You're* Robin Hood. I knew it wasn't Chip."

"Last weekend, I was irritated to find that he was wearing the same costume I was. It was my fault for telling him, I guess." He held up a corner of the black cloak. "I moved on to Zorro, which wasn't all bad. The sword that comes with this costume is impressive, even if it's made of plastic."

"I practically told you my life story and I don't even know your name."

He took her hand, kissed it, and in the British accent said, "Dale Holbrook, at your service m'lady."

"Pleased to make your acquaintance, kind sir. My name is Victoria Merrill, but you can call me Tori."

"I like that better than Little Bo Peep."

"Me too." Tori looked down at her hand in her lap, which he was still holding. "So if you're Chip's brother, you're here because your family is sponsoring this whole thing, right?"

"The money goes to the fund my family set up to benefit local children's charities."

"So you have to deal with this every year?"

"I don't always attend." He rubbed at the side of his black mask. "But I have been to quite a few. You're right that there seems to be more screaming and crying this year. But the people who organize this event love Halloween and their enthusiasm is contagious. Some of the scare actors have been doing this for a decade or more."

"I guess I'm not a big fan of Halloween. I don't like being scared or wearing costumes."

"Pretending to be someone else for a while can be fun."

"Is that why you're wearing a mask?"

He leaned closer to her ear. "Let me clue you in on a little secret. As a vendor, you're supposed to be wearing one too."

"I know. I think I lost it the first night when I was trying to find a place to change. It was an awful pink thing." She tugged at a dark brown tendril of hair that had fallen out of her topknot bun and into her face. "Today, I was in a rush and I left the bonnet at home."

"If it helps, I think your real hair is prettier than the plastic blonde curls."

"That's nice of you to say." Tori pushed her hair behind her ear and discovered a piece of hay, which she removed. Was he actually flirting with her? "Thanks to the rain, it's a mess."

"Heavens to Murgatroyd."

Tori twirled the stalk of hay in her fingertips. "You sound exactly like the cartoon character. I don't even remember what his name was."

"Snagglepuss. He was pink and exited stage left a lot."

"Yes! You really know your cartoons."

He leaned over, plucked another piece of hay from her hair, and handed it to her. "When I was growing up, I spent a lot of time watching TV and imitating cartoon characters."

"I would have thought you'd have been playing with all those toys your family makes. Sleds in the winter, wagons, swing sets, tricycles, puzzles, and who knows what else."

"I did have good toys. But I had a pretty bad wipeout while sledding, so I was a little less into snow-related activities after that happened."

Tori grimaced. "Ouch. I suppose so."

"While I recovered, I spent a lot of time in my room drawing and watching TV. In my family, being the first-born son is a big deal. As the second son, I think I was looking for a way to be noticed. I started doing imitations of Harvey the Penguin and it snowballed from there, so to speak."

Tori laughed. "Very punny, but now I have to hear you say something as Harvey."

"How fast can you go on an Avalanche Snow Coaster? Thiiiis fast!"

"That's amazing. You sound exactly like the commercial."

"It *is* the commercial."

Tori shoved at his shoulder. "Why didn't you say that Harvey is you before?"

"You didn't ask." He put his hand to his chest. "Now you know about my small contribution to the family business."

"I don't know how small it is. Everyone knows Harvey. Maybe our company needs a mascot like that. Kid's cereal is a bunch of nasty corn syrup and food dye, but having Tony the Tiger, Toucan Sam, or the Rice Krispies elves on the box is what sells it."

"That may be true, but you need to start with a product kids don't throw at you."

Tori turned to look at him. "Thank you! You're the first person who has listened to me."

"You said you're testing. What if you test something else?"

"I've been thinking the same thing, but I'm worried my partners won't agree. They're convinced this idea is the *one*. They keep saying that all businesses have risks and I shouldn't worry. But if we go into manufacturing with a product that kids don't like, I'm doomed."

"Doomed sounds pretty tragic. You'll think of something. You're smarter than the average bear."

"Thanks Yogi. But I'm not a millionaire like you are. This will take every last cent of my savings and it may not work. And now I'm fighting with Hope—someone I've been friends with forever."

"First, I'm not a millionaire. Second, you do know that business partnerships often destroy friendships, don't you?"

"According to who?"

"Business books." He picked a piece of hay from her skirt and threw it on the ground. "Partnerships are the most likely type of business entity to fall apart. It's often better to set up as a sole proprietor or corporation."

"I *was* a sole proprietor, and it was too hard doing everything myself."

"Corporations have drawbacks too, but they offer various protections."

Tori gave him an appraising look. "Now that I've met Chip, I'm guessing that in addition to being Harvey, you're the business genius behind the company."

"Nope. That's my father. I have almost nothing to do with the company operations at all."

"Then how do you know all this? And why are you here?"

He narrowed his eyes. "You're starting to shiver. Maybe we should go back inside."

Tori glanced around. They'd been talking for ages. Hope was going to be incredibly pissed off at her disappearance. "You're right. I should be handing out candy to my unappreciative audience."

They were still holding hands and Dale pulled her up from the bale of hay. "Allow me to escort you through the Crypt of Demons and the Demented Circus."

"Oooh, my hero."

"There's no need to fear, Underdog is here."

Tori burst out laughing because he sounded exactly like the cartoon. "You really need to stop doing that."

"Why? You have a beautiful laugh. And I'm getting the impression you don't laugh often enough."

Taken aback by the comment, Tori wasn't sure what to say in response. He was probably right. What did that say about her? "I suppose I have a lot on my mind."

He gave her hand a friendly squeeze. "That's no reason not to laugh. The next time a kid throws candy at you, throw it back."

"I can't do that! It would be rude."

"Maybe so. But it might be fun to see what happens."

Tori pursed her lips. "You're kind of an odd duck, aren't you?"

"Disss…spicable."

"You do a great Daffy Duck impression."

"Not compared to Mel Blanc, but he had a lot more practice."

"Who's Mel...whatever you said."

"He was the voice of Daffy Duck, Tweety Bird, Bugs Bunny, Sylvester, Porky Pig, Sylvester, Foghorn Leghorn, and other Loony Tunes and Merrie Melodies cartoon characters. In other words, my childhood hero. Who was yours?"

"I didn't have one. A chef maybe? Julia Child?"

He said in a high-pitched French accent, "Ah, food is love! *Bon appétit.*"

Tori giggled. "Okay, now you're just messing with me."

"Maybe a little. You need to lighten up. The Haunted Barn is supposed to be fun."

"Sure. *Fun.*"

~

Dale escorted Tori through the never-ending parade of screaming zombies and howling children back to her Candy Land stand. She introduced him to Hope, who looked more than a little frazzled, but was curtly polite. After a courtly bow to the two women, Dale vanished into the fog.

The rest of the evening was strained, but Tori managed to refrain from throwing chocolate at children or Hope. Once again, she was completely exhausted by the end of the evening. Who would have thought giving away chocolate could be so taxing?

The next morning she slept late. While puttering around the kitchen, she reflected on the conversation she'd had with Dale the night before. Maybe they did need to consider different candy ideas. She grabbed four of her many cookbooks off the shelf and sat at the table with her coffee.

As she flipped through pages, she took a few notes. Tonight, maybe she'd broach the idea of testing other options with Hope. It couldn't hurt to talk about it. They still had two more weekends of the Haunted Barn to get through, after all.

That evening at the Candy Land Stand before Tori could say anything about testing, Hope announced that she'd talked to Morgan the night before, and he wanted her to find more investors. So she was going to talk to other vendors to see if she could rustle up interest. Tori handed her a small basket of candy and survey forms. "Please ask them to taste it first."

Hope disappeared from view and Tori sat at the table. A little girl in a princess costume walked up to the table, took a piece of candy, and ran away before Tori could say anything. Oh well.

She got up to rearrange the baskets so that grabbing and running would be more difficult. A dark form emerged from the fog and she smiled at Dale, glad to see someone above voting age.

With a flourish of his cape, he took a chocolate and unwrapped it. "What's up, Doc?"

"So far, nothing but a nefarious princess and a wascally wabbit dressed like Zorro."

He chuckled and walked around the table to take a chair. "Looks like you've been ditched by your partner again."

"The other partners in this enterprise have decided they need more investors. Hope is off on a money mission."

"Money is good, but it doesn't fix everything."

Tori returned to her seat and absently handed a fistful of candy to a small dragon wearing oversized green, scaly shoes. He clumped away after she wished him a happy Halloween.

She turned to Dale. "I was thinking about what you said as far as trying other ideas."

"Did you come up with anything?"

"Not yet. I spent some time looking at cookbooks this morning. I planned to talk to Hope about it, but she ran off. I might do some experiments this week." She handed out some more candy to a kid who might have been dressed as a chicken. Or a pigeon. Hard to say. "I'm sick of thinking about my business. Tell me more about Holbrook and life in the toy biz."

"I'm not involved in the toy business, but what do you want to know?"

Tori gazed into the fog. "I'm not sure. How did the company start? What was it like growing up the heir to a toy company? It sounds like every kid's dream."

"I'm not the heir of anything. Assuming he decides to become a responsible adult and run the company, Chip would be the heir, not me. As for how the company started, my grandfather grew up in Iowa and that's where he started the company. He and my grandmother made the early sleds, which became popular in the state. They had a tiny factory, but my grandfather actually hated Iowa, so as soon as they could afford it, he moved Holbrook to the East Coast."

"How did it end up here?"

"My father expanded the company. When he married my mother, he added another manufacturing facility in Gleasonville. The official reason was to be close to a ski resort for testing and to have manufacturing closer to both coasts. But the truth is my mother grew up in the area and she wanted to be near her family."

"Is your mom involved in the business?"

"She was involved in marketing for a while, but got out of it."

"How come you're not involved?"

"Long story." He unwrapped a piece of candy. "Every family has a black sheep. That would be me."

"You don't seem like a black sheep. Chip made it sound like he was the black sheep after his big engagement fiasco."

"In my case, it's more that my father and I don't get along. We had a big fight when I was younger, and we only recently started talking again."

Tori handed out more candy to kids. "What was the fight about?"

"You're not a reporter, are you?"

"Of course not. You know all about my current business, such as it is."

"Then why are you asking all these questions?"

"You're easy to talk to and willing to sit here and watch me hand out candy, which has to be boring."

"I'm not bored. See that kid over there? I think he's dressed as a garden gnome. People-watching is interesting. You didn't answer the question."

"Okay, how about I'm talking to you because my best friend is mad at me? Or because all these kids just want to take candy and flee. Or maybe because I've learned that zombies aren't good conversationalists."

He laughed. "I guess I can't argue with that. Uuunnnnnhhhh, brains. Want to eat more brains."

"See what I mean? Disgusting *and* deadly dull. Ick."

They both looked up at Robin Hood, who leaned over the table, grabbed a chocolate, and unwrapped it. "Hi Tori. I, um, sorry I didn't call this week. I got super busy."

Tori offered a polite smile. She'd completely forgotten he'd said he would call. "That's okay. I was busy all week making candy."

Dale leaned over and in a Sylvester voice whispered, "Suffering succotash. What a toad."

Tori burst out in a jolt of laughter. "I'm, uh, I'm sorry. Please have some more candy, Chip. I know you like these."

He grabbed a fistful and pocketed them. "Don't mind if I do. Hey Bugs, I need to talk to you."

"All right, Chipmunk." He gestured toward the door. "I'll meet you at the barn office in a few minutes."

Chip left and Tori attempted to stifle a giggle. "Oh my God, you guys are Chip 'n' Dale. How did I not think of that before?"

"Well, you figured it out about fifteen years before Chip did. He hated the name Phillip and my father is Phil. So I suggested Chip. Unfortunately for both of us, it stuck." He grinned. "I told you I watched too many cartoons."

"I think I'm getting a feel for the black sheep part of your personality. If you want to set up a brothers strip tease show, you're all set. Chip 'n Dale as the Chippendales."

"This probably won't come as a surprise, but a number of writers at tabloid magazines came up with that idea long before you did."

"Oh yeah, Chip's a star of supermarket magazines, isn't he?"

"His fiancée, Sienna Martell, was the bigger star. I think he enjoyed riding her coattails until he didn't."

"I've never heard of her. Am I supposed to know who she is?"

"She's a wannabe actress and singer, but odds are you've never seen a single one of her movies or TV shows. She's definitely D-list. Or lower. Maybe Z. The thing that's more interesting to the tabloids is that she's completely loaded because her family owns the Martell toy company."

Tori frowned. "I've heard of the company, but not Sienna. I guess I'm not reading enough gossip rags while I'm standing in line at the grocery store."

"Apparently, not."

~

Dale took another piece of chocolate from a basket and unwrapped it. "These things are annoyingly addictive. I don't understand why the elementary school set isn't gobbling them up."

"They aren't cool." Tori shook her head. "I'm not sure what makes chocolate cool, but whatever it is, these don't have that elusive elixir."

"How come was Chip supposed to call you?"

"Hope invited him to my house for dinner last week."

"Is he one of her targets to become an investor?"

"Yes, but it didn't work out. He didn't seem to know what she was talking about. And then she ditched me." Tori crossed her hands and set them in her lap demurely. "Things went downhill from there."

"He can be kind of a louse, but he didn't..."

"No." Tori held out a basket to a short kid dressed as a fire hydrant. Was he truly eight years old? Maybe he was small for his age. "The evening ended when Chip spilled espresso all over the floor."

"In addition to being a louse, he's also kind of a klutz."

"I noticed. And a slob. He tracked mud inside and it got everywhere. Even my dog was repulsed."

Dale rubbed at the side of his mask. "So I know I don't know you very well, but why does your friend keep ditching you? That doesn't seem particularly, well, friend-like."

"In this case, she thought she was setting me up. But I told her Chip was not the Robin Hood I'd met earlier."

"You mean me?"

"Well, I know it was you *now*."

Dale grinned. "So wait, let me get this straight. She thought she was setting you up with me?"

"I told her I met Robin Hood." Heat rose on her cheeks, and Tori knew they had to be traffic-light red at this point. Good thing it was so dark in here. "And I might have mentioned that it was nice of you to scrape me up off the dead zombie."

"Aww, this is getting cute."

She giggled. "Cut it out. You and Chip are about the same height and build, so it took a while before I was sure it wasn't you."

"So now that you're sure Chip and I aren't the same person, I suppose I should ask you what his intentions are? And yours."

"*Intentions*? What is this? Victorian England? I don't know what he thinks, but I have no intentions. Inviting him over to my apartment wasn't my idea, remember?"

"So then is it okay if I ask you for your phone number?"

Tori tried to repress a huge grin, so as to retain some semblance of nonchalance. Talk about not being cool. No wonder she was incapable of making cool candy. She had zero cool, but to be fair, it had been forever since anyone had expressed any interest in her or asked for her phone number, so she was out of practice. "Sure."

"Unlike my brother, I will call." He ran his index finger over his chest in an x. "Cross my heart."

"I'll probably be making candy again, so I'll be at home."

"Sounds good. I have to go see what Captain Chipmunk wants. Have a safe drive home. I'll talk to you later this week."

He disappeared into the fog and Tori shivered. She was oddly lonely all of a sudden. But feeling alone in the middle of a crowd was silly. Where was Hope? She stood and foisted a basket of chocolate toward a kid dressed as either a gerbil with an extreme case of mange or an Ewok with no fashion sense. Despite the mantle of thick fur, the kid managed to gobble down the chocolate. Tori asked, "What you think?"

Whatever the child's response might have been was muffled by the costume, so Tori gave up interrogating and sat back down.

Much later, Hope returned and plopped down next to Tori. "I've talked to everyone, and no one wants to discuss money."

"I can imagine money is a delicate subject to bring up when everyone around is screaming and crying. Sort of like having a chat during a stock-market crash."

"You're hilarious." Hope grabbed a piece of chocolate and unwrapped it. "When was the last time you went running?"

"I didn't have time last week." Tori pointed at the chocolate as Hope popped it into her mouth. "I was making those, remember?"

"You're getting that edge to your voice that means you need to slap on your running shoes. Anxiety is rolling off you in waves."

"That's because we need to talk."

"About what? We *are* talking."

"I'm serious. This candy idea isn't working. Adults like the candy, but kids don't. I'm not sure why, but I need to come up with something else that kids think is cool."

"But Choco-critters are yummy." Hope held out a chicken. "And come on, they're totally cute."

"Apparently cute doesn't sell. Cool sells."

"What's cool?"

"I have no idea. That's what we're supposed to be finding out. But extracting exactly what constitutes 'cool' from a nine-year-old is turning out to be a challenge."

Hope rested her elbows on the table. "Okay, let's think about this. What else do kids like other than chocolate?"

"If you believe the commercials, cereal and peanut butter."

"How about chocolate and peanut butter?"

Tori proffered the chocolate basket to a mini Darth Vader and turned back to Hope. "Have you ever heard of Reese's Peanut Butter Cups? I think they've got that idea pretty well covered."

"I suppose so."

After more banter that included a slew of incredibly lame ideas, they ran out of steam and focused on unloading the last of the candy on disinterested children.

As they were packing up, Tori said, "I'm going to work on some new candy ideas this week. If you think of anything, let me know, okay?"

Hope assured her that if lightning struck and she had an epiphany for the coolest candy ever, she'd call. By the time they finished packing, Tori was concocting a wide range of doomsday scenarios in her mind, which all came back to the same fact. She never should have given up her store.

Bright and early Sunday morning, she drove to the kennel to retrieve Ginny. She rang the buzzer and Joel emerged from the house carrying the dog. Tori couldn't help but smile at the sight. Clearly, Ginny had these folks wrapped around her furry little paw.

Joel put Ginny on the ground so she could walk the last three steps and say hello to Tori. She wagged and wiggled her round body in unadulterated glee.

Tori crouched down. "Don't you look pretty! All fluffy and clean."

"Mia said she was good about being groomed." Joel said as he handed Tori the bill. "But you probably know she doesn't like being alone."

"No, she doesn't." Tori pulled her checkbook from the dark recesses of her purse. "She got a little too used to going to work with me. I guess she's a little spoiled."

"Keeping her in the kennels is too disruptive for the other dogs."

"I know she can be a little loud." Tori braced herself for the inevitable statement that they never wanted to see Ginny again. It certainly wouldn't be the first time the dog had been banished from a canine-related business because of her behavior. "I'm sorry."

"We've been keeping her in the house, but we're going to have to charge extra from now on."

Tori exhaled a sign of relief. "Do you mean she can come back? Really? Are you sure?"

"She's scheduled for two more weekends. I'm just letting you know that it will cost more because having her inside creates extra work for us."

"Oh thank goodness. The extra charge is fine. I don't mind. It's okay. I'm so happy she can stay."

Joel pointed at Ginny, who was looking up at them with a smug expression on her furry brown face. "I'm afraid she's not getting much exercise though. She has declined to attend the afternoon walks."

"She hates exercise. I tried taking her running with me once. It was the first and last time."

"That's easy to imagine. We'll see you on Friday."

~

When Joel walked through the front door, Kat and her friend Maria abruptly stopped talking to wait for the inevitable barking to subside. Kat was curled up in her typical spot at the end of the sofa, with her legs snuggled under the afghan that had been her constant companion since she'd come home from the hospital.

Maria stretched her arms above her head and stood up. "It's been good to hang out, but I'm going to have to get going, girlfriend. Tomorrow is Monday, and unlike you, I've gotta get ready to return to the working world."

"Hey, I've been working. Sort of. A little." Kat glanced at the pile of books topped by a yellow legal pad with the feeble ideas for the article that was going nowhere.

"I'm also a little worried my feline roommates might have trashed my apartment by now. If Scarlett has taken out her bad attitude on my curtains again, I'm gonna have to get drapes made of chain mail or something."

"I thought since you got her a playmate, she wasn't climbing the curtains anymore."

"Adding another cat made it a contest, and Quincy is hard core." Maria put her hand on her hip. "Remember gym class when you had competitions to see who could climb those stupid ropes to the ceiling fastest? It's like that. Except with claws."

Joel walked to the sofa and handed Tori's check to Kat along with the receipt. "Your furry pal is on her way home, and I broke the money news to Tori."

"I need a vacation." Maria pointed at him. "I wish I had someone to do my job for me for a while. I don't suppose you'd like to work in an ad agency when you're done here."

"Nope."

Kat glanced down at the papers. "Ditching work is even better when it means I can avoid talking to people about money. I'm too wimpy."

"Tori was fine with it," Joel said. "I'm going downstairs to do some work before the next walk. Let me know if you need anything."

As Joel thumped down the stairs to his office, Maria sank back down on the sofa next to Kat. "You know, I can be critical, but the engineer is being awfully nice about your incapacitation. I mean, let's face it, we've both seen men complain like babies about getting stuck with extra work."

"I think that applies to all genders." Kat rearranged her afghan over her knees. "And it's not like he had a lot of choice. He's stuck with me. This falls into the worse and sickness part of the marriage vows."

"Well, you could have told all those people they have to take their dogs somewhere else."

"I offered, but he said we didn't need to."

With a sigh, Maria leaned her head back so her huge brunette curls splayed against the back of the old sofa. "I guess I can't imagine the whole concept of being with someone forever and putting up with all the better or worse and sickness. And after what happened to you, I'm wondering if I'll ever have kids myself. The biological clock is ticking and unless something drastic happens, time's gonna run out on me."

"I'm definitely going to break the family tradition of unplanned pregnancies. I thought you didn't want kids."

Maria sat up and looked at Kat. "I don't know. Every time I see parents in Kmart dealing with their screaming children, I say a silent thank you to the science geeks who invented birth-control pills. So normally, I'd say *no thanks* to offspring."

"But now?" Kat pulled the afghan up over her stomach. It wasn't like Maria to be this serious. Something was definitely bothering her.

"I don't know. You're not having kittens. And now Sara and Zack *are* having a kid, even though he still is a kid. Or acts like one anyhow. It's a lot to think about. Change is in the air."

"I suppose that's true."

Maria flopped back again. "I don't know. I'm feeling off my game. Lonely maybe. Seeing you in the hospital, well, it freaked me out. I mean, you could have died."

"Well, not exactly…"

"If you'd been alone, maybe you could have. And I realized, no one would drive me to the hospital like the engineer did." She looked at Kat. "And he yelled at people for you and sat by your bed. Who would do that for me?"

"I would."

Maria put her hand on Kat's knee. "I know you would, girlfriend. But you wouldn't be there. You'd be here."

"Probably. I don't get out much." Kat pulled the pencil and legal pad from the stack. "The fact that I'm a reclusive writer who lives miles from town is an issue."

"You even boarded my cat. And yet there are still no viable men on my dating horizon." Maria looked down at her nails. "Maybe I should get a dog and solve the problem once and for all."

"Oh please, not that again. People meet people every single day. You just need to run across someone who can see who you really are."

Maria raised her eyebrows. "What's that supposed to mean?"

"Sometimes you come on a little strong."

"I beg your pardon?"

Kat twirled the pencil in her fingers. "It's not a bad thing, but it might make it more difficult for a guy to see that you have an incredibly kind, generous heart."

"I think you're making up this unicorn dude. Because the men I've met aren't looking at my heart." Maria swirled her hand in a circular motion in front of her chest. "They might be looking in the general vicinity, but it's more external."

Kat laughed. "You know what I mean. Joel saw past the insecure weirdo that I present to the world at large. How he did that, I'm not entirely sure. But he did. For whatever reason, he understood who I am inside. And a lot of people think he's this quiet, humorless guy who's even a little intimidating. When I realized he was actually kind, smart, and funny, I melted into a big puddle of goo."

"That's for sure."

"Yeah well, I'm just saying you need to find someone who thinks you're great because you're you."

"Good luck. I've looked, and no dice. It's wearing on me." Maria tossed her curls behind her shoulder. "Lately, I've found a guy who likes Italian food more than me and a guy who thinks televised sports are more interesting than me. Seriously, how come it's so hard to get someone's attention?"

"That proves my point."

"How?"

"When you really connect with someone, you'll know." Kat put the pencil down. "Being around that person will be easy because you can be yourself. You won't have to pretend to enjoy something like watching football or eating Italian food every day when you don't."

"You're confusing me." Maria pointed at her. "Is this some type of bizarro riddle? Because you know I hate riddles."

"It's not a riddle. I'm saying that if you meet the right person, you'll want to be together all the time. That unicorn will think you're so amazing, he'll want to be around you."

"To enjoy my fabulousness, you mean?"

"Exactly."

"Well, if this unicorn exists in Alpine Grove, he's pretty well hidden. It might take a rainbow-hued sparkly miracle to find him. Right at this moment, this burg is tapped out of available men that I haven't either dated or rejected because they're disgusting."

"People move here all the time. You never know. The other day, Tori told me she had dinner with someone she met at the Haunted Barn."

"Yeah, we'll see. Maybe I should attend more social events. A barn full of ghouls doesn't sound like a great place to meet people, unless there happen to be smokin' hot farmers there too. But thanks for the consoling words, girlfriend."

"I've had a lot of time sitting here on the sofa, thinking about life, love, and procreation lately."

"Yeah, I guess you have."

Chapter 5

Tribble Trouble

At the grocery store, Tori knew she was approaching the end of what she thought of as the Ginny Window of Tolerance. Four hours was the maximum amount of time she could leave the dog in her apartment before Ginny decided she was done being alone, lost her marbles, and started barking and howling like a possessed hyena. One time when Tori's car broke down, her landlord threatened eviction after every single neighbor had complained about Ginny.

Of course, it wasn't like Tori could complain too much. Ginny liked routine almost as much as she did. Keeping things orderly with defined routines and schedules made Tori feel like she was in control of her life. She had lists detailing the lists she needed to make. Maybe it was weird that even her lists had lists, but it helped. It wasn't Ginny's fault if all this structure had rubbed off on her. Perhaps the old saw about dogs ending up like their humans was true.

At a glance at her watch, Tori shoved her cart into the checkout line. The basket was filled with every ingredient she could think of adding to candy. She'd come up with something cool to give away to hypercritical children if it killed her. The idea for the ultimate fabulous kid-approved candy was out there somewhere, and she was going to find it.

When she got back to the apartment, Ginny looked surly, but hadn't moved into full-blown anger meltdown yet. After a quick journey around the parking lot for her bathroom break, the dog retired to her dog bed. Tori examined her list of candy ideas and considered what to tackle first. She was startled from her ruminations by the sound of the phone ringing.

She grabbed the cordless phone from its cradle and a happy little shiver skittered through her when she heard, "Hi Tori, it's Dale."

Tori waved her hand at Ginny in excitement and mimed, "It's him!" as she leaped around the kitchen. Ginny stood up to see what the fuss was about, but she determined it didn't involve food, so she spun around twice and re-curled herself into a ball within her cozy bed.

Working to assume her most casual voice, Tori said, "Hi, how are you?"

"I'm good. Have you figured out the holy grail of chocolate yet?"

"Not exactly, but I went to the grocery store, and I have a lot of ideas I'm going to try out, starting today."

"That sounds promising. I was calling because I'd hoped maybe we could go out somewhere this week."

Tori beamed at Ginny. Egad. She might have an actual date! "I'm making candy, but not all day."

"Well, unfortunately, I can't. I found out I have to go to Los Angeles. I'll be back this weekend, but I'm leaving tonight, and I didn't want you to think I forgot about you."

"Oh. That's too bad. Okay."

"But I'll see you at the Barn. And I'm not doing anything right now, except packing, so tell me about your ideas."

"I was looking over my list, trying to figure out what to make first. I got bananas for chocolate banana cream treats.

A bunch of sugar and butter for toffee and brown sugar and corn syrup for caramel. And I have strawberries, almonds, marshmallows, malted-milk powder, jalapenos, and Tabasco."

"I'm not so sure about the last couple."

"I know. I was getting desperate. A kid said he was eating eyeballs. I'm not sure why or how that could be good, so I went for a few novel flavors. Maybe kids like fiery hot stuff. I won't know until I give it a try."

"That sounds scientific. And a bit like you're using trick-or-treaters as lab rats."

"I doubt they'll care. I have to do something. I'm struggling to figure out how kids think."

"When I was a little kid, I worried about ceiling fans chopping off my head and my hand getting cut off by automatic car windows."

"That's gross." Tori poured the bag of sugar into a ceramic canister. "I think you had an overactive imagination."

"So you're saying when you were little, you weren't afraid of anything at all?"

"Well, when I went to the city once, I was worried about things coming out from manhole covers. That was probably from an urban legend or story I heard about alligators hiding in sewers."

"You never worried about getting sucked into an escalator? Or the things that live in floor vents?"

Tori put the strawberries into a pretty sky-blue ceramic bowl on the counter. "Nothing lives in floor vents."

"Are you sure? Do you really know what's down there?"

Tori glanced down at the floor. "I rent this place. How should I know?"

"Every kid is scared of something. You expect me to believe that you weren't?"

"Okay, I had issues with seaweed. I worried that it would act like tentacles that could yank me down and drown me." She poured the bag of almonds into a glass Mason jar and put it into the pantry next to the walnuts. "I still don't like it much."

"So you have no problem with spiders?"

"Nobody likes spiders."

"I used to dream that they'd crawl in my mouth and choke me."

"Yuck. Why are you telling me this?"

"You said you didn't know how kids think. I'm giving you insight."

Tori held up the bottle of Tabasco. It was hard to envision a nine-year-old version of herself thinking it would be yummy. Maybe he had a point. "You're telling me what kids are afraid of, not what they like or what they're thinking."

"Okay, here's a conundrum that bothered me for a long time. What happened when Pinocchio hit puberty?"

"He got older?"

"His nose grew when he lied. Other things have been known to grow when young men reach a certain age. The poor guy must have thought he told the worst whopper ever."

Tori burst out laughing. "A *whopper*?"

"Sorry. I couldn't help myself. But didn't you ever wonder?"

"Actually, no. I didn't."

"Okay, how about Wile E. Coyote? How come he never stopped shopping at Acme? Clearly their products were unreliable."

"This is you watching too many cartoons again, isn't it?"

"Probably. But they make you think. Here's another one. What's a sprocket? George Jetson worked at Spacely Sprockets. What the heck did that guy do? What was his job? All we know is that he carried a briefcase. What if he was really a spy?"

"Although that's interesting, I'm not sure what it has to do with candy."

"All I'm saying is that you might consider weird ideas. Go beyond your normal boundaries. Lots of little kids don't worry as much about what other people think as they do when they get older, so their minds are going in twelve different directions."

Tori picked up the Tabasco again. Maybe it wasn't such a bad idea after all. "That's a good point. I'm not quite sure what to do with it, but I'll think about it."

"Are you going to be around tomorrow night?"

"I think so."

"I'd rather talk to you than watch the cars go by on the freeway. Is it okay if I give you a call or send you an email? I have to work weird hours when I'm in LA."

"Sure." Tori gave him her email address with a bit of trepidation. She liked Dale, but if he made grammar or spelling mistakes, she'd think less of him. Or if he typed in all caps. Or worse, *no* caps. Only lazy people were uncouth enough to avoid using the Shift key. Although she couldn't share these thoughts out loud with anyone, she still thought them loudly. "If you have any more insights into the mind of children, please share."

"Will do. Talk to you soon."

Tori hung up the phone and grabbed Donna, the double boiler, from her cabinet and Temperance, the thermometer, from the drawer in preparation for the typical chocolate-melting routine. She went through the familiar tempering process, considering what Dale had said.

Hope often said Tori was rigid. How could someone like her come up with a fantastic, wildly creative candy idea that kids would like? She was way too boring and regimented.

She grabbed Stella, the spatula, and when she turned to check the mixture in the pot again, it was at a roiling boil. She snagged a potholder and snatched the pot off the burner. What had she done? What was *wrong* with her?

Had it been *that* long since she'd had a date? Or even been interested in someone? She hadn't messed up tempering chocolate in years. Maybe a decade. So far, it appeared the only thing that had melted smoothly was her brain.

~

By the next day, Tori had managed to create a small assortment of somewhat strange candy. Even if she managed to come up with the most delicious confection ever created, it wasn't going to make one whit of difference without a cool marketing gimmick. That was Hope's jurisdiction, but when Tori mentioned it, Hope said she needed to come up with the candy first. It was a chicken-and-egg problem. Too bad chocolate eggs had already been done to death for Easter.

Early in the morning, Tori called her bulk chocolate supplier because she'd gone through quite a bit in the tempering fiasco. He said he'd get the order processed ASAP and email her the receipt later in the day.

She flipped the power switch on her cranky desktop computer. She'd bought it for the store, and unlike a fine wine, it had not aged well. Much like a watched pot, it was better to leave the thing alone to grind through its startup sequence, rather than watch it plod through its paces like a geriatric turtle.

Tori leashed up Ginny for a visit to the great outdoors. Because the weather was getting colder, the small dog had zero interest in loitering, so it was a short excursion.

Ginny curled up in her dog bed, but Tori couldn't settle down enough to focus on cooking. Her brain was buzzing a mile a minute with all the things that needed to happen for this business to work and all the things that might go wrong. The odds of all the stars aligning perfectly was precisely zero. Worse, she had no control over any of it. Nothing she could do would force kids to like something they didn't. Although her logical mind kept saying she needed to relax and let events unfold, the rest of her body wasn't buying it. Hope was right. She needed to go for a run.

Tori went to the closet and got out her running shoes. The fact that they had a thin layer of dust on them was a sign she hadn't run in far, far too long. And that her cleaning regimen was completely out of whack. Now that she didn't have a weekly service to help, she'd somehow missed the closet. The last time she'd failed to be meticulous in dusting was when she'd moved back home to Gleasonville after leaving her position as a chef. At the time, she'd attributed the oversight to the stress of moving and finding a new company she could trust to clean her apartment. But maybe shutting down her store and being thrown into new situations had affected her more than she'd realized. It was time to get her act together, starting right now.

She sat and tied her shoes, which felt sadly unfamiliar. This run was likely to be extremely unpleasant. But it was necessary for her sanity. Running was one of the few ways she could stop the incessant chatter in her head. Only serious physical exertion forced her to completely disconnect from her thoughts. For her, spiraling predictions of impending doom couldn't coexist with bodily exhaustion.

After a few stretches, she gave Ginny a pat, grabbed her keys, and headed for the pavement. Outside, the cold air slapped her face as she took off, the wind causing her eyes to tear up. The sound of her feet hitting the asphalt turned into a rhythm coordinating with the pounding of her heart, and the wheezing of her labored breathing as she gasped for air. How had she let herself get so out of shape? This was sad.

She waved at another runner as they passed on the trail through the park. How come other runners always looked calm and collected when she was sweating like a pig and barely able to take another step? She slowed to a walk and put her hands on her hips, continuing to stroll while she waited for the stitch in her side to subside. Clearly, this would be one of those walk-run hybrid type expeditions.

Looking up at the crisp blue sky, Tori tried to remember the last time she'd gone for a walk. She used to run every day, but she'd gotten out of the habit. Except for driving to Alpine Grove and the Barn, she'd barely stepped beyond the parking lot of her building in weeks.

Walking Ginny to her favorite patch of grass didn't give Tori the opportunity to experience the seasons. Now it was fall, but she'd more or less missed out on summer entirely. She hadn't spent enough time outside to feel the breeze, smell the flowers, or listen to the birds. To be fair, 1997 had been a year full of changes, and she didn't do well with change. The year had an inauspicious beginning, which should have been a hint of things to come. After all, who got dumped on New Year's Day? That was just plain rude. Apparently, Leo's resolution had been to stop dating her, and he'd made good on it the first day. What a guy.

Dale was actually the first person she'd met in a long time who didn't seem to think she was a controlling fruitcake. It was a nice change of pace, and she found herself reflecting upon many of the things he'd said and the many voices he'd used. His ability to imitate cartoon characters cracked her up, which probably meant she was shallow or silly, but how could you *not* laugh at Daffy Duck?

It was a little odd that she had no idea what Dale actually looked like. Although she knew he was tall and had dark hair, she didn't know what color exactly. His hair might be dark brown or black and his eyes could be dark blue, brown, hazel, or something else. The lighting was so bad in the Barn, who could tell? Seeing him in daylight without a mask would be nice.

Presumably he looked something like Chip, who she had seen in the light. That was promising. And Dale was a lot nicer and more interesting. Not to mention amusing. But why was he in Los Angeles? He'd never said. But he did call when he said he would, which scored big points with her.

If he did send her an email that would be telling. Her ex, Leo had been a writer, and Tori discovered that she found literacy extremely sexy. She was secretly hoping Dale could put words together without coming across like a dolt.

She waved at another runner. The stitch in her side was gone, so she had no excuse not to resume running. As she launched forward, it didn't feel as awful. That was progress. No sprint was ever as bad as the first one. Everything would be better from here on.

By the time she finished the loop through the park, Tori could barely muster a coherent thought anymore, so the run had done its job admirably. She walked through the door to her apartment and went straight for the shower. It was apparent even now that she would be incredibly sore tomorrow.

After a restorative scrub, she gave Ginny a treat and settled into the desk chair in front of her creaky old computer. She logged into her email, which contained the receipt for the chocolate. The price had gone up since the last time she'd ordered. Perfect.

The next email was from an address she didn't recognize. Who was Taz? When she opened it, she quickly figured it out.

Hi Tory/Tori/Torrey/Torie,

Isn't it odd that I don't know how to spell your name? Maybe that's why Victorian etiquette included calling cards. That way you didn't look like a boorish oaf when you wrote a letter to someone you'd just met.

In any case, in the absence of a card or an email address that includes your first name, I'll simply avoid using your name at all.

Please don't be offended if in the course of
this email, I just say, "hey you."

    So, hey you, how is the candy business?
I continue to be intrigued by the list of
ingredients you rattled off the last time we
spoke. I'm thinking, of course, specifically
of jalapenos. In my mind, the only use for
jalapenos is as a vehicle to transport copious
quantities of cream cheese into your gullet.
I'm unclear how this cultivar of the species
Capsicum annuum could possibly augment candy
in any palatable way.

    Sadly, as I predicted, I will be working
into the wee hours of the night, so I won't be
able to listen to your melodic voice explain
the nuances of pepper pungency. However,
I'll try to call you later this week, if the
starship troopers who run the facility deign
to let me out.

Tori laughed as she shook her head. Dale had no problem
on the literacy front, but starship troopers? What the heck
was he doing there in LA?

Although she might be acting a little like a sappy,
sentimental thirteen-year-old, she was officially intrigued by
Dale and she couldn't wait to find out. Her fingers flew across
the keys as she typed her reply.

～

The next morning, Tori went for another run. As predicted,
she was sore, so it was a slow, stumbling run, but she was still
proud of herself for getting out there and making herself do
it. With all the uncertainty in her life these days, she needed
to be consistent about something.

After her shower, she turned on her computer and found no email from Dale. Ginny was looking at her expectantly and Tori crouched down to pet her fuzzy ears. "Sorry, no food and no email. We can be disappointed together. And now it's time to invent more incredibly cool and fantastic sweets for the wee zombies."

She spent the next few hours creating chocolate banana cream treats and chocolate seashells with a dash of sea salt for authenticity. When she was done, her feet hurt, and she parked herself in front of the computer, grateful for an excuse to sit down.

She checked her email and acknowledged the little thrill that shot through her at the sight of another missive from Taz.

```
Hi Tori,

    I enjoyed your extremely detailed
description explaining how malted milk balls
are created. You may think less of me,
but in the spirit of complete honesty and
transparency, I had absolutely no idea what
went into those things. I will never look at
them exactly the same way again.

    Watching cars go by on the freeway gives
a guy a lot of time to think, and even though
we may not be in the same general vicinity,
I'm enjoying this chance for us to get to know
each other.

    However, email is an imperfect medium, and
I won't be back in town until Friday, which
seems like a long time. I feel like I should
ask you out on a date because there's been
an expression of interest on both sides. So
```

it seems like the right time. And if I were
there, I would.

Since I'm not there, I'm considering
another idea. Tonight, I don't have to
work for a change, so let's go on a date.
Okay, maybe it's not exactly a date because
we're not in the same city. But there's
prearrangement if I call you at a particular
time. So perhaps we can consider it a phone
date. We can be together auditorially if not
physically.

Do you have a TV? If you do, we can watch
something together, which would be the next
best thing to going to a movie together.
Bonus: we can yell at the screen and not
offend other moviegoers.

On that pleasant note, I'll call you at 8
pm, unless you tell me not to. At least with
email, if you reject my overtures, you won't
see the despondent expression on my face.

Tori looked down at Ginny. "I'm pretty sure this is weird, but I'm going to say yes anyway. That may mean I really like this guy. Or I'm lonely. Or desperate. Or all of the above."

Ginny wagged her tail a few times to acknowledge the statement, and Tori began typing her reply. Another advantage of a phone date was that she didn't have to get dressed up or put on makeup. How often did you get the chance to go on a date wearing grungy old sweatpants?

That evening at precisely eight o'clock, the phone rang and Tori jumped to pick it up. Dale said, "Flip to channel nine. There's a *Star Trek* marathon happening tonight."

Tori grimaced as she grabbed the remote control and pressed the channel button. "Hello to you too."

"This will be great."

"Oh wow, this is the old *Star Trek* with Captain Kirk."

"I know. And it's the 'Trouble with Tribbles' episode. Mute the sound."

"What?"

"If you don't have a mute button, lower the volume as much as you can. Watching TV without the sound is a blast. You have to figure out the story through the visuals alone."

"Why would we want to do that?"

"Because it's fun to make up your own dialogue."

"Um…"

"See, right here. Chekov is talking." Dale continued in a Russian accent, "Captin, we are approaching Deep Space Station K7. Look at that mother."

Tori laughed. "What? I can't read lips, but I'm sure he didn't say that."

"We made it, Captin. Would you look at that planet! We're close enough to smell alien feet." He switched to a credible impression of William Shatner. "Chekov. You. Must. Settle. Down."

"Hey, Spock is pointing at something. What's he saying?"

"Captain, this is the location of the battle of Donatu Five. Sensors show that Sherman's Planet has fur. An excessive amount of fur. But that is not logical."

"That can't be what he says."

"Why not?" In a female voice, he continued. "Captain, I'm picking up a priority-one distress call."

"How many times have you seen this episode?"

"Maybe a couple." He went on in Kirk's voice. "We. Need. To. Save. Them."

"I think William Shatner wouldn't appreciate this."

He said in Spock's voice, "I'm going to be typecast forever. I was a respected actor once. I performed Shakespeare. Now it's star date 4523.3 and I'm dealing with little fuzzy monsters that eat and constantly reproduce. What's wrong with my life?"

Tori laughed. "Okay, I'm even more sure Leonard Nimoy wouldn't appreciate this either."

"We need to guard the quadrotriticale and make sure it gets to Sherman's Planet. Hey Uhura, check out this cute tribble."

Tori pointed at the TV "Hey, there's a Klingon battle cruiser."

"See! Now you're getting into the spirit." He said as Kirk, "Koloth. You. Suck."

"Kirk did *not* say that."

"Maybe not. But he might have thought it. Let's face it, Kirk isn't the most sensitive guy."

"I think McCoy is concerned about food here. The tribbles are eating everything."

"Dammit, Jim. I'm a doctor, not a nutritionist!"

Tori laughed. "Beam me up."

"He would never say that. Bones was not a believer in the transporter. He didn't want his molecules scattered all over space."

"I can't believe what a serious Trekkie you are."

"*Star Trek* is a cultural phenomenon, and one of the most influential science-fiction shows in the history of television."

"If you can get past the plastic rocks and cheesy acting."

"But the franchise continues, and there are conventions. *So* many conventions. The fact that you know what a transporter is shows how the show has been infused into the fabric of society. NASA even named its first space shuttle Enterprise."

"I'm sorry, but your geek side is showing."

"Spock also made being a nerd seem cool for the first time. I'd like to point out that right now he's figured out that the grain is poisoned."

"Logically, that means there must be something in the grain. But the poor little tribble died."

Dale said in the Kirk voice, "Bones. Find. Out. What. Happened. To. This. Varmint."

"Kirk would never call a tribble a varmint." She pointed at the TV. "Oooh, look at that. The little guys really don't like Klingons, do they?"

"Nope. Tribbles have good taste." He chuckled. "You actually haven't seen this episode before, have you?"

"I don't think so. I'm not sure anyone has watched as much *Star Trek* as you have."

At the end of the episode, Dale said, "So now pretend we're walking out of the movie. I'm supposed to ask you what you thought about it. So what did you think?"

"I liked it, but I'm worried about what happened to the tribbles. It's a little vague."

"The furry varmints do okay. In the animated series that followed the original show, the guy who wrote the tribble episode created a sequel where the tribbles end up becoming a pest on Klingon planets. There's also a time-travel episode on Deep Space 9 about the tribbles, but I don't want to give anything away."

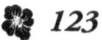

"Your knowledge of television is encyclopedic."

"So as a first date, how was it? Do you think there's potential for a second one?"

Tori grinned like a goof. "Definite potential."

"Great. How about an in-person date at the Haunted Barn on Friday?"

"I'll be there. Are you going to be Zorro, Robin Hood, or someone else?"

"Unknown. I'm sure you'll figure it out though."

Chapter 6

Pirates & Puzzles

Tori spent the rest of the week making candy. She created candy of every type she could think of and a few she probably shouldn't have thought of, but made anyway.

At this point, she'd completely lost perspective on what might taste good to the procession of costumed kiddies that passed by her table at the Haunted Barn. Over her many years as a gourmet chef and chocolatier, she'd taken pride in her refined palate. But all that gustatory acumen didn't help when your primary consumers willingly ate things like candy corn and Starburst. Anyone with any reasonable discernment knew those candies tasted like sweetened plastic.

In addition to her chocolate banana cream treats and the salted chocolate seashells, she created soft toffee caramel, strawberry-flavored almonds, jalapeno dark chocolate, Tabasco chocolate, marshmallow-coated chocolate, malted milk balls covered with dark chocolate, strawberry-toffee caramel bites, and multiple types of biscuits coated with chocolate.

In an email to Dale, she described her experience with baking peanut butter biscuits and how Ginny liked to supervise. As she had pointed out to Hope, peanut butter was one thing kids supposedly liked. And if Reese's could make a fortune off PB, why shouldn't they? And covering a crispy peanut butter biscuit with chocolate was different enough that they shouldn't get sued by the giant candy conglomerate either.

The dog had hidden in the bedroom during the jalapeno-related processes, but she returned to the kitchen for the adventures in peanut butter. Tori had to admit that the crisps did smell great while they were baking. Unfortunately, Dale pointed out in an email that lots of kids had peanut allergies. He probably had a point, so after she dipped the biscuits in chocolate, she packed them away in a box so she could make sure to include a big warning label. Causing an allergic reaction would be bad for PR.

Although she had gone running every day, by Thursday, she was feeling frantic about the potential reaction to all this bizarre candy. How could she sell something she didn't like herself? After pulling the last set of honey biscuits from the oven and setting them to cool, she picked up the phone and called Hope.

After a few pleasantries, Tori dove in. "I'm making candy that even *I* don't like. This isn't going to work."

"You're over-thinking again, aren't you?" Hope said.

"Maybe. But I've made every type of candy I can think of. What if kids hate them all?"

"That's impossible. With this many choices, statistically they'll have to like something. Probability is on your side."

"But what if they don't?" Tori touched the top of a small biscuit, which was perfectly browned on the edges. Eight minutes was the magic baking time.

"We'll think about that later. Pack everything up and we'll see how it goes this weekend."

"Hope, what if this business doesn't work? I'm getting scared. What am I going to do?"

"Calm down. Remember when you got that perm in high school?"

Tori nibbled at the edge of a warm honey crisp. "Of course I do. I looked like an electrocuted squirrel for weeks. Never again. Thanks for bringing up that special memory."

"You lost your mind about it and there wasn't a single thing you could do except wait for your hair to calm down."

"It was horrible. I still have a couple of the hats I bought to cover it up. So what?"

"There's nothing you can do about this either. You can't control everything, Tori."

Tori leaned against the counter and surveyed the cooling racks scattered across the counters. "I've given up my store. What am I going to do if this doesn't work?"

"Something else. You were a brilliant chef and there's never going to be a shortage of restaurants. You can always go back to that."

"Are you forgetting the job almost killed me?"

"Not every restaurant job has to be like that. I'm sure there are places that are better managed and less stressful."

When Tori hung up the phone, her mood was worse, not better. Even though Hope was her best friend, she was wrong. Hope had never worked in a restaurant. Tori had, and in her experience, all restaurant work was stressful. It was only a matter of degree.

The next day, she made the trek up to Alpine Grove again to drop off Ginny. Throughout the drive, she relived the conversation with Hope in her mind repeatedly, except saying all the things she *wished* she'd said. Unfortunately, Tori was a lot more eloquent in her mental retellings than she ever was in real life.

Hope had been her best friend since first grade. They'd met the first week of elementary school and had been inseparable ever since. Well almost. Hope's marriage to Morgan had put a bit of a strain on their friendship, but they always promised to remain loyal to each other no matter what. Various men had come and gone in their lives, but their friendship remained constant.

They'd survived Hope's first marriage and the various disastrous relationships Tori had endured, such as her ill-fated romance with Augustin. He'd been a fantastic chef, but a rotten boyfriend. The only thing she missed were the glorious meals Augie had created. It was the one time in her life someone had been willing to cook for her. Of course, she'd been compelled to assist in the process and offer suggestions, which weren't necessarily well received by Augie. Fighting about food was not *très bien*. Oh well. *C'est la vie.*

When Tori arrived at the kennels, it was oddly quiet. She got out of the car and was startled when Joel emerged from the door of the kennel building.

He smiled, "Right on time. How is our favorite house guest?"

Tori went to get Ginny from the car. "She's happy to be back. I think she knows when we're getting close. She stands in the back seat and tries to look out the window."

Once Tori put her on the ground, Ginny ran to Joel, who crouched down and rubbed her ears. "Hi there." He took the dog in his arms and turned to Tori. "So you're picking her up on Sunday morning, right?"

"Yes. I'll be so happy when this event is over. I can't believe they run it every weekend for the whole month."

"I've never been, but I guess it's a big deal."

"It is. There are so many people, and it's exhausting."

"People like Halloween." Joel stroked the fur on Ginny's head slowly, and she leaned back onto his chest, obviously enjoying the attention. "I've heard there was a Halloween event at the North Fork Lodge a long time ago. When that ended, the Haunted Barn became the new thing to do."

"I love that it's so quiet here. While I'm at the Barn, I've found myself wishing I were here with Ginny, instead of in that madhouse."

"Well, it might be quiet at the moment, but there tends to be a lot of barking."

"I suppose that's true. But it's better than people screaming and chain saws, ghost noises, and undead clowns muttering." Tori waved her arms in exasperation. "It's hard to explain how weird it is. The whole experience feels out of control, and I hate it."

"Then why are you doing it?"

Tori was a little taken aback at the quiet, rational way he made the statement, but it was a valid question. "It's part of the business plan my partners and I came up with to test candy."

"I see."

"It's a new opportunity and I'm trying to be positive, but I'm afraid the kids hate the candy. It's a lot of changes for me, and I'm not good with change." Tori paused. Why was she blabbing to this person? "I'm sorry. You probably have other things to do."

"It's okay. I think I told you, I quit a programming job, but now I'm doing something new. When you've done something for a long time, doing something different can be hard."

"But you seem so calm. My emotions are all over the place. First I'm afraid, then angry, then worried. I'm a mess."

He raised a single eyebrow. "Well, if Ginny could talk, she'd tell you that I yell at my computer a lot."

Tori reached to pet Ginny. "What's the new thing you're doing?"

"Accounting."

"I'm terrible with numbers. The accountant I hired to do the books for my store hated me."

He readjusted Ginny in his arms. "Actually, it's forensic accounting, which involves following money trails to see if anything seems off. It's basically looking for indications of fraud or embezzlement."

"So it's kind of like solving a mystery?"

"I think of it more as a financial puzzle. It's different from what I used to do, but I think I'm starting to get the hang of it."

Tori gave Ginny a final pat. "I hope I can get the hang of my new business before I lose my mind."

~

Kat looked up from her computer at the sound of small dog claws hitting the wood flooring in the entryway. Joel followed Ginny through the kitchen to the dining room table. Ginny put her front paws up on Kat's chair and she stroked the soft fur between the dog's pointy ears. "You're back."

Joel leaned over to give Kat a quick kiss. "Maybe she'll help you finish your article."

"I need all the help I can get. Maybe she can help me figure out why this software hates me. I'm so behind, and the stupid program keeps crashing."

Joel sat at the table and pulled Kat's yellow legal pad off the stack of books. "Nice doodle."

"You look exhausted. Are you getting any sleep at all?"

"I'm fine." He set down the pad. "You're the one who is supposed to be resting."

"I'm resting a lot. In fact, my sleep is all screwed up because I keep taking naps." She got up and sat in his lap. "Every time I wake up in the middle of the night, you aren't there."

"I told you that I'm logging into the accounting system at night."

"I know you're working late on the dead accounting thing, but you still have to sleep."

"*Forensic* accounting. I think I'm starting to figure out what's going on."

"But you look terrible."

"Thank you." He moved to stand up. "I need to go walk a pack of dogs now. Could you relocate?"

"No." She put her arms around his neck and looked into his eyes. "I want to talk to you."

"About what?"

"About you. I'm worried."

"Isn't that what you do?"

"I know I always say that, but this is more than my normal worrying. You're working late, but then you're not sleeping. How can you not be tired? And like I said, you look exhausted."

"I'm having trouble going to sleep, that's all."

Kat gave him a fixed stare. "We sleep in the same bed. It's not just about *going* to sleep."

"Don't give me that look."

"Then tell me what's going on with you. Why do you keep getting up at two or three in the morning?"

"Sometimes I have bad dreams and I can't get back to sleep. It's no big deal."

"What are the dreams about?"

"Why does it matter?" He tried to pull her arms off his neck. "I have to walk dogs."

Kat clasped her hands together along with his ponytail. "I'm not leaving until you tell me."

"Let go of my hair." He grabbed at her arms. "Ow. Cut it out."

"No."

"I can't remove you without hurting you."

"I know." She gave him an evil grin. "Isn't it great?"

"No. It's not."

"Tell me what you're dreaming about that keeps waking you up." She kissed his lips. "I love you, but you realize your tendency to 'clam up' is what makes your sister insane."

"Thanks for bringing that up. Fine. If you must know, it's a recurring thing. I keep dreaming about the accident that killed my parents."

"You said your sister had bad dreams about the accident, but you never said *you* did."

"I haven't for a long time." He pulled her arms down and this time she let him. "When I try to go back to sleep, I lie there worrying that I'll go back to the dream. So I get up."

"I'm sorry. Why do you think this is happening now? Is it because I was in the hospital?"

"Maybe. I don't know."

"Is there anything I can do?"

"I think you just did." He smiled and gave her a kiss. "I should probably tell you stuff like this."

Kat shot her fist in the air. "*Yes!* Score one for me." She wrapped her arms around his neck again. "But if you need to talk to someone else, like a professional, that's okay too. I mean, it might involve me, and I understand if you want to talk to someone else."

"I don't think that's necessary. When Tori dropped off Ginny, I was thinking she seemed like she needed someone to talk to. I do have someone to talk to, so I should."

"The next time you wake up in the middle of the night, let me know, okay?"

"I don't want to disturb you. You're still healing."

"I'll heal better if you sleep better."

"Okay. It's a deal. Can I go walk dogs now?"

Kat gave him a kiss and got up from his lap. "Have fun."

Kat returned to her article, watched the software crash a few more times, and with a loud and unladylike curse stood up and walked to the kitchen. Time to forage for snack food. Being upstairs made it easier to procrastinate. Having an office downstairs meant normally she had to go upstairs to access food. But now it was all right here. How convenient. Not to mention fattening.

She opened the refrigerator door, looking for inspiration, but was interrupted by the phone ringing.

Maria said, "Hey, how's my favorite invalid?"

"Bored. Procrastinating."

"It must be a Friday thing. No one else is here and I have a bunch of crap filing to do that I don't want to do. But I need advice."

"Any time."

"So I decided to go to that Haunted Barn thing in the hope of finding my own Robin Hood. Or maybe Tarzan. A half-naked hulky guy would be nice."

"Sounds good. Why do you need my advice?"

"It turns out there's a regional shortage of Halloween costumes. That Scare Wear place is pretty much the only game in town. It's huge, but they're cleaned out. The only costume left that fit me was a nun outfit."

Kat laughed. "You're wearing a *habit*? This I have got to see. You absolutely have to take pictures."

"Shut up. This isn't funny. At least the flying nun had the wing-like things on her hat. This costume isn't even that good. It's all black and dreary. This was not the look I was going for when I drove all that way to a costume store."

"I can't quite imagine you in a nun outfit." Kat suppressed another giggle. "Get thee to a convent."

"They had a cute cheerleader outfit, but it was a size miniscule. There was no way I could fit the girls in there."

"Yeah, you don't want to give the zombies too many thrills."

"It was either the nun or a cow outfit. And the Holstein bovine motif was not going to happen. Should I just give up on going?"

"You should definitely go to the Haunted Barn. Why not? If you can't face being a nun, you could always make your own costume. Maybe do something with those wooden shoes. You could be Heidi or something."

"I don't sew, and I gave those shoes to the thrift store to make sure I never have that kind of fashion accident again. I suppose I've got no choice but to look all pious and pure. Ugh. I wish you could go with me. We could do a whole *Sister Act* thing."

"No way. I'm recovering, remember?"

"You're feeling better, right? And for the next few weeks you have to remain celibate, which adds realism."

"Don't remind me."

"You sure you don't want to be a nun with me?"

"Very sure. It's not my job to solve a problem like Maria. You can do that all by yourself."

Maria laughed. "Okay, stop the presses. That works for me. I can totally run with the *Sound of Music* concept. Maybe I'll find myself a baron. He was kind of a jerk, but he redeems himself. When he sings 'Edelweiss' I cry every single time."

"I know. Me too."

~

As she worked with Hope to haul boxes from her car to the barn, Tori tried to sound positive about the many new types of candy she'd created for kids to try out. She might not actually *feel* positive, but Hope didn't need to know that. Hope might eventually get completely fed up with Tori's anxiety attacks, and Tori didn't want to make her friend regret going into business with her.

In a secret corner of her mind, Tori was also looking forward to seeing Dale again. Unlike Hope, he didn't dismiss her worries as type-A free-ranging anxiety. And sometimes he offered suggestions.

A rather hefty bald man ran by them, yelling at the top of his lungs that there was a guy inside the barn with a chain saw. Tori grinned at Hope. "I'm guessing it's his first night."

Hope nodded as she pulled the lid off a box. "Definitely a Haunted Barn virgin."

Tori set the last box on the table. "I think the worst part of this is the constant noise."

"I know. Even after I get home, my ears are still ringing. When I talked to Morgan Saturday night, he asked why I was shouting at him."

"If it were all kids, it might be quieter. But the adults are incredibly loud. Last weekend, a woman let out a bloodcurdling scream and I swear she had to be in her eighties."

"How much candy did you make?" Hope pulled candy from another box. "I keep finding different things."

"I labeled them, so you can tell what's what." Tori held up a box. "I got a new label-maker. Isn't it great?"

"Nice. But the candy isn't all packaged. I thought we agreed that it should be wrapped in foil."

"I didn't have time. And the foil I got was sized for the Choco-critters. Some of these things are the wrong shape." Tori held up a small peanut-butter round dipped in chocolate. "I realized we haven't been smart about this test. We need to get these kids to tell us what they think while they're here. If they take the candy home, we don't learn anything. Candy that isn't wrapped isn't going to travel well, so we have an excuse to tell them to eat it now. Also, these have peanut butter, so we have to make sure kids know that. I made them before I thought about nut allergies."

"People are giving out Snickers bars, so it shouldn't matter."

"I know." Tori ate the chocolate-peanut-butter crisp. "A kid yelled at me for not having them. Everyone knows Snickers have peanuts, but our stuff is new, so we have to be careful."

Hope offered a melodramatic eye roll. "Fine. Whatever. I think that's all of it. Does everything look okay?"

Tori walked to the front of the table and straightened two baskets that were out of place. The Candy Land stand was seriously stocked this time. "It looks okay to me. Remember that you have to be proactive and find out which types kids like."

"Right, Mom. Got it the first twelve times you said it."

Tori was settling back into her seat behind the table when the barn doors opened and the hoards of costumed people flowed inside. A burly man in a strikingly unflattering Spider-Man outfit grabbed a piece of chocolate, popped it in his mouth, and spat it out. "Jeez, what's in that?"

Tori pointed at the label. "Tabasco."

"That's disgusting." He walked away shaking his head.

Hope reached over the table and took one from the basket. She nibbled an edge of the candy, frowned, and stuck her tongue out at Tori. "This is grotesque. What were you thinking?"

"It's an experiment. Spider-Man's opinion doesn't count. Neither does yours or mine. We're too old. We need to find out if kids like it."

Hope shuddered. "Ugh. Maybe kids are picky, but they still have taste buds."

A couple dressed as a pair of dice walked by holding hands. A scare actor leaped out from behind a post and the dice people shrieked, lurched to one side, and rolled onto the ground.

Hope said, "Bummer. Snake eyes."

Continuing to roll on the floor, the dice clearly were having trouble righting themselves, so Tori went over, grabbed their hands, and dragged them to their feet. After thanking her, they ventured down the foggy aisle, glancing around themselves furtively.

When Tori returned to the table, Hope was explaining to a boy in a skeleton outfit why he should try a strawberry caramel nugget. He obligingly took one from the basket and chewed for a while. He spat the masticated goo into his hand and gave it to Hope. "This sucks, lady."

Hope held out her palm to Tori. "How would you like to dispose of this?"

Tori extracted a plastic bag from one of the boxes under the table and held it out. "I'll go find a garbage can."

Hope deposited the goo. "Bye."

Tori wandered into the fake fog, dodging scream-team members, crying children, and various other creatures of the night. So far the experiment wasn't going too well. If this business didn't work, she would have to face the ugly concept of earning money some other way. Perhaps she shouldn't have pinned all her hopes on this one idea. She was completely out of her element. It was difficult not to think wistfully of the shiny immaculate counters and soothing classical music at her gourmet chocolate shop.

Finding a garbage can proved to be more difficult than she'd expected. No wonder the place was such a mess. Once darkness fell, the attendees couldn't see how filthy the floor was, so people probably didn't care. Sure it was a barn, but the dirt below her feet had considerably more mysterious and probably revolting things floating around than it had last weekend. Eww.

Tori leaped at the touch of something on her shoulder, hurling the bag of goo into the darkness. Whoops. She turned and found herself facing a pirate. "Excuse me, did you need something?"

"Aye, maytee. I seek a striking candy-selling wench who be dressed in pink."

Tori peered more closely at the masked face. "Dale?"

"In the flesh, me hearty."

"I'm so glad to see you. Nice hat."

"I'm partial to the feather, meself. Are ye lost again?"

"Maybe a little. I was looking for a garbage can, but that's no longer an issue."

He put out his arm as an invitation. "So ye be sinkin' into this mire like a grungy deckhand."

Tori grasped his forearm. "I beg to differ on the grungy aspect. I'm perfectly clean, but the mire on the floor is getting pretty nasty."

"Are ye wee reef monkeys enjoying yer candy?"

"Two people have spit it out so far, so no. Things are not looking good." She squeezed his arm. "I'm so happy to finally see a friendly face. Well, sort of. Maybe someday I'll see you without a mask."

"Dumpin', pukin', scallywaggin' an' mutinizin'. That be how we sail. And the evening is young, me lass."

Tori caught a glimpse of a man walking a dog and jerked on Dale's arm. "Hey, look at that guy talking to the nun. How come he can bring a dog? I thought they weren't allowed. Why am I spending a fortune boarding Ginny every weekend?"

"That be the swashbucklin' knave who owns this place. The dog's name is Muttley, and he lives here."

"Oh. I guess that does make sense."

Dale said in his normal voice, "I don't think you'd want to bring your dog anyway. From your description, she sounds a bit set in her ways."

Tori smiled. "That's true. It's why I'm paying so much to board her. Apparently, she's too good for lowly dog kennels, and they're letting her stay in their house."

"Great Oden's Ghost, that's mighty kind of them."

"It's in their best interest to keep Ginny content. She has a little barking problem."

"Methinks it's not so little."

Tori shook her head. "The sound makes your ears bleed. I can't describe the noise, but it's absolutely awful."

When Tori's table was within view, Dale said, "I must be going, but I'll see you on the morrow."

Tori let go of his arm and squinted to try to determine his expression. "I thought, well, you said the other night, we might spend some time together tonight."

"And so we have. And so we will." With a swish of his huge cloak, he disappeared into the fog.

Tori was surprised by his abrupt departure. What was that about? Had she said something? More than a little disappointed at being summarily ditched, she sat down next

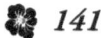

to Hope with a thump, crossing her arms and scowling at a small hockey player who hustled by without stopping.

Hope turned to look at her. "I wondered what happened to you. How long does it take to find a garbage can?"

"Not long enough."

~

Tori spent most of Saturday reorganizing her kitchen in an effort to stop thinking about business, candy, overly picky kids, and Dale. Everything in the kitchen had been labeled, organized, and shiny, but she still was anxious about the upcoming evening.

During their phone date, Dale had made it sound like he wanted to spend time with her, but after last night's brush-off, she was wondering if she'd completely misinterpreted his interest. It was extremely difficult to hold any type of serious conversation amid the mayhem of the barn. Most of the times they'd talked for any extended period, they'd either been on the phone or outside. If she managed to find Dale this evening, she planned to drag him out of the building to get some answers.

After donning the hideous pink dress again, Tori ran out to her car. Heavy black clouds loomed over the west where she was headed. Maybe rain would keep people at home. That wouldn't be the worst thing to happen. Then she'd have only one more weekend and Halloween itself to deal with, and this testing phase would finally be over.

When she got out of her car at the barn, the air was heavy with moisture and ozone. The wind was picking up, and it smelled like rain. When she stepped inside, she looked up at the sound of the rain hitting the huge roof like pellets. A boom crashed outside followed by a flash of light, splitting the dark sky. Tori hustled to her table, glad to get away from the door. A stream of other vendors followed her inside. No one was interested in dawdling in the parking lot during a thunderstorm.

Tori started setting up and was joined by Hope a few minutes later. She shook the rain off her red cloak and put it back on. "This is one doozy of a storm."

Both women glanced toward the doorway at the sound of another massive thunderclap. Tori set out a basket. "Maybe they can ease off on the scary lighting and noise, since we have the real thing."

By the time the doors opened to the public, the most violent storm energy had subsided and it had evolved into a solid, soaking rain. Soggy ghouls wandered through the crowded barn, annoyed that the corn maze and other outdoor attractions were closed for the evening. The aisle was wall-to-wall costumes, some of which didn't smell particularly good. Tori and Hope handed out candy, but it was so claustrophobic, they didn't bother trying to get any opinions. The wet, surly attendees were hungry and seemed willing to eat almost anything. Hope announced that she was getting a headache and was headed to the ladies' room. Tori nodded absently to acknowledge her departure and continued to foist candy on anyone who would take it.

At a light tap on her shoulder, Tori turned around and smiled at Dale, who was still running with the pirate look.

He returned her smile. "Ahoy, matey. May I join you?"

She gestured toward the empty chair next to her. "Have some candy."

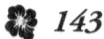

"Shiver me timbers, that's a lot of grub." He took a morsel from a basket. "What be this?"

"They're all labeled, but I think that's a Tabasco chocolate marshmallow cream."

"Blimey!" He coughed and covered his mouth with his hand. "That hornswoggled me tongue. For real, that be."

"I'm guessing that's not good. Try something else.

"Curse the monkey's paw. 'Tis a terrible shame, but I've eaten mere moments ago."

"Sure."

He pointed at the baskets on the table. "Perhaps ye could suggest a small bonnie one."

"The chocolate seashells only have a little salt."

"Chocolate and salt?"

"It's better than you might expect. And definitely better than anything with Tabasco. I don't like those."

Dale squinted at the shell-shaped candy. "Then why did you let me eat it?"

"You grabbed it, not me. This is all your fault anyway. You get what you get."

"*My* fault? How?"

"You said I needed to make different candy."

"I suggested testing other options, which is an obvious thing to do if you're not getting positive results. You're the one who chose what to make. I may have mentioned that Tabasco sounded weird."

Tori stopped herself before she blurted out something nasty. Lashing out at everyone wasn't helping anything. "I know. That wasn't fair. I'm just upset and tired of shouting. All this noise is driving me crazy."

Dale leaned closer to her ear. "How about we talk later, once this place has cleared out a little?"

"That would be great."

He stood up. "I'll stop back here around ten."

Hope finally returned from her extended journey to the ladies' room, and they returned to handing out candy. By nine thirty or so, the crowds were thinning and Tori was starting to look around, hoping to see Dale emerge from the fog.

She proffered the basket of chocolate banana cream treats toward a young boy in a bulky green dinosaur outfit and absently offered up her typical spiel about providing his thoughts on the candy. He opened the jaws on his toothy mask and popped the treat into his mouth.

Looking over her shoulder for Dale, she jerked back to see what was wrong with the dinosaur. He'd launched into an extreme coughing fit. Hope ran around the table to him and Tori was going around her side when he projectile-vomited all over the table, himself, the candy, and everything else in the vicinity.

Someone dressed as an angel, who Tori assumed was probably his mother, appeared from the fog and yelped, "Jimmy! What did you eat?"

Tori volunteered, "It was a banana cream with chocolate. He's not allergic to anything is he?"

The dragon pointed at the table. "I ate that candy over there. Did you see the erectile vomiting? It was so cool!"

The angel put her arm around the dragon. "Jimmy, please stop saying that. I keep telling you the word is *projectile*, not erectile."

"Is he okay?" Hope asked the angel.

"Yes. I knew we shouldn't have come. He has asthma and when he coughs too much, sometimes he vomits."

Jimmy looked extremely pleased with himself. "It was so totally erectile."

"Projectile!" The angel yanked the dragon away. "We should get home. I'm sorry about the mess."

Tori and Hope faced the table, which was exuding a foul, nauseating odor as the vomit settled into place. Hope said, "I'll go find a bucket and paper towels."

"I'll throw away, well, everything." Tori rummaged around in the boxes under the table and found plastic wrap. She tore off a couple of pieces and put it over her hands. She gingerly picked up baskets and dumped the contents into a box, which if she'd had her label maker, now would be labeled *trash*. She threw the baskets into another box, for washing at home. Yuck.

Dale came up next to her and wrinkled his nose. "What happened?"

"Another negative reaction to the merchandise."

"Someone actually threw up?"

"The dinosaur's mom said he has asthma." Tori swiped at her forehead with her sleeve. "This is awful. I feel like crying."

"I'm sorry." He put his arm around her shoulders and held a small furry object out in front of her. "Maybe this will cheer you up. I brought you a present." He squeezed it, and it made a soft trilling noise.

"Is that actually a tribble?" She looked up at his face. "Where on earth did you get that?"

"Not on Sherman's Planet. Or the Klingon home world. I thought it could commemorate our first date."

Tori smiled up at him. "That's so sweet. I want to touch it, but I'm covered with dragon barf."

"It stopped raining. I need to stop by the office, but how about I meet you outside when you're done here?"

"Okay. See you later."

Chapter 7

Scars

After returning with a bucket and cleaning materials, Hope helped Tori hose down the table. She offered to take the baskets home and wash them, maybe because Tori was obviously so upset about having to throw away all the candy that she'd spent hours upon hours creating.

Tori visited the ladies' room, and once she didn't reek of dragon vomit anymore, she went outside. Dale was leaning against the door of the barn waiting for her.

She smiled. "The fresh air feels so good."

"Rainwater fresh." He handed her the tribble. "For you. I think you've earned a little cuddly fuzziness after this evening."

Tori held the stuffed tribble in her hands and squeezed, so it made the soothing tribble noise again. "You didn't answer my question. Where does someone acquire a tribble in these parts?"

"You don't. I was in Los Angeles, remember? If you want something TV-related, you can find it in Hollyweird."

"Well, your timing was great. Tonight was rough, and I'm sorry I snapped at you. I enjoyed our first date, even though I'm not much of a *Star Trek* fan."

"I did too." He took her hand and they strolled toward the parking lot, Tori cuddling her tribble to her chest.

She pointed with her tribble at the sign for the corn maze. "Have you gone through it yet?"

"I did, although I will say it's easier if you've already seen the layout."

"That sounds like cheating."

He gave her a friendly nudge. "I'll let you in on a little secret. You get to cheat when your family sponsors the event."

"How did all this get started? I mean, I grew up here, so I've known about it, but not how it came about."

"I think I told you my mother's family lives here. They were friends with the Jensens. My father met Clint Jensen years ago. Their farm was struggling, particularly in the winter. There used to be a Halloween event in Alpine Grove, but they stopped doing it. It had been successful though, so it gave Dad the idea for doing the Haunted Barn as a charity PR thing for Holbrook."

"Hope would call that a win-win idea. Your family helps raise money for charity, gets great press, and a local farmer benefits too."

"After Clint Jensen died, his son Bob took over. He's the nicest guy you'll ever want to meet, and he loves putting on the event. The rent we pay for the venue helps keep the farm going through the winter."

"I've been so focused on my problems, I haven't thought about how this helps the community."

"Bob grew it beyond anything Dad ever imagined. It wasn't a massive event when I was a kid, but it's huge now. Hotels sell out for all the weekends. Thousands of people show up, and we've been able to give hundreds of thousands of dollars to the foundation."

Tori gestured toward a crowd of people still milling around. "I'll vouch for the thousands of people. It might have been more fun when I was a kid, but I never wanted to go."

"You grew up here, right?"

"My parents owned Merrill's."

"I'm not familiar with it." He shook his head. "I only lived here when I was really little. When my parents got divorced, Chip stayed here, but I went to live with my mom in Los Angeles. I only came here occasionally."

"Your parents split you up?"

"They gave us a choice, and I wanted to get away from here. Going with my Mom seemed like an adventure."

"Was it?"

"That's a long story." He squeezed her hand. "So what happened with the candy before the dragon barfed? Did you find something that kids liked?"

Tori stopped at her car and dropped his hand. "No, and I feel sort of sick."

"You didn't eat one of the Tabasco marshmallow things, did you?"

"No, and I don't mean literally sick, although my stomach does feel a little queasy. I need to tell Hope that this isn't going to work. We need to dissolve the partnership. I'm not sure how to say that to her. And when I do, then what?"

"You still have one more weekend. And then Halloween after that for your big finale."

"I'm out of ideas." She spread her arms out wide. "I've made every candy I can think of, and we've learned exactly nothing. The only feedback I got was that you hate Tabasco and a few other kids hate various other candies."

"The salty chocolate thing wasn't terrible."

"That's not exactly a ringing endorsement, and you're too old anyway. I need a kid to tell me something is actually good. Not one has."

He put his arm around her shoulder. "Hey, it will be okay."

Tori knew she was working herself up into a full-bore anxiety snit complete with high-pitched squawky voice, but the facts were the facts. "No, it's not okay!"

"Is there anything I can do to help? Maybe help you look through recipes? Brainstorm ideas? I don't know."

Tori took a deep breath. She couldn't talk to Hope about this yet. First, she had to think it through. "I'd like that, but I have to get home. I'm so exhausted, I'm not thinking straight. And I have to get up early to drive up to Alpine Grove to pick up my dog."

"How about I go with you? I'm looking into real estate up there and I wouldn't mind driving by a couple properties if you don't mind."

Tori turned toward him and looked up at his face, which was largely covered by the black mask. "I'd actually get to see you in daylight in normal clothes."

"Don't get too excited."

She grinned. "You're not a vampire or something, are you?"

"Not as far as I know. It's a long drive. We can talk about it, and you'll figure something out."

"I hope you're right. I don't understand why you're being so nice to me."

"I like you, and you haven't rejected me yet."

She gave him her address, and he promised to meet her at her building promptly at seven thirty in the morning. "The kennel pick-up hours are pretty strict, and they're already being nice about letting Ginny stay inside the house."

"I'm curious to meet this little dog." He took Tori's hand. "I hope she's as captivating as her owner."

Tori looked up, surprised by the comment. Captivating was not a word anyone had ever used to describe her before. He gazed into her eyes and moved his hand slowly up her arm, along her throat. With his arm, he gently pulled her to him. The kiss was slow and smooth, and Tori wrapped her arms around his neck, enjoying the warmth of his lips. When she could breathe again, all she could think was "Wow."

She must have said it out loud too because Dale said, "Yeah. Wow."

Although she couldn't see him well in the darkness, he seemed sort of startled. Tori said, "I don't think I've ever kissed a pirate before."

"That's probably wise. They tend to be disreputable scallywags."

"I've dated worse."

Dale laughed. "I'm sure there's a story there, but it's getting late. I'll see you in the morning."

"Until then, ye scurvy dog."

～

When Tori exited her apartment building the next morning, she found Dale leaning against the wall near the door reading a book. He looked like a bookish college professor, clad in faded jeans, a gray sweater, and a green windbreaker. When he looked up and peered over his glasses at her, Tori smiled and tried not to overtly stare at the long scar that slashed across his left cheek. Smaller, whitened strips of scar tissue curled around the socket of his left eye. Seeing his deep-set, soulful eyes behind the wire-rimmed glasses clearly for the first time, Tori was glad that whatever had battered his face had missed his eyes. Their deep brown color was almost exactly the same as a seventy-percent cacao bar of dark chocolate, flecked with tiny bits of hazelnut.

Tori pulled her car keys from her purse and offered a polite smile. "You're extremely punctual, and I had no idea you wear glasses."

"It's from the sledding accident."

"I...what?"

He gestured at the left side of his face. "The scars. Believe me, you aren't the first to notice."

"I'm sorry. I didn't mean to stare. It's just that I've never seen what you look like before. It must have been horribly painful."

"Not great for Holbrook company PR either."

Tori unlocked the car and they got in. "How old were you?"

"Five. I was in kindergarten." He pulled on his seatbelt. "So where exactly is this kennel?"

Tori pulled a business card from her purse and handed it to him. "It's way out in the trees. I know how to get there now, but when they gave me directions, I probably scribbled down two pages of notes."

"Huh, that's interesting."

"What?"

"Nothing. I might know someone who lives near there."

Tori gave him a curious glance. "Where in Alpine Grove do you want to go after we pick up Ginny? She loves car rides."

"I have a couple of addresses we can drive by. They're north of town, so they might be out by the kennel."

"If so, it's likely to be remote."

"I prefer to think of it as quiet and private."

"So you're looking at what the real estate agents might call pastoral estates or forested retreats for escaping the modern world?"

"Pretty much." He chuckled. "I think you've been reading the same listings I have."

"After I left the restaurant life, all I wanted to do was get away. Returning to Gleasonville helped, and my little apartment is fine, but I'd love to have one of those pastoral estates with a gigantic farm kitchen. Unfortunately, I'd need to win the lottery to make that happen, since my big business opportunity is looking like more of a bust all the time."

"Have you had any ideas?"

"Not one."

He rubbed at the scar on his cheek. "We're supposed to talk about that, aren't we?"

"Does it still hurt?" Tori blurted before thinking. What was she doing? She had absolutely no tact whatsoever. "I'm sorry."

"Don't apologize. Last night you thought you were kissing a dashing pirate when it turned out it was Frankenstein. That's bound to freak anyone out a little."

"That's not true." Tori was completely mangling this conversation. She paused before continuing, trying to collect her thoughts. "I keep thinking about what it would be like to have a terrible accident at only five years old."

"It makes for an unusual childhood, I suppose. I had lots of operations up until I was eighteen, then plastic surgery for revision on my scars. It's much better now than it was."

"You look fine to me." Actually better than fine. Seeing him up close in daylight was revealing. Sure he had scars, but he was still Dale. "I'm sorry to bring this up. You probably don't want to talk about it."

"We're supposed to be talking about kids and what they think. I might not be the best source of information though. Because of the accident and surgeries, my childhood wasn't totally normal. I spent a lot of time alone."

"I suppose you would have. In my case, I was busy helping my parents. Because they were at the store all day, I spent a lot of time alone too. And if I hadn't learned to cook, we might have starved."

"That explains your career choice."

"Food is the one thing I'm good at. Whether or not your childhood was different from other people's, you made a good point about how kids often can be scatterbrained and unfocused." Tori glanced at him. "That's the antithesis of me, so it's hard for me to put myself in their shoes."

He took off his glasses and cleaned them with his shirt. "Here's a less charitable observation: kids can be mean. As you might imagine, I had a hard time in school. I was teased mercilessly and started making jokes to cover up how I felt. I couldn't stand how I looked, so I started doing cartoon impressions because it made the other kids laugh. I forced myself to look in the mirror and practiced making faces, so I could tell jokes at my own expense."

"Well, you certainly are good at impressions. And you got a job being Harvey the Penguin."

"Maybe you shouldn't worry quite so much about what the kids said about your candy. It's possible they were trying to impress their friends by being mean to the lady in the pink dress."

"But if they really liked something, they'd get excited, wouldn't they?"

"Maybe. Probably."

Tori turned her gaze from the road momentarily to glance at him. "But no one did. Not one positive comment."

"There are a whole lot of distractions at the Haunted Barn."

"So after weeks of testing, we've learned nothing." Tori squeezed the steering wheel more tightly. "What should I do?"

"That's up to you and your business partners."

"You're not helping here."

"Sorry."

They rode for a while in silence. Dale seemed lost in thought, content to stare out the window at the scenery. The leaves on the deciduous trees were turning, and it was a glorious fall day. The sky was a brilliant blue, and it was as if the storm the night before had scrubbed everything clean, making the colors more vibrant.

Tori's thoughts churned and spiraled down into a vortex of despondency. She would have to suck it up and have a hard conversation with Hope. A conversation that would be extra difficult because Hope wanted the business to work too. After she married Morgan, she'd quit working and was excited about doing something related to marketing again.

Bailing out wasn't only going to leave Tori in the lurch. Hope would have to find something else too.

Distracted by her ruminations, Tori almost missed the turn to the kennel. At the sign, she abruptly turned, and Dale lurched in his seat. "Sorry. You'd think after so many trips I'd know where the driveway is, but it always sneaks up on me."

"Look at these trees. They're gigantic."

At the kennel, Tori parked and they got out of the car. She rang the buzzer, and he wandered off, looking up at the massive evergreens that surrounded the parking area.

Joel emerged from the house and strolled down the driveway carrying Ginny, who seemed to be enjoying the ride.

Dale returned from his forest explorations and stood next to Tori. "Does your dog have some sort of disability?"

"Nothing beyond being lazy and spoiled."

He laughed. "Ah, okay. I get the picture."

Joel set Ginny down on the ground and Tori crouched down to say hello to her dog. She waved at the men. "Joel, this is my friend, Dale Holbrook."

Joel shook his hand. "It's nice to meet you in person."

Dale said, "Same here. I thought I recognized the address on the business card."

"My wife inherited the house, and I helped build the kennels." Joel pointed at Ginny. "And yet, after all that work, some of our guests are pickier about their accommodations than others."

"When Becca showed me your cabin, she mentioned you had done other construction work." Dale gestured toward the kennel buildings. "I guess this was what she was talking about."

Joel said, "I was planning to call you with an update this week. Our dog-walker will be back at work and I'll have more time. I've found…"

"Maybe I can give you a call about that later." Dale said.

Tori continued petting Ginny in silence, evaluating what the two men might be talking about. Clearly, they already knew each other. Was Dale the client Joel had mentioned before? And if he was, why did Dale need forensic accounting?

⁓

After Tori gave Joel her check and they said their goodbyes, she loaded Ginny into the car and got into the driver's seat. She turned to Dale. "So where to now?"

Dale pulled a piece of paper from a pocket in his jeans. "There's a place not too far away from here, I think. But I don't know the back roads. Probably the best thing is to get back to the highway and head south a little ways."

"I'm sort of surprised you know Joel. Is he doing forensic accounting for you?"

Dale rubbed at his scar. "How do you know about that?"

"We were talking about my business challenges, and he told me he quit a project he didn't like and was doing something new. Are you the new client?"

"Not exactly."

"What exactly is it, then?"

"Probably something I shouldn't talk about with you."

Tori looked away from the road briefly to glare at him. "Are you in some type of trouble? Are you being investigated? Because if you are, I would like to know. *Now*."

"No, I'm not. Not in any way, shape, or form."

"I've spilled my guts to you about my business, and yet I don't even know what you do for a living, other than that you are the voice for Harvey the Penguin sometimes."

Dale ran his fingers through his hair. "Okay, I'll tell you. But you have to promise not say anything about this to anyone."

"Okay, my lips are sealed. I'm listening."

"Normally I have nothing to do with Holbrook beyond the occasional Harvey commercial. But my father encouraged me to attend the Haunted Barn this year and asked me to keep an eye on Chip. That led to finding out about issues related to the company."

"Accounting issues?"

"Among other things." He pointed at a sign. "I think you need to turn there."

"What other things?"

"This makes my family seem like the ultimate soap opera, but I blame Chip."

"For what?"

"For being a jerk. Dad wasn't too pleased about having Chip's romantic life splattered all over the tabloids, so he asked me attend the Barn and keep him from hitting on unsuspecting costumed women."

"Is that why you asked about his intentions toward me?"

"Partly." He smiled. "I had more selfish reasons too. You're way too nice to have to deal with the likes of him."

"Thanks, I think. What does this have to do with accounting?"

"At first, I thought they just wanted me to keep Chip from doing something dumb that would put his name in the papers again. His love-em and leave-em reputation is justified, but he was still irritated that Dad sent me to keep an eye on him. Like I said, I don't always go to the Haunted Barn, and Chip knows Dad sent me to act as his babysitter. I was even less excited about it than Chip was."

Tori turned onto the highway heading south. "But you did it anyway. How come? Tell me where I need to turn."

"It's the next road off to the left."

"So why are you here?"

"I've been looking at real estate in Alpine Grove."

Tori waved her hand in exasperation. "I know. You told me that before. I mean why were you willing to babysit, and what does it have to do with accounting?"

"I found out there were unexplained changes in financial metrics."

"What?"

"That's accounting-speak for signs of embezzling."

"You think Chip is stealing from the company?" Tori jerked her attention from the road momentarily to evaluate his expression. "Are you serious?"

"I'm not sure it's Chip. I'm not a numbers person, so I needed someone smart to look over stuff."

"How did you find Joel?"

"My real estate agent talked to an appraiser who lives in a cabin Joel built. The place is a lot like something I would like to buy. It's small and simple, so it's perfect for a single guy like me."

"And the embezzling?"

"Right. Anyway, Becca told me Joel was good at what she referred to as computer stuff. That sounded promising, so I gave him a call. It turns out he's a programmer, and he explained what he could look at, so I figured he knew what he was doing."

"Today he made it sound like he found something."

Dale pulled off his glasses and rubbed his eyes. "I hope it's not Chip. Part of me thinks he's not that smart or sneaky. But I honestly don't know. I'm tired of thinking about Chip and angry for letting myself get sucked into this mess."

"Thanks for telling me. I wish there was something I could do to help."

"It's kind of a relief to talk to someone about it. Well, other than Joel. I didn't tell him about suspecting Chip. I just asked him to look for anything off." He pointed at the cross street ahead of them. "Turn left up here. It's supposed to be a couple miles up the road. The address is 170."

Tori slowed and turned onto the gravel road. They scanned the numbers on the mailboxes that stood like sentinels at the ends of the long driveways. A For Sale sign was jammed into the grass next to the mailbox for 170, and Tori pulled the car over to the side of the road. "This is it, but there are too many trees to see much of anything."

"Do you suppose I'll get shot by a privacy nut if I walk down there?"

"Shooting people would discourage prospective buyers. It seems pretty quiet, and I think the house is behind that clump of pines. Ginny and I can go with you. We look pretty harmless."

Dale looked over at the back seat. "I think you'll have to wake her up."

They got out and Tori put Ginny on her leash. "I'm sorry, but you have to walk. I'm not carrying you."

Ginny glared at her but followed as they started down the driveway. The driveway curved, and a house came into view. Or what was left of it. Tori looked at Dale. "I think this one is a bit of a fixer-upper."

The roof was caved in, possibly from a long-ago snow storm, and it appeared that the place had been abandoned for years.

Dale said, "I think that is more than I'm willing to take on. Abandoned houses like this one make me sad."

"How come?"

"It's not like the cookie-cutter tract homes you see all over LA. Someone built this house, and it was what they wanted or what they could afford. For all we know, it might have been someone's dream home."

Tori smiled. "I didn't realize this before, but you're kind of a softie, aren't you?"

"I don't know about that, but I spend a lot of time thinking about stories. All houses have stories."

"I think the story has ended for this one."

"Maybe so. Or someone will have a vision for putting it back together. Or tearing it down and starting over. I don't think that person is me though."

"Well, no matter how cheap it is, I can't afford it, so it's not me either. Shall we go to the next place on your list?"

He handed her a piece of paper. "I had to draw a map for this one."

"So that dotted line is a logging road? Getting there could be interesting."

"It might be better to think of it as an adventure."

"I hope my poor little car can survive it."

～

Tori stopped the car. "I don't think we can go any farther. Are you sure this is the road?"

"I'm not even sure this *is* a road." Dale peered out the window. "I think I need to be a little more specific on my requirements. Can you imagine what this would be like in the winter?"

Tori shook her head. "You said you wanted privacy."

"I'd prefer not to have to use a sled-dog team to get to my house." He pointed at a clearing full of tree stumps. "Bad access and a clear cut is not my idea of a pastoral retreat."

"Okay, let's see if I can turn around." Tori slowly did a twenty-nine point turn on the narrow quasi-road. "I should take my car in for a tune-up to apologize for this trip."

"I'll pay for it. The word *remote* has new meaning for me now."

Once they were pointed back down the hill, Tori asked, "I feel silly asking this after spending so much time talking to you, but where exactly do you live?"

"Well, I used to live in Los Angeles. The neighborhood where I lived was getting incredibly noisy. A club moved in nearby and it became party central. I ended up talking to a real estate agent who listed my condo at a ridiculous price, figuring it wouldn't sell. Then it did. So I put all my stuff in storage and traveled over the summer."

"How come you didn't buy another place?"

"I was feeling restless, so I decided to take a little time to think about what I wanted to do next."

Tori stopped at a stop sign. "Speaking of not knowing, where are we going?"

"The next house is closer to town. Head back to the highway."

"So my next question is what do you do that you can take three months off? And how can I get a job like that?"

He laughed. "Work too hard for a lot of years, maybe?"

"I did that! First I got so burned-out I got sick, then I tried something else and burned-out again because I couldn't get ahead. I have no trouble working hard. I do seem to have trouble being successful though."

"What's your definition of success?"

"Well, the typical answer would be to make a lot of money, I suppose."

"Money helps." He pointed at a sign. "The turn is up ahead."

"It does, but I think my answer would be not having to work as much. For years, I've had no free time. I haven't taken a vacation, since, well, ever."

"I came to the same conclusion. I worked incredibly hard to become independent of my family's business and be successful in my own right."

Tori stopped at another stop sign and shifted in her seat to face him. "You honestly don't have anything to do with your family's company?"

"Nothing except being the voice of Harvey every once in a while. I was able to use that to get into voice-over work. It took years, but now people *invite* me to participate in projects. I don't have to scrounge for work anymore."

"That's impressive." She drove through the intersection, continuing down the rural road. Where were they going?

"This year, I realized I can actually pick and choose the projects I want to work on. And that if I leave LA and move to a place with a lower cost of living, I only need to do one or two projects a year to make ends meet."

Tori took her hand from the wheel and shoved at his shoulder playfully. "Okay, stop it. I'm officially completely jealous now."

"I still need to earn a living, but I want to explore other interests and get out of LA. When I came up to talk to my father about the Haunted Barn, I visited Alpine Grove, and everyone was incredibly nice. After I went back to LA, it struck me how different Alpine Grove is, and I thought, 'hey, why don't I move there?' So I am."

"Assuming you can find a house you can get to that has a roof."

He chuckled. "Yeah, who would have thought it would be so difficult? I think that's the road where you need to turn up there. The address is 1201."

Tori parked and unloaded Ginny. She clipped the leash back on and set her on the ground. "Yes, I know. More walking. You can do it."

The house was set reasonably close to the road and appeared to be occupied, so they walked down the road to see the side of the house.

"Is that part of the chimney that's sitting on the ground over there?" Tori pointed at a pile of rocks and cinder blocks. "That's probably not good."

He took her hand and they walked down the road to check the other side of the house. "The chimney could be fixed, but this doesn't feel right."

"That's vague. What do you mean? This what?"

"The house is okay I guess, but I can't imagine myself living here."

"Why not?"

"It doesn't feel right."

Tori shook her hand in his in frustration. "You just said that. I think you're going in circles. Buying a house should be a rational decision and that's not particularly logical."

"Haven't you ever had the experience where something just felt right?" He pulled her into his arms, swirling her around almost like a dance step, so she was pressed against his warm chest, the leash wrapped around her legs. Unprepared for the sudden move, her heart fluttered and did a little flip when he kissed her. She wrapped her free arm around his waist and lost herself in the warmth.

Ginny interrupted the moment with a long, agonizing howl that segued into hysterical barking. They broke apart, glaring at the dog.

Dale leaned in closer again, so their foreheads were touching as Ginny proceeded to lose her canine mind.

Tori crouched down, disentangled herself from the leash, and tried to calm Ginny, but the dog wasn't having any of it.

A voice from the yard said, "Hey you, get off my lawn. I don't want no dog pooping in my yard."

Dale waved and said, "No worries, mate, we'll get it sorted. What's the John Dory?"

The bald man rubbed his head. "Huh? I told you. Get off my lawn!"

"Eh, give us a fair suck of the sauce bottle, mate."

Tori stood up and leaned toward Dale. "What the heck does that mean?"

As he waved to the man again, Dale whispered to her, "I'm not sure, but I'm betting he doesn't know either. Saying pretty much anything with an Australian accent makes it sound friendly."

"Shut up that dog and git off my land!" The old man waved his cane at them. "And you better stay gone."

"Crikey, we'll do the Harry. We're just on walkabout. Keep your dunders on, mate."

They walked back to the car, Tori dragging Ginny, who was expressing her displeasure at the entire experience by doing her best imitation of a boat anchor.

Tori said, "Your aversion to buying that house is making more sense to me now. We weren't on his lawn. We were on the side of the road. It's public property, and we weren't trespassing at all."

"I think that guy is a few stubbies short of a six-pack, but I don't blame him for wanting Ginny to shut up."

"I told you her barking is awful."

"You weren't lying. I'm definitely crossing this place off the list. I'm not sure there's enough sage in the world to get rid of mean-old-guy juju."

They got back into the car and Tori leaned over to kiss Dale. Ginny jumped up in the back seat and barked in Tori's ear. She whirled around and shook her finger at the dog. "*No!* That's enough. Go lie down."

Ginny looked startled for a moment, but spun around twice and curled up in a tight ball, facing the back of the seat.

Tori leaned over again and kissed Dale's cheek. "I'm *so* sorry about that."

Dale glanced at the back seat and gently placed his hands on the back of her neck, rubbing her jaw with his thumbs. He whispered, "Shhh," before kissing her lips slowly and thoroughly.

She closed her eyes and savored the experience. When she opened them and was able to breathe again, she said softly, "Maybe we could go somewhere without Ginny."

"How about if we go on a real date tomorrow night? In person, and someplace where they serve food and don't allow dogs."

"I'd like that."

Chapter 8

Jolly Good Chocolate

Tori spent most of her Monday going through more cookbooks and pondering new ideas for candy. It was becoming difficult to find options that she hadn't already either made or ruled out for good reason.

By the time she went downstairs to the lobby of her apartment building to meet Dale for their date, she was downright depressed about her options. She pushed open the door just as Dale drove up alongside the curb in an expensive gray sedan. Maybe a Lexus? Audi? Whatever it was, it indicated there was serious money to be made in voice-over work. If he was loaded, why was Dale looking at such trashy real estate? At least he'd figured out that being on time scored big points with her.

She got in the car and sank into the plush leather seat. "Nice ride."

"If I actually move to Alpine Grove, I need to trade this in for something with four-wheel drive."

"Are you having doubts about moving?"

"I don't know. When Joel called his place a shack, I thought he was kidding. Now, I'm not so sure. He said he did a lot of work on it, and I'm thinking I should ask if he built the whole thing."

"Have you considered buying land and building a house? Or moving somewhere else?"

He stopped at the end of the driveway and leaned over to kiss her. "Where do you want to eat?"

"Well, there's Amigas, but I'm not in the mood for Mexican. The Pine Tree Bistro used to be good, but after their chef moved to Oregon, it hasn't been the same. Or there's the Granite Grill, but the new chef there is, well, you don't want to know about that whole disaster. The steakhouse out on the highway is absolutely awful. DiMaggios is new, but when I tried their chicken, I was appalled. That place on Fifth, Jonah's Fish House, must get their fish from the old fish home because it's practically inedible."

"How about The Gourmand? Chip mentioned he went there once, I think."

Tori scowled and tugged at her seatbelt. "No, you don't want to go there. They've had a lot of turnover, and it's completely mismanaged. The service is terrible."

He lifted his hand from the steering wheel and rubbed at his scar. "I didn't realize this decision would be quite so difficult."

"Sorry. Unfortunately, I know about the chefs or how the kitchen is run at a lot of restaurants."

He stopped at a traffic light. "I don't know where we're going. Don't you ever eat out?"

"Not very often. Because of the business, I'm trying to save my pennies and what I can make at home is better than almost anything I can get at a restaurant in Gleasonville anyway."

He pointed at a green awning as they drove by. "How do you feel about coffee?"

"I love coffee. But aren't you hungry?"

"Yes, but if there's no place you're willing to eat, I think we're at an impasse."

"I know! Let's go to the grocery store."

He chuckled. "Well, that's romantic. The ambiance of the cereal aisle is a major turn on."

"The expensive grocery on Seventh Street has all kinds of delicious cheeses and munchies."

He flipped the turn signal indicator. "You want to eat at the grocery store?"

"Not exactly. I'd make something for you at my place, but I'm afraid Ginny might pitch a fit."

"I'd like to avoid having that experience again."

"We could have a picnic somewhere or take food to your place." Tori paused. "Where are you staying?"

"I'm sleeping in a room at my father's house, but I'm trying to spend as little time there as possible. Chip lives there, and the fewer hours we are in the same building, the better."

"Ah, okay. So a picnic it is. Let's go to the grocery store." Tori clapped her hands together.

"I've never seen anyone get so excited about buying food."

"The deli there is excellent with lots of gourmet Italian antipasti. We can get stuffed peppadews with mascarpone and ricotta, truffled three-bean salad, pepperoncini-pickled cornichons, pancetta, marinated peppers and olives. Oh, and they bake their own bread and pastries. The cheese selection is incredible, and there's a salad bar too. You'll see."

"I'm getting the impression you shop there a lot."

"Not as much as I'd like to. It's expensive, but sometimes I have to splurge."

Tori leaped from the car when they arrived at the designer grocery store, excited to see what was new. Dale followed her through the aisles as she evaluated her options. The store was probably her favorite place in Gleasonville, and the fact that she didn't have to worry about the prices for a change was liberating. She held up a jar. "Oh my god, I haven't seen this since I've been back here. This curry is amazing if you're in a rush and don't have time to make a sauce from scratch."

"I'll take your word for it."

Tori set the jar down. Dale was being patient, but he'd already said he was hungry, so he was probably getting weary of her many foodie proclamations and exclamations. "Sorry I got distracted. I think we have everything."

When they exited the store, they were greeted by gray looming clouds. Tori looked up at the sky in dismay. Fall weather was unpredictable at best and downright crummy at worst. "I'm not sure our picnic idea is going to work out."

"I think the temperature dropped ten degrees while we were in the store."

"This is silly. We should go back to my apartment. I don't know why Ginny was being such a problem yesterday. When Chip and Hope had dinner at my place, she was fine."

"You'd think if she could put up with Chip, she could put up with me."

Tori giggled. "Well, she did bark when he spilled espresso all over the place."

"Who wouldn't? I'll do my best not to be a clod."

They returned to the apartment building and ran through the drenching rain to the door with the bags of groceries. In the elevator, Dale shook his hair like a dog, set down his bag, and slapped his hand on the red stop button. Tori looked over at him in surprise. "What did you do that for?"

"I'm planning ahead." He took her bag from her arms and set it on the floor, then pulled her into his arms. "I want to make sure I get my good-night kiss in case I'm driven from your home by your dog."

After giving her a rather phenomenal kiss, he released her and pulled the stop button back out. "Onward."

"That was enjoyable, but you're not supposed to press that button if it's not an emergency. What if it calls the police?"

"It doesn't. There isn't even an alarm. This is an old Otis elevator from the sixties or seventies. If it were a newer building, I'd be more worried."

"How do you know that?"

"From watching too many old TV shows. And occasional experimenting."

Tori picked up her bag again and offered up a small request to any canine gods nearby to keep her dog from losing her mind again.

When they entered the apartment, Ginny was curled up in her dog bed. She raised her head sleepily at Tori and closed her eyes again. She jerked awake at the sight of Dale and ran to the door, barking as if a demon had arrived and the world was in danger of imminent doom.

Tori set her bag on the table and grabbed the dog mid-stride. Ginny made a loud "oof" noise as Tori hauled the hefty dog into her arms. "I refuse to let you hold my apartment hostage. Get over it." Tori stared at Ginny, who was clearly not pleased by this uncharacteristically stern behavior from her human.

Tori stroked Ginny's head. "I'm going to put you down now. Can you behave?"

Ginny glared and didn't offer up any type of response. Tori set her on the floor and the dog stalked off to the bedroom.

Dale said, "Maybe she'll get used to me."

"I have no idea what her problem is, but I don't like it." Tori took her bag to the kitchen. "I can defrost an eggplant Parmesan I made and I have a California wine that's a blend of Cabernet Sauvignon and Merlot that would be a great complement. It's a dense red with aromas of chocolate, black fruit, and other earth tones."

"Whatever you say."

~

Tori handed Dale a glass of wine. "Here's to our first real in-person date. I'm sorry about Ginny."

They clinked glasses, and Dale sat down on a bar stool in front of the counter that connected to Tori's galley kitchen. "You actually made all that candy here? How did you do it in this tiny space? You can barely turn around in there."

Tori was busy digging out platters from a low cabinet so she could serve the fun appetizers from the grocery store. She stood and pointed at an empty bookshelf. "It's not ideal. But I donated all my books—well except cookbooks—to the library. I use the shelves as a space to cool the candy, which helps. This kitchen is part of why it takes all week to restock for the Haunted Barn. I have to do small batches."

Dale sipped his wine. "This is good."

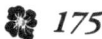

Tori took a sip and set a tray of antipasti on the bar in front of him. "I do like a classic red blend. We got off on a food tangent, and you never said if you're interested in moving somewhere other than Alpine Grove. I mean, why not Gleasonville? Your family is here."

He took off his glasses and set them on the counter. "That's not a point in its favor."

"Alpine Grove isn't that far away."

"I know. But it's far enough to avoid getting tangled up in Holbrook bureaucracy. I've tried to stay away from it and it bothers me that I'm getting roped back into their, uh, stuff."

"You mean with the Haunted Barn and Chip?"

"I should have known better. And I'm sure you've noticed that Gleasonville isn't like it was when we were kids." He waved his glass for emphasis. "It's changed. I'm not sure how or when it happened, but over the years it evolved from a farming community into an ocean of strip malls."

"I suppose that's true. The little neighborhood where my parents store was located is now filled with fast-food places, chain stores, and a parking garage."

Dale poured more wine into his glass. "That's depressing."

"The area where my little chocolate shop was located is still cute, but they were talking about tearing down a bunch of the old houses and building a shopping center. The owner of my building was thrilled because it gave him an excuse to raise the rent."

"Even more depressing. But from what you said, it sounds like you were ready to give up the place anyway."

"I was tired, and that storefront was the least expensive place I could find. With the higher rent, the numbers didn't work, no matter how much I wanted them to."

"You could have moved."

"I don't want to go back to the city."

He drank the wine and set down the glass. "I know what you mean."

"The idea of having a business model where I didn't have to have so much direct customer contact was appealing too." Tori nibbled on a stuffed pepper. "Of course, then Hope had the bright idea of testing at the Haunted Barn. No one ever threw up at my candy store."

"I'm glad to hear that."

Tori got out another bottle of wine. "I think this will go better with the antipasti. So you said that you only have to work on one or two projects. What's next?"

"I read a script for a movie that started filming in June. They wanted me to do a bunch of voices for the CGI parts, but I don't think I can face it. There are more animated movies that are likely to be coming up, so I don't need to do it."

Tori poured the wine into his glass. "What's it about?"

"Did you hear about the new *Star Wars* movie? There's been chatter about it for a long time."

She pulled more appetizers from the grocery bags. "Not really. I always wanted to know what happened to Luke Skywalker and all his friends after *Return of the Jedi*."

"This movie won't tell you. It's the first installment of a prequel trilogy. I'm probably violating some contract by telling you, but it's set thirty-two years before the *Star Wars* that we all know as *Star Wars*. That movie will then be called *Episode Four*. But it stinks. The script is so bad, I think I'm going to take a pass. I absolutely hate it."

Tori laughed. "So tell me how you really feel."

He swirled the wine in his glass, watching it whirl around. "Sorry. Sometimes the movie business brings me down. I thought the *Empire Strikes Back* was a good sequel. But most of them aren't. Hollywood spends an incredible amount of money rehashing and redoing the same movies over and over again. How hard is it to find a new story?"

"So if you're not doing the crappy *Star Wars*, what are you doing?"

"I haven't decided yet. I've got a pile of scripts to read. They're in the car. Work is a good excuse to get out of the house. I drag them to the library to force myself to sit and read."

"When you're not looking at falling-down real estate that is."

He laughed. "Right now, my life consists of reading bad stories, looking at bad real estate, and tripping over people in bad costumes. No wonder I want to escape to a remote retreat."

"Except they tend to have maintenance issues."

"I suppose. If I weren't working as much, I'd have time to fix a few problems. But I draw the line at putting on a new roof. What do you do with your free time? What are your other interests outside of candy and food?"

Tori hated it when people asked this question. "Other interests? What are those?"

"Oh, come on." He took a sip of wine and widened his eyes at her in theatrical shock. "Don't you have hobbies? Activities? Sports? Games?"

"Nope."

He set down the glass. "What do you do for fun?"

"Cook. Organize things."

"That sounds suspiciously like work if you're a chef or chocolatier."

Tori leaned over the counter to examine his eyes more closely. "Are you okay?"

"I feel sort of dizzy. I think I'm probably drunk. To be honest, I don't drink much because alcohol isn't great for your voice. I can't remember the last time I had any type of liquor. I guess I probably should eat something. How's that eggplant doing?"

Tori looked at the timer. "Ten more minutes. I'll get you some water."

"Thanks. So what *do* you do when you're not working? I've been thinking about all the things I'll have time for if I'm not working all the time. I heard the old theater in Alpine Grove is being restored and there's a theater troupe. That might be fun to get involved with."

"That sounds suspiciously like work if you're involved in making Hollywood movies."

"It's not the same. Voice-over work is sitting in a little booth in a studio wearing headphones and drinking gallons water or decaffeinated tea. Live theater is different."

Tori gathered silverware and walked into the dining area to set the table. "I suppose."

He swirled the bar stool around to face her. "You didn't answer my question. Suppose the candy business takes off, what do you plan to do? You said you haven't taken a vacation. Where would you go?"

"I can't think that far ahead. Right now, I'm trying to figure out how to get out of this partnership. I think creating candy for kids is not something I want to do after all."

"Are you sure? I thought you were going to find a different candy."

Tori set down a fork and paused. "Maybe it's because of the dragon barf, but I don't want to be involved in the corruption of a minor."

"Chocolate as a gateway drug?"

"You know what I mean. Sugar is bad for kids. I think I've made a terrible mistake." She waved a spoon at him, gesturing toward the table. "Please sit down and I'll get the eggplant Parmesan."

Dale grabbed his water glass and stumbled to a chair. "How much wine did I have?"

"I'd say too much." Tori leaned over his shoulder and kissed his cheek. "I have a lovely couch you can sleep on tonight. There's no way I'm letting you drive home."

He looked over at the sofa. "It looks appealing. But I don't have a toothbrush."

"I have a package of six because I rotate them out every three months."

"How organized." His gaze followed her as she sat. "You're an intriguing woman. You plan your toothbrush schedule, but are compassionate and flexible enough to let a disreputable scallywag like me crash on your sofa."

"I'm a mystery, even to myself."

～

The next morning, Tori rolled over and opened her eyes. Virtually every morning, the first thing she saw was Ginny, curled up tight in her little bed, contentedly snoring. But this morning, the bed was empty. Where was she? Ginny was *always* in her bed when Tori woke up. Was she having a problem? Did she need to go out? Tori got up and went into the living room.

Dale was tangled up in the sheets and blankets on the sofa, and Ginny was nestled up to his chest. His arm was encircling her like a fortress and they both were fast asleep. Tori tip-toed back into the bedroom, turning to take one last look at the scene. Ginny knew she wasn't allowed on the furniture, but Tori's heart melted a little nonetheless.

After heading to the bathroom and going through her morning routine, everyone else remained asleep, so Tori returned to her bedroom with a couple of cookbooks. Although the date with Dale had been enjoyable, she was now behind on her candy-invention program. Maybe she should make a few more Choco-critters and give up on trying anything new. She flipped through a few more pages in search of inspiration. Nothing. With only a few days of testing left, perhaps it was time to give up on determining what eight-year-olds deemed cool and just make candy.

Making a wide variety of Choco-critters was time consuming. Of the various other options she'd tried out, she liked the salted seashells and the peanut butter biscuits covered with chocolate the best. The little peanut butter discs were the size of nonpareils and smelled fantastic while they were baking. Even better, she'd gotten a massive vat of PB on sale. And she'd get to use her label maker again to alert people to the potential allergen.

A thud came from the living room and Ginny ran into the bedroom and settled into her dog bed. Tori got up and leaned over to pet the dog. "Yes, I saw you on the sofa. Don't try and pretend you weren't up there."

She walked out into the living room where Dale was still tangled up in the sheets, but sitting up. His clothes were beyond wrinkled and he looked rumpled and scruffy. Perhaps he wasn't a morning person.

He rubbed his face with his hands and looked up at her. "I feel like death."

"You don't look too great either." She sat next to him. "Why didn't you tell me you don't drink?"

"I don't have anything against imbibing. I'm not a teetotaler or striving to re-institute Prohibition or anything." He rubbed his eyes with his thumb and index finger. "I was hungry and sort of nervous and well, who knows? Ugh."

"What about all those Hollywood parties I'm always reading about? If you believe the tabloids, they're swimming in alcohol."

Running his fingers through his hair, he arched his back and rolled his shoulders. "It's Hollywood. Everything is all about appearances. No one invites the seriously non-telegenic voice-over guy to red-carpet events."

"That's too bad."

"Not to me. I prefer to remain anonymous. Which I was until Chip pulled me into his PR disaster. He mentioned something about family problems related to the company, which led a reporter to dig into our family lore for a story about my 'tragic accident.' Chip is such a toad."

Tori laughed. "I think you may have mentioned that before."

"It's not easy being green."

"You do a great Kermit the Frog voice. But toads aren't green."

"How about calling Chip a troglodyte then? As far as I know, they aren't a particular color." He stood up and stretched his arms over his head. "I need take advantage of that brand-new blue toothbrush you gave me last night."

"I'll make breakfast. You'll feel better once you have some food."

Tori decided that pancakes were in order. She pulled Millie, her trusty Kitchen Aid, from the cabinet and happily busied herself mixing pancake batter.

When Dale returned, his clothes were still wrinkled, but he'd obviously washed his face and calmed down his hair. He walked into the small kitchen and looked over her shoulder at the batter. "You don't have to go to all this trouble. I'll be fine with some coffee."

"It's no trouble. The coffee is in the pot over there. Help yourself."

He navigated around her and poured a cup. Setting it aside on the counter, he waited for the mixer to stop. Tori looked up, and he pulled her into his arms and kissed her.

From below them, Ginny let out a horrendous yowling, wailing noise. Tori gasped, shoved Dale away, and yelped, "*Ginny*! You have to stop that."

Ginny turned around and stalked through the doorway into the living room.

Dale leaned against the counter and folded his arms across his chest. "That's enough to give a hung-over guy a heart attack."

"I don't know what's wrong with her. When I woke up this morning, I came out here, and she was sleeping on the sofa with you. What happened?"

"I think I become *persona non grata* when I touch you."

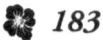

"What? No. That's ridiculous."

"Is it?" Dale reached for his coffee and took a sip. "I hate to pry, but when was the last time someone was here?"

"Well, I told you Chip came over for dinner. Ginny spent most of the evening in the bedroom, but came out to beg for food."

"So Chip didn't make any moves on you?"

"No, he said he'd call, but then he didn't. Which was fine with me."

"I'm glad the troglodyte kept his hands off you, but when was the last time a guy *didn't* keep his hands off you?" He smiled. "Other than me, that is."

"Eight hundred and ninety-two days ago."

"But who's counting?"

She took the bowl off the mixer and used Stella the spatula to fold a cup of blueberries into the pancake batter. "There's been a bit of a drought in my romantic life since I moved to Gleasonville. No one—other than you—has stayed over or even kissed me since I broke up with Augie in LA. And that was before I adopted Ginny."

"No wonder she's jealous. All of your attention has been focused on her."

"No it hasn't. I work a lot."

"You said you took her to the store with you."

"I did, and she was a very good girl." Tori pulled out a pan from the cabinet. "I suppose I was so focused on getting the store going that there wasn't much time for a social life. It seems a little pathetic, in retrospect, but I was busy."

"Now that you've given up the store, you have time."

"But I'm afraid I've made a horrible mistake and am going to end up homeless because I can't come up with marketable candy to make this new business work."

"I think you're exaggerating." Dale turned toward the doorway of the kitchen where Ginny was sitting and glaring at them. "I'd give you a hug, but I think your dog would flip out."

Tori turned the stove burner off and set the pan aside. "This is absurd."

"What do you want me to do?"

She took his hand and pulled him out of the kitchen to the sofa. "Sit down."

He complied and looked up at her. "Now what?"

Tori picked up Ginny and set her on the couch next to Dale. She sat on the other side of Ginny and took Dale's hand in hers. "We're going to have a conversation and she's going to watch us."

He covered her hand with his and caressed her palm. "Okay. What do you want to talk about?"

"I'm a mess."

"That's quite an opener. You seem fine to me."

"I'm serious. I'm a walking romantic disaster area. My last relationship imploded spectacularly. All of my neurotic behavior drove him away. You're nuts to be interested in me, and I can't figure out why you're here."

"It's not that complicated. I met you. I liked you. I wanted to keep seeing you. So far, you haven't rejected me. Since I still like you, I'm hoping to see you more often."

"Even if a relationship with me is likely to be doomed?"

"Right now, it seems like the biggest problem we have is sitting between us." He leaned over Ginny and tucked his index finger under Tori's chin, pulling her toward him until their lips were less than an inch apart. "Now what?"

"I'm not sure." Tori put her arms around his neck and looked down at Ginny, who was staring up at her. She looked into Dale's dark eyes again. "I like you too, but I always screw up relationships. My track record is *really* bad."

"Mine isn't great either. But your lips are really soft. I like how they feel."

"I'm overwhelmed with my business problems. I feel trapped like I have no way out, and I'm not thinking clearly. I'm so confused. I feel like I'm missing a sneaky business trick that would make everything work."

He kept his eyes locked on hers. "What if all you need is someone you can tell these things to? What if I'm that someone?"

"Maybe you are." Tori put one hand on Ginny's head and kissed him.

They both looked down at the dog, who gazed back at them in silence.

~

After Tori finished making the pancakes, she and Dale sat at the table and dug in as Ginny looked on. If there was one thing Tori knew, it was that food solved countless problems. And if it didn't solve a problem, it distracted you from it, which was the next best thing.

Dale scraped the last of the boysenberry syrup from the plate with his fork. "I'm starting to understand why you became a chef."

"This is nothing. Anyone can make pancakes."

"That may be true, but these are possibly the best pancakes I've ever eaten."

Tori took his plate into the kitchen. "Flattery about my cooking is appreciated, but I have bad news. I spent all of Monday woolgathering, trying to come up with ideas for candy, so I'm way behind for this weekend. I need to work."

He sat on a bar stool and set his coffee mug on the counter. "You mean make candy?"

"That's my work, yes."

"Can I help?"

"As you've already pointed out, only one person can be in this kitchen at a given time." Tori spread her arms to demonstrate the narrow space. "I don't see how you could help."

"I could sit here and keep you company." He sipped his coffee. "Or be a taste tester."

"I'm giving up on trying something new, so you've probably already tasted everything." She pointed at him. "Also, I have to keep my work area clean and you're not."

"I've been rejected for a lot of reasons, but being dirty is a new one."

"I'm not *rejecting* you. I have to work. It's nothing personal. Don't be sensitive."

He pressed his hand to his chest. "Hey, I'm a thhen-thitive guy."

"Sorry Daffy, but you're wearing yesterday's clothes and you haven't showered."

"Holy dirty underwear, Batman. You do realize I could fix that, don't you? I could go home and change."

"Oh, well, yes, I suppose that's true." Tori splashed her hand into the soapy water in the sink. "And I do have running water here too."

Dale walked around the counter into the kitchen and pulled her hands out of the water. "Do you want me to leave? I will if you do."

Tori looked up, scanned his face, and shook her head. After being lonely for so long, she was afraid to admit she didn't want him to go anywhere. It was comforting to have someone to talk to who didn't chastise her for constantly being an overwrought worrier. "I have extra towels. And a huge, wonderful terry-cloth bathrobe."

"It's not pink and frilly, is it?"

"I hate pink. It's a utilitarian blue bathrobe. And there's a washer and dryer in that closet over there."

"Saved by modern appliances and terry cloth."

"It's been a long time since anyone has wanted to spend time with me." She put her arms around him and leaned her cheek on his chest. "I'm glad you do."

He stroked her hair. "Absolutely. And I'm curious how you make candy."

Tori got Dale her enormous snuggly bathrobe and towels, and he disappeared into the bathroom to take a shower. She finished cleaning up the breakfast dishes and got out all her favorite tools, appliances, and ingredients. First up was creating the little peanut butter crisps that she'd dip in chocolate.

She threw all the ingredients into Millie the mixer and let the machine do her thing. By the time Dale returned from his shower to his kitchen surveillance post on the barstool, Tori was in the middle of rolling out the dough. Ginny found the process fascinating and was supervising from her typical spot in the kitchen doorway.

He pointed at the small circular pieces of dough lined up in orderly rows on the cookie sheets. "I thought you were making chocolates again. I'm no expert, but even I know that's not chocolate. What is it?"

"Before the dragon barfed all over them, I created peanut butter crisps dipped in chocolate that I thought came out well."

"I don't think I tried those."

"You'll get your chance because soon there will be a whole lot of them."

While she worked to create tiny cookies, Tori had fun chatting with Dale about cooking. Amazingly, he seemed to be genuinely curious about how she created candy and how chefs managed to keep everything flowing smoothly in a busy restaurant kitchen. Most people were only interested in the end result of all the work, not the work itself.

She pulled the cookie sheets from the oven and carefully removed the little discs onto cooling racks that she then carefully carried to the bookshelf. Dale waved his hand at her. "I want to try a naked one."

"They aren't cool yet."

"I'm willing to risk it." He left the barstool and walked to the bookshelf. "They smell way too good to wait for the chocolate."

"I have about two hundred more to make."

He plucked a disc from the rack and flipped it back and forth in his hands. "Okay, they might be a little warm."

"They're better with the chocolate coating."

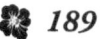

He examined another one, holding it up to his nose. "They're cute and tasty too."

Ginny jumped up and hit his bare calf with her claws. With a yelp, he stepped backward and the small disc went flying into the dining area. Ginny ran after it and gobbled it down.

Tori set down her spoon. "Ginny, behave yourself. You know you're not supposed to eat the merchandise."

Dale bent to examine the scratch on his leg. "Ouch."

Ginny snuffled at Dale's leg, searching for more flying foodstuffs. He reached up, grabbed another disc, and held it in front of her nose. "Sit."

Ginny plopped her rear on the floor like a perfect obedient dog, wagging her tail and looking expectant. He gave her the disc, and she ate it as if she were starving and it were the last morsel of food on the planet.

He stood up, ate another disc, and looked down at Ginny, who was doing her best imitation of Velcro. "I think your dog is obsessed with these."

"Well, she can't have them after they've got their chocolate coating. Chocolate is bad for dogs. I still have several batches to make. Then I need to temper the chocolate and dip them. It's going to take all day."

Dale grabbed a few more discs and walked back to the bar stool, pausing to give Ginny a few commands and rewarding her with peanut butter thrills.

He popped the last disc into his mouth. "I read somewhere that chocolate triggers feelings of relaxation, intoxication, and pleasure."

"It didn't seem to have that effect on the screaming children at the Haunted Barn. People who came into my store were more appreciative."

"Don't you like chocolate? I haven't seen you eat much. And last night you made dinner, but you hardly ate anything."

Tori gestured toward the kitchen with Stella the spatula. "I spend a lot of time tasting, not eating."

"Eating more chocolate might lower your stress level. It's supposed to release serotonin. And it has antioxidants too."

"Why are you telling me this?"

"Chocolate stimulates physical desires and lowers inhibitions."

"Where did you read that?"

"Probably a trashy magazine at a doctor's office, or while I was waiting to get a haircut." He ran his fingers through his wavy hair. "It might have been a while ago."

"When you own a chocolate shop, everyone tells you stuff like that. Chocolate is good for you. Chocolate is better than sex. I've heard it all before."

"So is it true? *Is* chocolate better than sex?"

"I'd have to say that it depends on the chocolate. And the sex."

"You said you use the expensive designer chocolate. Is that better than sex?"

"Probably."

"Are ye sure, luv? Might I try a bit o' this magical elixer o' joy?"

Tori laughed. The British accents killed her. "Sure. After I've made the other four hundred and eighty cookies I have to bake first."

"Well, that'll take a bloomin' long time."

"Fine. I'll melt a little bit of chocolate in the microwave so you can try it."

"Jolly good, luv."

Tori got out a block of her thin-formula chocolate that she used for dipping and molding. "This is a Belgian sixty-percent cacao dark chocolate with a well-balanced flavor."

"It calls t' ye seductively, don't it? There'll be moments of bliss 'ere soon."

Tori chopped a piece of chocolate off the huge block and cut it up. "You do realize that this is going to set me even further behind schedule, don't you?"

Dale got up and walked into the kitchen to observe more closely. "Yay, but it's garn ter be so good, luv."

The microwave beeped and Tori pulled out the glass measuring cup. She turned to get a spoon from a drawer and when she turned back around to face Dale, he glopped a blob of chocolate on her lips with his fingertip and grinned. "Yum."

She licked the chocolate off her lips. "That's not very hygienic."

"But very sexy." He ran a chocolate-laden fingertip down her neck and followed with his tongue. "Mmmm."

As tingles shot down her spine, Tori managed to gasp. "What are you doing?"

"Experimenting. Better than sex, they say? Maybe yer've just been doin' it wrong, then? So shall we find out?"

Tori's hormones overruled her responsible brain. Would anyone actually care if there was less candy for the kiddies this weekend? Probably not. She tugged at the terry-cloth ties of the bathrobe, pulling him toward the doorway. "I think we should find out. But not in the kitchen."

"Brilliant, luv."

Chapter 9

Cocooning

Much later, Tori was lying in bed curled up alongside Dale. She ran her hand down his arm. "Why didn't you say something?"

"Would you? 'Hey, you know those scars? They aren't just on my face. Wait until you see the rest of me.' It tends to be a real conversation stopper."

"I suppose so. I'm sorry. That was an insensitive thing for me to ask."

"Everyone has scars. Mine are just easier to see."

"That accident must have been a lot worse than I imagined."

"I don't remember much about it. I broke my right femur, and between the trees, the road, and the sled itself, I lost quite a bit of skin, I guess."

"It sounds so terribly painful." Tori traced a scar and rested her head on his chest. "I have trouble even thinking about that type of thing. As a chef, you see a lot of people cut themselves with knives. And I was terrible about it. Seeing blood or people in any type of pain makes me physically ill. I can't stand to watch scary movies. It's why I hate all the gross decorations at the Haunted Barn too. All that blood and gore upsets me."

"And you called *me* a softie."

"That was more about being sentimental. In my case, it's being a coward, really."

"It's a good thing you didn't want to be a doctor or a nurse."

Tori giggled. "No thanks. I'd be the worst nurse ever."

"Another advantage is that you don't have to spend time in hospitals. I'll be happy if I never see one again."

"I'll bet. Nurses also have to be able to do math. After my parents broke up I almost flunked algebra in high school."

"My parents split after my accident. At the time, I didn't understand what was going on. But I've read divorce isn't that unusual when children die or are sick or disabled in some way."

"You said you went with your Mom to LA. I was thinking about how different that would be." Tori sat up and pulled up her knees, wrapping her arms around them. "In my case, after they got divorced, I lived with both Mom and Dad, just not at the same time. They live close to each other and still see each other all the time."

"How come they got a divorce?"

"I don't know. Maybe they had trouble working together. Owning the store was a grind. The work was all day, every day. I knew that when I started my chocolate shop, but I figured I had all this background, having practically grown up in retail, so I'd be smarter about it. Turns out I was wrong. On the other hand, I also knew when to cut my losses and give up."

Dale sat up, put his arm around her, and kissed her cheek. "From the expression on your face, I'm thinking there's more to the story."

"They lied." Tori looked at him and something in his eyes compelled her to continue. "I don't know why I'm telling you this."

"What did they lie about?"

"Everything. I mean, here's little dependable Tori, taking care of the house and making dinner. I tried to help them, do my homework, and not cause any trouble. I think everything is going okay, but then suddenly it's not, and they announce they're getting divorced. What was that about? I was old enough to realize what they were saying was a lie. All they said was that Dad was moving out, and I'd spend time with both of them. But there was no reason why."

"You said they had joint custody. So you did spend time with both of them. I don't understand where the lie is."

"They didn't tell me the whole truth. To this day, I don't know what actually happened. They won't tell me. A lie of omission is still a lie."

He put his hand on hers. "Maybe they thought it was better for you *not* to know."

"But that's not fair." Tori looked into his eyes. "They weren't telling me the truth about something that affected every aspect of my life."

"There's no way for you to know what happened to their marriage."

Tori balled up the sheet in her fist. "But why did they have to lie about it? I tried so hard to keep everything running at home. I tried to fix it. And I thought it was working."

He hugged her tighter and gave her a kiss. "You know that's impossible."

"They were so busy with the store. I kept thinking if I just had worked harder, they would have more time to work things out. But it didn't happen and Dad moved out. I missed having him around."

"You saw him when you stayed at his place."

"I did, but it wasn't the same." She pointed at the blue terry cloth draped over the chair. "That bathrobe was his. I stole it because I missed him so much."

"I was wearing a stolen bathrobe?"

"You should be honored. It's one of my most treasured possessions. I think you're the only person other than Hope who knows how angry I was. How angry I still am in a lot of ways."

"I get it." He pushed her hair back from her face. "Divorce is hard at any age, but when you're a teenager everything seems magnified. Sometimes I think back on how I let myself freak out about so many things when I was younger. People would stare or I'd hear comments like 'he'd be cute if it weren't for those scars.' Or I'd suspect that people were only interested in me because they thought I'd inherit a fortune. At that age, thoughts like that can mess you up."

She smoothed the sheet back out over her legs. "I don't know what I would have done without Hope. She was and is my best friend. She calls me on my crap, and I've always felt like I could tell her anything. But with this business I feel like I can't. Now it feels like I'm lying to her and betraying our friendship."

"You told her you had concerns, didn't you?"

"Yes, but I need to tell her that it won't work. I keep putting it off. Instead I organize a closet or pull out my label maker and alphabetize my spices."

Dale grinned. "I have to say I've never had that response to anything."

"When I'm stressed or unhappy, I organize things." She gestured toward the closet. "The other day I made labels for my clothes hangers and organized my wardrobe by color. I need to face the fact that my career has been making me miserable for a long time. And since Augie dumped me, I've been lonely. Even worse, I'm still angry about my parents lying after all this time."

"If you know this, what are you going to do about it?"

"I don't know. Tidying up has always been my go-to option. But it hasn't helped. I haven't figured out what I need to do to make myself happier."

He gave her a kiss. "Can I offer a bit of unsolicited advice that you'll think is hard and you probably won't like?"

"Gee, that sounds fun."

"Talk to your parents. Forgive them. Life is too short not to."

"I've tried talking to them before. It never works. They still treat me like a child and give me the same old lies."

"My situation is different from yours. My parents had an extremely nasty divorce, and looking at it now, I think my mother more or less prioritized me over her marriage. Anyhow, custody arrangements were angry and contentious, so holidays were a nightmare. I never wanted to spend time with Chip and my father. I loathed both of them."

"But you still had to spend holidays with them?"

"I did, except when I was having surgeries or otherwise engaged with health stuff. And I hated it."

"It doesn't sound as if you like Chip any more now. You refer to him a toad and a troglodyte. Why are you telling me this?"

"My mother died a year ago. I spent most of the year before that taking her to chemotherapy and countless doctor visits. I finally felt like I could repay her for all the time she spent with me in hospitals. And for taking me to LA in the first place. She did it because the best plastic surgeons were there."

"I'm so sorry about your mother."

"She was a great person. When we were at oncologists and chemo treatment centers, we talked a lot, and she shared some of her regrets. One of them was saying awful things about my father when I was around. He and Chip aren't terrible people. We're just different. She said I should forgive them."

"It doesn't sound like anyone lied to you though. All I want is the truth. Why should that be so hard?"

"It's a long story, but my father wrote me out of his will. Until recently, we hadn't talked for a long time."

"It sounds like you don't like him either."

He rubbed at the scar on his cheek. "Here's another question. What would you do if you knew you only had a year to live?"

"I don't want to think about that."

"No one does. While I was waiting around during Mom's chemo treatments, I thought about it a lot. I decided I wanted to work less and live more."

Tori raised her eyebrows. "Is this a hint?"

"That's what *I* decided. All I'm saying is that you should think about what you want."

"I already told you that my goal is more or less the same as yours. I want to figure out a way to make money where I don't have to work eighty hours a week. That's why I thought this candy business with Hope was such a great idea."

"But now you're just as sure it's not. So it's time to move on and figure out something else. After Mom died, everyone told me I shouldn't make any major decisions, but I listed my condo. Then, it sold. I figured it was the universe telling me to get on with my life."

"So you're saying I should forgive my parents and get on with mine?"

"I told you it was something you wouldn't like."

Tori leaned her head against his shoulder. "I can't say I do. But I'm running out of things to organize and label."

~

Tori spent the next two days with Dale, mostly in the kitchen or in the bedroom. After years of living alone, it was strange to spend twenty-four hours a day with another person. But for reasons she didn't quite understand, he was easy to be around. He could be quiet and self-amused, content to read scripts on the sofa with Ginny, who oddly enough had decided he was now her favorite human. It helped that whenever Tori indicated a willingness to slip off to the bedroom, he gave Ginny a peanut butter disc, and suggested that the dog take a little nap because after Tori returned from behind the closed bedroom door, she'd be much more relaxed and in a better mood. He wasn't wrong about that and Ginny seemed to realize it too, content to snooze in her dog bed.

Dale was willing to help wash dishes or package candy into boxes. When Tori insisted that he wash his clothes again, he didn't seem to mind. While she was cooking, he was happy to watch and ask questions or leave her alone if she was anxious. It was so nice to have someone to talk to and share meals with who appreciated her culinary skills. It was almost like when she was growing up before her parents got divorced. While she was cooking, they'd all be in the kitchen chatting with a dog looking on, keeping an eye out for any handouts.

Somehow Dale seemed able to sense her mood. And when she moved something to put it back in the right place, he just looked at her, but didn't say anything. He was so easy to talk to, the poor guy now also knew practically her entire life story. Not to mention all her worries and hang-ups. It wasn't like her to share so much personal information, and her emotions were tangled into a knot. Was she setting herself up for disaster again?

If this wasn't a fling and she was actually starting to care for Dale, it could be a problem. In her rational moments, she thought that idea was utter nonsense. But when he looked at her with those dark, expressive eyes and her hormones took over, she wasn't so sure.

Friday morning, Tori was making breakfast, and Dale was sitting at the counter reading one of his scripts. He flipped a page. "So the scene is a muddy parking lot in front of a depressing gray manufacturing building. Workers are walking inside and our hero is a rabbit who is walking along with the crowd, holding his metal lunch box and having an argument with a squirrel."

"Since it has bunnies and squirrels going to work, I'm guessing this is a cartoon."

"Quite so, m'lady. So our friend the bunny says, 'I haven't lost my temper. I know precisely where it is and what to do with it.' So now my question is, should he be Yokel bunny?

'Ah haven't lost mah temper. Ah knows precisely whar it is an' whut t'do wif it.' Or maybe he should be Cockney bunny. 'I 'aven't lost me temper. I know precisely where it is and wot ter do wiv it.' Or perhaps mutant Swedish bunny. 'I hefee't lust my temper. Hurty flurty schnipp schnipp! I knoo preceesely vhere-a it is und vhet tu du veet it. Um de hur de hur de hur.'

"I don't know about that one."

"Maybe Valley-girl bunny? 'Gah, I haven't like lost my temper. I know fer sure where it is and like what to do with it.' Or snooty Shakepearean bunny. 'I haven't did lose mine temper. I knoweth precisely whither 't is and what to doth with 't.' Okay, nope. Forget that one."

"*Definitely* not." Tori waved her spatula at him. "No wonder it's taking you so long to finish reading through these scripts. How do you come up with all these different voices?"

"Listening, mostly." He set down the script. "Airports are great for that. Suppose the studio says they need a Midwestern accent. All I have to do is go to an airport and hang out in baggage claim after a flight has landed from Chicago."

"Why baggage claim?"

"People are waiting around for their suitcases. Most of them aren't stressed about making a connection or angry about missing a flight. They've gotten where they're going. Often they're talking about what they're going to do next when they get home or on their vacation."

"That's interesting. I never thought of that."

"People have regional dialects and different speech patterns. For example, you sound like this, 'My name is Tori, and I'd like to have a successful business that doesn't require working eighty hours a week.'"

Tori paused in her cooking activities to frown at him in horror. "Do I really sound like that? Oh my God, I *do* sound like that, don't I? How did you make your voice sound like me?"

He flipped to another page in the script. "You speak quickly and you have a sort of breathless cadence, probably because you move around a lot and you're often anxious or worried about something."

"Please, please, promise me you won't use my voice for cartoon characters."

"As you wish."

"Okay, that's the guy from the *Princess Bride,* isn't it?"

"Westley, otherwise known as the Dread Pirate Roberts." He grinned. "You're catching on, luv."

Later that afternoon, Tori pulled her awful pink costume from the closet and packed the last of the candy into her banker's boxes. Dale had to leave to go change into his costume for the Haunted Barn, and she had to drop Ginny off at the kennel.

He helped her drag the boxes down to her car. On the last trip, she got Ginny's things and clipped on her leash. Dale picked up another box of candy. "I should probably say something eloquent about your hospitality and how much I enjoyed being here over the last few days. I'm not particularly eloquent though, so I'll just say thanks for letting me invade your space. It was fun."

Instead of opening the door, Tori grabbed the box from him and set it on the floor next to Ginny. She wrapped her arms around him and hugged him hard. "I can't believe after all this time with me, you didn't want to go running for the hills."

"Why would I do that? You fed me fantastic food, we had amazing sex, and your dog doesn't hate me anymore. It was great."

She looked up at him. "You know every wretched, unflattering thing about me. I'm a neurotic, hyper-organized workaholic."

"And I'm a disfigured loner with a warped sense of humor who watches way too many cartoons. What's your point?"

Tori wasn't sure. Maybe she was feeling vulnerable. "I guess that I'm, well, I'm going to miss you."

"You'll see me in a few hours at the Haunted Barn."

"It won't be the same. For the last few days, we've been in this little warm, sexy cocoon. I wish it didn't have to end."

"It doesn't, if you don't want it to." He leaned to kiss her. "After the Haunted Barn, I could return. And maybe bring a change of clothes this time."

"I haven't wanted to ask, but isn't your family wondering where you are?"

"As long as I show up for the Haunted Barn, no one much cares when I come and go." He released her and picked up the box. "It's a big house, and I don't particularly want to see Chip. My father is out of the country at the moment with his wife. That's why he asked me to babysit Chip."

Tori giggled. "You're not doing a very good job of it since you haven't seen him in days."

"That's not the worst thing in the world. I'm a better person around you than I am around him. My absence from the ole homestead is me trying to be a better person and enjoy myself for a change."

"If you say so." Tori grabbed Ginny's leash. "We should get going."

He leaned to give her a kiss and whispered, "Parting is such sweet sorrow, m'lady."

～

After one final heart-stopping kiss next to her car, Dale walked to his swanky automobile and drove away. Tori had no idea where the Holbrook family homestead was, but he turned south. She put Ginny in the back seat of her car and headed in the opposite direction toward Alpine Grove.

She reflected on what she'd said to Dale about being wrapped in a sexy cocoon. The time they'd spent together had been easy, and best of all, she'd felt appreciated. It was far different from her experiences with Augustine. When she'd spent time with Augie, she had to be "on" all the time. On their dates, she was supposed to be the perfect chef with answers to any culinary questions he might ask her. The fact that Dale didn't know much about cooking was an unexpected blessing. Being involved with someone who didn't know much about the nuances of flavor or spicing was a relief.

Meals, in particular, were a lot more enjoyable when every last detail of the food wasn't analyzed. Arguing about food had been exhausting and gave new meaning to the term food fight. Augie also had taken every opportunity to detail his latest cooking fetishes. One evening, she actually avoided serving pickled asparagus as a side dish because she knew it would spur yet another conversation about his latest peppery pickling spice revelations.

It also didn't hurt that Tori found Dale incredibly sexy. He could be achingly tender or wildly exciting, and Tori had trouble keeping her hands off him. Even better was that the feeling was clearly mutual. Heck, at this point, even Ginny

liked him. She glanced back at the dog who was curled up in the back seat.

By now, Ginny undoubtedly was wise to the fact that they were going to the kennel yet again. Thankfully, there was only one more weekend and then Halloween itself. The light at the end of this long tunnel was finally visible, and the end of the month was nigh. All Tori had to do was suck it up and deal with annoying costumed people for three more days, and it would be over.

The discussions with Dale about the recent changes he'd made in his life had led Tori to ask herself a few hard questions. And not only about her business. If the new candy biz became successful, would she be happy? She always thought that if she simply tried harder and worked harder, she'd be happy. But mostly it had led to burnout. Career success was important, but was it enough? What did she want from the rest of her life?

Until recently, her day-to-day life had been so busy that it was easy to avoid asking, much less answering these fundamental questions. Sure, she'd been disappointed in her many failed relationships. But was she capable of maintaining a relationship with another human being long-term? Did she want to? And if she did, was Dale a candidate? Could she see herself falling in love with him?

On the positive side, he was sexy, easy to talk to, and seemed to be interested in her. The most obvious negative was that he had an unfortunate tendency to upset the routines that made up her life. This week, she'd made far less candy than last. She'd shirked her obligations, and there was no doubt that it was because of him. Her orderly life became disorderly with him in it.

Tori shook her head as if she could shake her confusing thoughts and emotions out her ears. The long drive to the kennel gave her far, far too much time to think. With a sigh, she flipped on the radio and tuned it to the one station that you could get in Alpine Grove.

By the time she arrived at the kennel, she'd listened to enough music that she wasn't a swirling mass of anxiety. Being surrounded by so many trees helped too. She got out of the car and looked up at the massive evergreens. A bird launched from a branch and she heard the whooshing sound of its wings flapping as it disappeared from view.

The door of the kennel opened and Joel walked out, followed by Kat. At the sight of the petite woman, Tori grinned, "I'm so glad to see you!"

"Thanks. It's good to be outside again." Kat walked to the car and peered in the window. "How's our favorite houseguest?"

"I think she's happy to be here." Tori unloaded Ginny, who walked around in circles wagging her long tail. "We had another big week of making candy, and I found out she likes peanut butter."

Kat looked up at Joel, who picked up Ginny and held her in his arms. Kat stroked the dog's head. "Is PB the way to your heart, Ginny? This is information I could use to my advantage."

Joel said, "Have you seen Dale lately?"

Surprised, Tori paused for a moment. How did he know? Wait, he couldn't know Dale had spent all week with her. "He should be at the Haunted Barn tonight."

"If you see him, could you ask him to call me?"

"Sure." Tori fiddled with her keys in her hands and almost dropped them. Running off now would be rude. "Is everything okay with his accounting project?"

Kat said, "Better now that Mia has returned, and he doesn't have to play with dead numbers in the middle of the night."

Joel glanced at her and raised an eyebrow. Turning back to Tori, he said, "I need to ask Dale a couple of questions."

"So are you looking at spreadsheet printouts or something?" Tori asked.

"He hacks into the system," Kat said. "Like a geeky vampire, roaming around at three in the morning."

"It's not hacking if you've been given a log-in." Joel readjusted the dog in his arms. "I have remote access."

"I suppose if your last name is Holbrook you can do what you want—even give access to vampire geeks," Kat said as she scratched Ginny behind her ears. "I can't believe you didn't fall asleep. But your office buddy has returned to keep you company."

"True." Readjusting Ginny again, he continued, "Tori, we'll see you on Sunday, right?"

Realizing this was her cue to leave, Tori stepped toward her car. How on earth did Dale, who professed to have nothing to do with his family's company, get Joel access into their systems? Something wasn't adding up here. How did Dale find out about the financial issues in the first place? Was Dale lying about his involvement with the company? If so, why? What was going on?

Kat said, "We'll see you then."

Shaken from her thoughts, Tori stammered, "Yes. Sunday. I'll be here bright and early."

"We appreciate your punctuality," Kat said. "Not everyone is quite as conscious of our pick-up and drop-off hours."

"That's an understatement," Joel added.

Returning her focus to the conversation at hand, Tori said, "I'm a stickler when it comes to being on time. I try to be prompt or a bit early for everything. If I'm late, it's probably because something happened that was beyond my control. One time I had a flat tire on the way to work and I almost had a heart attack. I don't understand those people who are habitually late for everything. How hard is it to calculate how much time it takes to get ready, how long the drive is based on typical traffic conditions, and how long it will take you to park and walk to your destination?"

Kat raised her eyebrows. "You sure take your appointments seriously."

"I'm sorry—being on time is a bit of a hot-button with me," Tori said. Not unlike lying and half-truths. She managed to muster a feeble smile. She must sound like a hysterical hyper-punctual lunatic. "Thank you again for taking such good care of Ginny. I need to get going."

She climbed into her car feeling slightly ill. If Dale had misrepresented his connection to his family business, what else had he lied about? Why was it so hard for people to tell the truth, the whole truth, and nothing but the truth?

∽

Kat and Joel stood and watched as Tori drove down the driveway. Joel set Ginny on the ground and shook out his arms. "I think this dog is getting fatter."

Ginny sat and stared up at them. Kat laughed. "You may as well carry her, or it will take us hours to make it up the driveway to the house."

"True." With a sigh, he hefted the dog back into his arms and started walking. "So it's probably not a good idea to talk about the forensic accounting project with Tori. I signed confidentiality forms, remember?"

"We didn't say anything she didn't already know. Dale told her what you're doing."

"Are you sure?"

"Positive."

"I suppose it's not like I'm dealing with top-secret classified intel. It's actually pretty tedious. A lot of it is going through logs. I have written a few scripts now, so it's going more quickly. But how did you know she knew about it?"

"I know I wasn't there, but you told me Dale cut you off because he didn't want to talk about the project in front of Tori. But today, she knew he was the dead accounting client."

"Good point."

Kat reached over and gave Ginny a pat as they walked. "Did you see the look on Tori's face when you asked if she'd seen Dale lately? Deer in the headlights."

"It wasn't that bad."

"Yes it was. She didn't say it, but I'm guessing she's seen a whole lot of him. I think he hasn't answered your emails or phone messages because he hasn't been home all week. It's completely obvious they're together now."

Joel chuckled. "You're taking nosiness to a new quasi-psychic level."

"I prefer to think of it as being observant."

He laughed. "Yeah, sure."

"As a writer, I am trying to become a student of human nature. But from afar because I'm an introvert."

Joel set Ginny down in front of the back door of the house. "Okay, you know the routine. It's time for the meet and greet."

Kat walked inside and shooed her dogs back, "Ginny has returned. Everyone, sniff and move on."

The requisite sniffing and wagging took place as all five dogs ascertained that they knew Ginny already. The phone in Joel's office rang, and he maneuvered through the canines to answer it. He said, "Hi Dale, how are you?" and shut his office door.

Kat walked into her office followed by the canine parade. Her computer had been returned to its regular spot downstairs, snuggled alongside her towering piles of books and printouts.

She pulled a handful of paper off the stack and started going through it. Lurking somewhere within the archaeological pile were the notes listing the problems she'd found while writing an article about a "new improved" software upgrade. It might be new, but improved was debatable, and she needed to compose a delicately worded email to her editor. They had two choices. One: give up on the article and pay her a kill fee. Two: tell the truth and risk the wrath of the Giant Software Company.

She pulled out the sheet of paper as the door across the hall opened. Joel thumped upstairs, undoubtedly on a mission to forage for food. After living with him for quite some time, Kat had learned Joel was a power snacker. He had

an enviable metabolism. If she grazed like that, she'd weigh four hundred pounds.

The phone rang and Kat picked it up, eager for an excuse to avoid her awkward email. She smiled at the sound of her friend Maria's voice. "Hi, how's it going?"

Maria said, "Well, I told you I met a farmer last weekend at the Haunted Barn, right?"

"Yes, he said you had lovely eyes."

"Well, that's because he couldn't see any other part of me thanks to the hideous nun tent I was wearing. I may have mentioned to him that I thought the whole vow of celibacy thing was a crock."

"Probably good to get that discussion out of the way."

"Yeah, he seemed to appreciate the sentiment. I know black goes with everything, but that nun costume is ugly. I prefer a bit more form-fitting attire."

Kat set her paper aside. That was an understatement. Form-fitting was Maria-speak for skin tight. Her favorite fabric was spandex. "So did Farmer Bob call you like he promised?"

"He did! And that's why I'm calling you. I have a wardrobe situation."

"How does that affect me? You hate the way I dress."

"I know. But Bob invited me to go riding. On a horse."

Kat laughed. "Thanks for the clarification."

"I'm not sure about this, girlfriend. Horses are big and I don't have suitable clothes. I need jodhpurs."

"I'm fresh out of those. I'm not even sure what they are."

"Riding pants. Breeches. I didn't know what they were either, but I looked it up online when I was at work. You need them to save your lady parts."

"Save them from what?"

"I'm sorry. I wasn't thinking. That's a sensitive subject."

"No, it's not." Kat tried not to roll her eyes. "I still have some parts left, you know."

"Okay, well, speaking of sensitive. Horseback riding requires sitting on a saddle. I've watched enough Westerns to think that can't be easy on my favorite lady parts. Jodhpurs have extra layers of fabric to avoid chafing. I don't like the sound of chafing anywhere near my nether regions, so I'm sure I need them. Horses are clunky, and I don't know how to ride."

"Wouldn't wearing pants suffice? Cowboys seem to wear a lot of denim and other heavy fabrics."

"But they're ugly. Jodhpurs are form-fitting and cute. But I don't know where I can find them locally. Mail-order will take too long."

"The shopping here is limited, so I have no idea. Did you try calling stores in Gleasonville?"

"Yeah, but it didn't go anywhere. I learned that feed stores don't carry clothes and clothing stores don't carry horse stuff."

"I don't know what to tell you. Wear pants. Live dangerously."

"I have leggings from my 80s Madonna phase. You know when she was in *Desperately Seeking Susan*, she wore those leggings and skirts all the time. I never quite was able to pull it off."

Kat reached down to pet Linus. Considering the various ways in which Maria might go for a Madonna look was unsettling. "Leggings tend to be pretty thin. That might be unpleasant."

"I'm not sure they still fit either."

"Don't you own a pair of blue jeans?"

"Of course not. I refuse to dress like a farmer."

"Even when you're going out with a farmer?"

"Hmm, I didn't' think of that. I guess you might have a point. He'll probably be wearing jeans, won't he?"

"Probably. They sell blue jeans at the local Kmart that you pretend doesn't exist."

"I can't believe I'm actually considering buying denim at Kmart. What has my life become?"

"Think of it as a learning experience. You're growing as a person. Having new experiences. Exploring new frontiers."

"I know you're silently laughing over there, girlfriend. I can feel it."

"Maybe a little."

Chapter 10

Focus Group Failures

The now-familiar scents of old hay and wood greeted Tori upon her return to the Haunted Barn. She walked through the massive wooden double doors, kicking up dust as she strolled down the main corridor to the Candy Land stand.

Although animals obviously weren't living in the barn during the event, the fact that the gigantic building had housed them for multiple generations was evident from the vague lingering odor of manure and straw that pervaded the space. Most of the spiders and spiderwebs were fake decorations, but not all of them were, so it was best to exercise caution near any walls, beams, or corners.

Clad in her Red Riding Hood cape, Hope was at the table setting up the display. Tori set down a box. "I'm so glad you're early. Could you help me with the rest of the boxes?"

Hope agreed, and they carted the candy inside and set it out in the baskets. They'd gone through the process several times now, so there wasn't much need for conversation.

When they were finished, Hope walked to the front of the table and pointed at Tori's peanut butter warning sign. "What's this?"

"It's to let people know that peanut butter is one of the ingredients in them. I had it out last week too."

"Why aren't there any Choco-critters?" She picked up a chocolate-covered peanut butter crisp and ate it. "Last week you brought all kinds of weird stuff. Now you only made two things. Why seashells? What happened to the Choco-critters?"

"They're a lot of work, and no one liked them."

"I liked them!"

"You're not our target audience. So last week I experimented and tried something else. That's a reasonable thing to do in business, isn't it?"

"Yes, but we didn't come to any conclusions. Why didn't you talk to me about what you were bringing this week? What are you thinking?"

"I told you we needed to try other candy options." Tori waved her arms in exasperation. "And I was busy this week."

They were interrupted by a bedraggled-looking mummy who stopped in front of the table. "Can I have one? I didn't get dinner and I'm starving."

"These have peanut butter," Tori said.

"Awesome." The mummy grabbed a fistful and wandered off.

Hope dove back into the conversation. "Why were you so busy that you couldn't make Choco-critters? Testing is fine, but Choco-critters are the basis of our entire marketing strategy."

"I wanted to make something easy. The mummy likes the peanut butter. Oh, and Ginny does too."

"Well good for her. She's not our target market either. What were you doing all week if you weren't making chocolate?"

"Making these! Dale likes them too."

"Dale who? You mean Dale Holbrook? *Really?*"

Tori looked down at her fingernails. "Yes. He's a nice person."

"Okay, now this makes sense to me. You never admit you actually like a guy unless you're sleeping with him." Hope chomped a seashell. "The salt is sort of weird."

"Kids might like it though. I brought them last week, but I don't remember anyone saying anything."

"How did you get involved with Dale anyway? Chip says he's weird and lies all the time. According to Chip, Dale is the black sheep of the family."

"They don't seem to like each other much. Their parents are divorced. It's probably a sibling-rivalry thing. I was an only child, but I'm guessing it's typical family stuff."

"I don't know. According to Chip, one time when he went to visit his Mom in LA, Dale took all of Chip's right shoes and hung them on trees throughout the neighborhood."

Tori frowned. "Do you know why?"

"Chip said it's because he's nuts. Another time, Dale took Chip's underwear and hung it on a tree under a ski lift at Snow Grove."

"Maybe they argued about clothing. We don't know the whole story." Tori didn't want to hear any more. She needed to find Dale. He had to be around somewhere. "I need to visit the ladies' room before they let everyone in and the screaming starts."

"Well, hurry up because I need to go too."

Although it was getting dark, the fog machines hadn't started running yet. The scare actors were milling around talking among themselves instead of leaping out at people, so it was relatively easy to navigate to the ladies' room. When she returned, Hope was talking to someone dressed as Robin Hood.

He popped a peanut butter disc into his mouth. "These are good."

"Tori experimented with many different types of candy last week, and those seemed to be popular. Try a seashell, Chip. They have interesting salty overtones."

"Don't mind if I do."

Tori frowned. That wasn't true. Nothing had been popular. And she didn't even get to save the leftover candy for this week because a dragon had barfed all over it. Hope was glossing over events, making it sound like they were being intentional about this, which was definitely not the case. She went behind the table and pulled a box of candy out from underneath the table skirt.

Hope said, "I'm sorry I had to leave early from our dinner the other night. It seems like quite a while since I've seen you."

He grabbed another piece of candy. "I should get going."

Something about his hand movement tickled Tori's memory, and she scanned the man's face. "What are you *doing?*"

He looked up in surprise. "Eating candy."

Tori stomped around the table. She had to give him credit. The impression was amazingly good. "Why are you pretending to be Chip?"

He raised his eyebrows and shrugged slightly. "Old habits die hard, I guess."

Hope leaned over the table. "I'm sorry for the misunderstanding. You probably had no idea what I was talking about. But you look a lot like Chip Holbrook."

"He ought to," Tori said, and turned back to him. "You didn't answer my question. What are you doing?"

Hope said, "If you're not Chip, who are you?"

Tori pointed her index finger. "This is Dale Holbrook. Chip's brother."

"Oh, Tori mentioned you." Hope said. "So did Chip."

Tori put her fists on her hips. "Are you sure about that?"

Hope made a face. "Maybe. So did you really hang Chip's tighty whities on a tree under a ski lift? And if so, why?"

"There's no proof that was me. And if it had been me, maybe I was making a statement," Dale said.

"Oh my gosh, I just realized you're Chip and Dale. Like the chipmunks!" Hope grinned widely. "I never thought of that before."

"That's Dale's fault too." Tori needed to speak with Dale alone. She grabbed his hand and yanked him away from the table. "We need to talk."

"Is something wrong?"

Tori stopped next to a stall filled with bales of hay and a repulsive fake zombie lying on the floor. She dropped Dale's hand, leaned against the old wood, and crossed her arms. "I told you everything. Absolutely *everything* about me. And now I find out you've been lying to me."

"Lying about what?"

"You said you had nothing to do with your family's business. But you're able to get Joel access into the company accounting systems. No one who isn't involved could do that."

He reached out to take her hand. "You don't…"

She slapped his hand away. "And now…*now*, you're pretending to be your brother. Deceiving my best friend. How could you? I trusted you. I thought I could tell you anything."

"You can…"

"No, I can't. I can't trust someone who is lying to me."

"Tori, this has nothing to do with you."

"But I told you how I feel about every little thing in my life. I thought you were being honest with me too. I'm such an idiot."

"Aren't there things you don't or can't say even though you want to? Things you wish were different?"

Tori glanced at a scare actor wearing striped criminal garb who was staring intensely at her. This was so embarrassing. She whispered, "I don't know. Probably."

He reached for her hand again. "Let me explain."

With a piercing squeal of the metal runners, the huge barn doors slid open and a hoard of screaming children dressed in a wide array of costumes barreled through the entrance, screaming at the top of their lungs. The hum of the fog machines started and the spooky music began, signaling the opening of the Haunted Barn.

Tori let go of his hand. "I have to go work." She turned and joined the stream of costumed people flooding into the barn, hurriedly brushing a tear from her eye.

Dale's lack of denial was all the explanation she needed. She was done with people lying to her.

⌒

Tori spent the rest of the evening hoping to avoid Dale and handing out candy to kids who had no comment. Children were as bad as movie stars or politicians. Heaven forbid they'd actually want to offer an opinion or make a statement on the record. One forest elf gave her a halfhearted, "It's okay," before running off. Even Hope was starting to understand the issue at hand. The pre-pubescent crowd wasn't enthralled by anything.

By the end of the evening, Tori was still feeling demoralized about her prospects for ever having a successful business. Hope was uncharacteristically quiet, which was never good. As they packed up the candy for the evening, Tori said, "Only two more days of this and we're done."

Hope put the lid on a banker's box. "I'm not sure what we've learned."

"Me neither. We need to talk about what we're going to do."

"I need to talk to Morgan."

Tori bent to put the box under the table and stood up. "What are you going to tell him?"

"I'm not sure." Hope pulled her red cloak over her shoulders. "I'll see you tomorrow."

Tori tucked the last of the boxes under the table and shook out the tablecloth. After arranging all the boxes into tidy rows and carefully covering them with the cloth, she walked toward the exit. What an exhausting evening. She was furious at Dale, and Hope was depressed. All Tori wanted to do was slide into bed and forget about her life.

She stepped out into the cool night and jerked to one side when Dale appeared next to her. He took her arm and echoed what she'd said earlier. "We need to talk."

"I'm tired. I want to go home."

"In a minute. At first, I didn't tell you what I was doing because I didn't know you. Then I did know you and it didn't seem important."

Tori stopped, shook off his hand, and turned to face him. "How could it not be? Part of who I am is that I need to know who is telling the truth and who isn't. Did you really put Chip's underwear in a tree?"

"Yes. Did I tell you about it? No. Why would I? Hanging underwear on trees rarely comes up in conversation."

"No it doesn't. But I don't understand why you imitated Chip. And now I'm guessing that the first night I met you, Chip didn't copy your Robin Hood costume. You copied his. How many other things do I *not* know?"

"I told you I was keeping an eye on Chip. I followed up with women I thought he might be hitting on to see if he had."

"Do you and your brother have bizarre issues with clothing or something?"

"Not exactly."

"Then *what* exactly? You said you were making a statement."

"First, let it be known that I was fifteen. Chip was seventeen. Have you ever heard of a wedgie?"

"Yes, I suppose so."

"You might not know this, but having your stupid brother hang you up by your underwear every single time you have to see him over the holidays gets old. I was tired of it, so when Chip went on a ski trip with his buddies, I stole all his underwear and wrote his name on the butt with a permanent marker. Then I went to Snow Grove and hung them on the trees under the ski lift. Chair 1 to be precise."

"You and Chip really don't like each other."

"We don't." He spread his arms wide. "Are you happy now?"

"No, I'm not. But I'm extremely busy and I need to go."

"What are you so afraid of? How is spending ten minutes talking to me going to make a difference?"

"This is my business we're talking about. It's important."

"I understand that. What I don't understand is why you're afraid to talk to me."

"I'm not." Tori tugged at the scratchy ruffle on her sleeve. It was torn and had been bothering her all night. "I already told you. I'm afraid the business isn't going to work."

"So you'll do something else."

"But what?"

"Whatever you want."

"You don't get it." Tori ripped the lace off the sleeve. "If this doesn't work, what will I do all day? I can't handle having nothing to do. I'm one of those people who thrives on being busy. In fact, while we're being honest here, I love scheduling and organizing and putting check marks on check lists. I'm like a little hamster running on his wheel, thrilled by my happy hamster busyness. And if you imitate a cartoon hamster now, I'm leaving no matter what you say."

"I only do chipmunks, not hamsters." He took her hand. "Spending so much time with you was amazing. I thought we had a connection. I don't want to lose that."

"I need to focus on my business. It's not going well, and we probably shouldn't see each other for a while."

"Why? You can still work. This week you spent a lot of time making candy. I was working too. But it was like that old saying, 'it's not the destination, it's the journey.' I read over scripts like I always do, but the journey was more fun because I was hanging out with you."

"Maybe so." Tori looked down at her hands, fiddling with the lace in her fingers. He wasn't wrong. It had been fun. Wonderful even. Possibly the best time she'd ever had with anyone, ever. But she hadn't gotten as much work done. She'd slacked off in her responsibilities and Hope had been disappointed in her. "I feel guilty about how little I accomplished. You already know I'm an obsessively organized, workaholic overachiever. I need to work and I can't be involved with someone I don't trust."

"You honestly don't trust me?"

"I asked you before and you didn't answer me. How did you get Joel access to the Holbrook accounting systems if you have nothing to do with your family's company?"

"That's complicated."

"In other words, you're not going to tell me. If I'm right, and I know I am, we have nothing to say to each other." Tori straightened, trying to steel her resolve. Although part of her wanted to burst into tears or heave herself into his arms like a slobbery lovesick Labrador retriever, she refused to let her emotions overrule her brain again. This was the right thing to do. "I need to go."

"I already told you that the relationship I have with my family isn't good. I didn't want to infect you with that toxic brew."

Tori shook her head. "I'm not sure I even know who you are."

"Okay, I get it." He looked up at the stars in the black sky. "Maybe you're right. I'm not ever going to live up to your level of super-human perfection. You can definitely do better. Aim high. If you ever decide that you're willing to give me a chance, let me know. If not, well, that's all, folks."

Without another word, he strode back into the barn and disappeared into the thinning fog. As she slowly walked to her car, the sick feeling that had been roiling in her stomach increased. In one evening, it seemed she'd managed to destroy both her business and her love life.

Even for her, this had to be some type of record.

~

The next morning, Tori dragged herself from the warmth of her bed and set to work creating a small batch of Choco-critters. After pondering her critter options, she settled on strawberry-flavored pigs. Maybe she was inspired by Dale's Merrie Melodies send off.

Her enthusiasm was low, but she'd made them so many times, she could melt chocolate in her sleep now. It was a good thing too because last night's slumber had been anything but restful. Her brain wouldn't shut up, taking the opportunity to repeat her angry conversation with Dale over and over in her head.

By the afternoon, the chocolate was cool, and she went through the process of wrapping the little critters in foil.

It had to be the most depressing cooking experience she'd ever had. The apartment was so empty and quiet, Tori could barely stand it. Without even the soft snorty sounds of Ginny snoring in her dog bed to keep her company, Tori's nonstop mind chatter might slowly drive her insane.

She picked up the phone and dialed her mother's number. The answering machine recited its spiel and Tori was trying to figure out what to say when her mother burst onto the line. "Hello!"

"Hi Mom."

"Tori! How are you? I haven't heard from you for ages. What's going on?"

"I've been working at the Haunted Barn. Right now, I'm wrapping lots of chocolates to give away."

"How fun. I hope the business is doing well."

Tori wiped a smudge of chocolate off the counter. "I'm not sure."

"I'm sorry honey, but I'm about to run out to lunch with a friend. Is there something you needed?"

"No, nothing. I wanted to…uh…see if you're okay."

"I'm fine. Are you? You sound upset."

"No, I'm fine. A friend told me about their mom being sick and I haven't talked to you."

"Oh my God, you mean Hope's mom? Is Gail okay? I need to give her a call."

"No, Mom, not Hope. Gail's fine. I was talking to someone else." Tori jerked on the phone cord. Talking to her mother always led to a misunderstanding. "Never mind. I just wanted to check in. You should go to your lunch."

They said their goodbyes and Tori hung up the phone, feeling worse than she had before. What a miserable day. If life was about the journey, not the destination, today's sad, lonely journey was headed toward a car crash at the Haunted Barn. It was likely to be an awkward evening. Ugh.

The phone rang, jolting Tori from her morose ruminations. She picked up the receiver and was greeted by her friend's voice. "Hi Hope. What's up?"

"So, I wanted to talk to you before we get to the barn. It's difficult to communicate there with all the screaming and noise. I feel like we haven't talked about the business in a while."

Tori tried to repress an audible sigh. "I know."

"You said you were going to do experiments, but I probably should have run your ideas by Morgan first. He's a bit upset that you've deviated from the business plan."

"Kids didn't like Choco-critters. They thought they weren't cool. I told you we needed to try something else. You didn't say I shouldn't test other options."

"I know." Hope cleared her throat. "But I, uh, probably should have."

"So what you're saying is that everything is Morgan's decision? Is that how this partnership works?"

"No. That's not it at all."

"Then what *is* it?" Tori hadn't seen Morgan in quite some time. Every time they met, she remembered why she and Hope didn't hang out much anymore. He was one of those people who dominated every conversation. Hope thought he was successful and fascinating. Although she never said it out loud, Tori thought he was more than a little arrogant and definitely full of himself.

"Morgan wants to make sure we network front-end relevance feedback resources. Without that data, we can't leverage scalable product manufacturing."

"Does that mean find more kids? We've already seen thousands of kids. You're reading this from a piece of paper, aren't you?"

Hope ignored the comment and pressed the point. "The kids at the barn weren't paying attention. Morgan said we need to do a better job of facilitating seamless communication with our focus group."

"You've got to be kidding." Tori waved her hand in exasperation, wishing she could smack Hope for simply parroting everything Morgan had said. She'd probably spelled facilitating wrong on her notepad. "Morgan honestly thinks a bunch of kids riding a sugar high in a gigantic barn are going to pay attention? Has the man ever gone trick-or-treating?"

"He's worried we aren't getting actionable information."

"Maybe not." Tori didn't want to have this conversation. "Was there anything else?"

"He said it's important to design semantic ballpark deliverables. Oh, and we need to visualize a result-driven downstream sales funnel. And extend our out-of-the-box dynamic bandwidth."

"Right. Let's get through this evening and maybe we can talk about it later. I need to get back to wrapping my Choco-critters."

"Did you make the strawberry ones?"

"Yes."

"Excellent. Those are my favorites. I'll see you later."

Tori hung up the phone and ate a piece of candy. It was entirely possible that she wasn't cut out for partnership. At least when she'd operated her own store, no one ever used words like actionable or deliverables. Sheesh.

That evening when Tori arrived at the Haunted Barn, Hope didn't mention their conversation, but she'd known Tori forever and practically the first words out of her mouth were, "Have you been crying?"

Tori frowned. Was it that obvious? She'd put on tons of eye makeup, but apparently not enough to fool Hope. It was pointless to try to avoid the issue. "Dale and I broke up."

"Good. You're better off without that guy."

Tori wasn't so sure, but they continued going through the typical motions of setting up without dwelling on Tori's latest romantic train wreck. The doors opened and even though handing out candy was the same as it ever was, it seemed uncomfortable, as if they'd just met instead of having been best friends since elementary school.

While dispensing candy, Tori also kept her eye out for Dale, who she desperately wanted to avoid. That was yet another conversation she didn't want to have. Although intellectually she didn't want to talk to him, another part of her was dying to catch a glimpse of him, even if it was only for a second. She wanted to see the little crinkles next to his eyes when he laughed. Hear the warmth in his voice when he made a random off-the-wall comment. Enjoy the melodramatic expressions of adulation for her latest cooking concoction. See the way his hair curled around his collar and stood up in twenty-five directions when he'd just awakened in the morning. Okay, maybe she missed him more than she wanted to admit.

Although the barn was crowded with noisy people, the evening dragged on as if it were being filmed in slow motion. Because it was the last weekend before Halloween, the number of people getting into the ghoulish spirit had increased. Little Bo Peep would never wear a watch, so in the spirit of authenticity, Tori had left hers on her dresser and there was no way for her to know what time it was.

Tori handed a Choco-critter to a kid dressed as a garden gnome and they both jumped at the sound of Hope letting out a squeal next to them. The garden gnome ran away and Hope flapped her arms like a bird taking off as she ran out from behind the table toward the great mountain of man approaching them. She leaped into his arms and he twirled her around.

Tori was significantly less thrilled to see Morgan. When it came to him, the culinary analogy about oil and water was apt. At six-foot-six, Morgan was hard to miss. With his massive frame and booming voice, he reminded Tori of the Jolly Green Giant. It was easy to imagine him holding up a can of corn, encouraging people to eat their vegetables.

Hope hugged her husband, bubbling over with joy. "I thought you weren't coming back until next week."

He planted a sloppy kiss on her lips. "I couldn't stand being away from you any longer, babe. And I wanted to see first-hand how our enterprise is doing."

Making a conscious effort to repress her emotions, Tori settled her expression into a polite smile. It sounded suspiciously like he was checking up on them. "Hi Morgan. It's nice to see you again."

"What's with the frilly ruffles on your display?"

"That was the only tablecloth Tori had," Hope volunteered.

"You could have bought something else if you didn't like it," Tori said.

Hope put her hand on her hips. "I thought you were going to do that."

"I was making candy, remember?" Tori said. "All day, every day."

"Ladies, let's not argue about this. The ruffles match that pink dress you've got, Tori. But aren't you supposed to be wearing a mask?" He wrapped a beefy arm around Hope. "I never would have thought Little Red Riding Hood could be so totally hot with a mask."

"I'm Little Bo Peep, who apparently likes pink." Once Halloween was over, Tori was going to burn this dress in a ceremonial bonfire. "I lost the mask quite a while ago."

Morgan didn't reply. He was too wrapped up in whatever Hope was whispering in his ear. She giggled and unwrapped herself from him long enough to hand a Choco-critter to a kid dressed as a Disney princess. "Let us know what you think."

The princess ran away without saying anything. Morgan handed a chocolate-covered peanut butter crisp to a short, round fireman and said, "Eat it and give me your impression of it."

The kid appeared to be paralyzed with fear at Morgan's command and obediently took a bite. "It's okay. I gotta go." He placed the rest of the disc on the table and ran away.

Morgan ate a strawberry pig. "These are good. What if we sell these exclusively? Call them Iggy Piggys."

Hope said, "I love that, sweetie. Let's see what the kids think."

Tori couldn't stand all this ooey-gooey business speak. "I still haven't seen the a-mazing corn maze. Maybe you two could hold down the fort for a while, so I can check it out."

Hope smiled up at Morgan. "Sure. Have fun!"

The last thing Tori wanted to do was visit the corn maze, but she couldn't bear any more of the amorous swooning and drooling. She hustled off toward the exit before Hope could change her mind.

This wasn't the first time Tori had been the third wheel. It's where you inevitably ended up when you had as many romantic disasters as she did.

~

Tori exited the barn, enjoying the crisp autumn air. It was nice to be away from the stuffy barn and lovebird central. She walked through a few "scare zones," fending off a few disappointed scare actors with snotty comments, and stopped at the entrance to the maze. According to the information, it was six acres of corn maze that was packed with so many twists and turns that it was "sure to get you lost."

Given that Tori could get lost in a parking lot, she was a little apprehensive about actually setting foot inside. The only good news was that she was unlikely to be returning to her candy duties for quite some time. Children under twelve weren't allowed in the maze, and supposedly it took about an hour to get through it. Tori suspected it would take her longer than the average twelve-year-old to make it out of the agricultural labyrinth.

She walked through the entrance into the maze itself, gazing up at the tall stalks of corn that formed the walls. From the outside, the maze looked like a typical corn field with densely planted corn stalks that were at least twice her height. Walls of corn stretched as far as she could see. She moved forward until she found a break in the corn that went in a different direction. She considered her options, but it was impossible to know what to do. Each passageway was identical to the next. It was corn, corn, and more corn. There was no reason to believe that turning left would be better than turning right or continuing straight ahead.

A teenager ran by her and disappeared down a passageway to her right. Should she follow him? No way. She kept walking, but slowed when a scream pierced the night from somewhere deep in the maze. Then a howling noise rose from somewhere to her left. She hit a dead end and doubled back to return to the last passage she'd walked by. The corn was impenetrable. What if she got so lost that she disappeared for hours and they shut down the Haunted Barn? Sleeping in a corn field at the end of October didn't sound like fun at all. Was it cold enough that she'd freeze to death? At the end of the evening, did someone run through the maze to clear out stragglers? They had to. People with a poor sense of direction—like her—could be in big trouble otherwise.

She kept walking, trying to figure out if there was any rhyme or reason to the maze. Everywhere she went led to a dead end with a hay bale, so you could sit and ponder the error of your ways. After the sixth dead end, Tori sat on the bale and crossed her arms. This was absurd. At this rate, she might never get out of this corn field.

It didn't make sense. Why was everything so complicated? Her life was falling apart, and now she would be trapped in a corn maze forever. A scream came from nearby and Tori decided to scream back. She took a deep breath and yelled, "I hate corn!"

Screaming and yelling was cathartic. Maybe those scream actors were on to something. She yelled, "I hate manufacturing build-out and front-end relevance. What the heck is that supposed to mean?"

She laughed, giddy at the freedom of yelling in a place where no one could hear you. If you're doomed to die in a corn maze, you should say everything you want to say. She shouted, "I'm not a food snob because I traveled thirty miles to purchase ripe strawberries. That's wanting quality, okay? Get over it, Leo."

She took a breath. "No one should ever eat packaged ramen noodles, no matter how cheap they are. They're disgusting!"

Standing up, she walked down the passageway. Maybe if she kept walking, she'd finally get out of here. "I *still* hate corn."

At another dead end, she sat on a bale of hay and screamed, "I hate this. Corn is evil. Let me out!"

Tears started to stream down her cheeks. "I don't care what anyone says. I am not a control freak. I'm *not!* I can't help it if I know the right way to do things. I hate kids who hate candy. What is wrong with them? I hate this corn. Why do I drive everyone away? I want to get out of here. Let me *out!*"

A masked person in green ran down the passageway at full speed. Tori was so startled, she jumped up off the hay bale and tripped over her own feet.

The impact of hitting the dirt knocked the wind from her lungs. Lying on the ground, she caught her breath and rolled onto her back. She spread her arms wide, closed her eyes, and whimpered, "I'm going to die here. I'm going to freeze to death unhappy and alone. It's the end. I know it."

At the touch on her arm, she jerked to a sitting position and found herself face-to-face with Dale. He smiled. "I think you're going to live."

Without thinking, she threw her arms around his neck. "I'm so glad you're here. I can't believe how much I missed you."

"I missed you too." He wrapped her in a warm hug. "I know it hasn't been long, but it sure felt like it."

"I'm so sorry." The sick feeling in her stomach melted away and Tori started to cry in earnest. "What you do with your family is none of my business."

He pushed her hair away from her face. "Hey, don't cry. You were right too. After all the time we spent together, I should have told you what was going on."

"I don't know what's wrong with me. I mean, who am I to judge about family stuff?"

He gave her a wry smile. "Nobody's perfect."

"I don't want perfect. I want you."

"Are you sure? Even my flaws have flaws. And you were right that I've been imitating Chip to make sure he's behaving himself."

"Has he been hitting on women after all that bad playboy press he got? I mean he's not that stupid, is he? He knows you're here and he should lie low."

"He might not be that stupid, but he is that horny. The guy thinks with his gonads."

Tori wiped the last of the tears from her eyes. "Did you find out anything?"

"Pretending to be Chip is draining, and I'm glad this event is almost over. I can tell you that I've talked to every single woman in this place, but you're the only one I actually *wanted* to talk to."

She hugged him hard and put her head on his shoulder. "I knew you were the right Robin Hood."

"That's brilliant news, m'lady." He gave her a bone-melting kiss and took her hand. "Would you like to get out of here?"

"Yes, but I'm hopelessly lost."

"I cheated, remember?" He pulled a piece of paper from a pocket in his tunic and unfolded it. "This is the corn maze layout. You're over here."

"That's pathetic. I didn't even get close to the exit. No wonder I felt like I was walking in circles."

"I'm glad I found you." He gave her another kiss. "All the screaming helped. Most people don't yell about food."

Tori squeezed his hand. "I might have needed to let off a little steam."

"I think that was more than a little."

Chapter 11

Be Afraid

Tori tugged on Dale's hand. "Do we have to go back right now?"

"You want to stay here in the corn maze? I thought you were screaming to get out."

"Now that I know I *can* get out, I'm feeling better. It's nice and quiet here, except for the occasional person looking for the exit."

Dale sat next to her on the bale. "Are you avoiding candy-agnostic children or the guy who looks like Andre the Giant?"

"That's Morgan, Hope's husband. It was probably hard to tell in the dark and fog, but he's actually much better looking than Andre. He is enormous though."

"I'll say. Why are you avoiding him?"

"I didn't say I was." Tori slumped down, wrapped her arms around him, and leaned her head on his shoulder. "But I am. Hope is different when she's around him."

"You don't like him, do you?"

"I didn't say that. But no, I don't."

Dale pulled a piece of straw from her hair. "Why not?"

"He's rich and successful, and I guess I feel like a failure by comparison."

"I think that says more about you than it does about him." He ran his palm across her hair and picked out more pieces of straw. "And from what you've said, you've been successful at almost everything you've ever done. Certainly anything involving food."

"Until recently, maybe so. Maybe I'm jealous that he takes up all the attention in any room."

"You mean Hope's attention."

"I guess. Hope quit her job after she married Morgan. He travels all over the world making corporate deals for airplanes. I never thought about how much a jet costs, but it involves astronomical amounts of money. Hope wanted to travel with him because it sounded exciting and fun. She liked it for a while, but she got tired of airports and hotel rooms. He didn't go to any of the sights with her. So this business was an opportunity for her to do something on her own again."

"And now you think it's not going to work."

She sat up again to look into his face. "I'm sure it won't. Or not with me anyway. Now they're saying we should only make chocolate pigs. Without any input from me. They don't care about my opinion."

"I doubt that's the case."

"I thought they'd start listening to me more once there was a product to talk about, but I see that's not going to happen. While I was lying on the cold, hard ground I thought about what you said about figuring out what I want."

"And?"

"I want out of this partnership." Tori ran her fingers through her hair, removing tangles and farm detritus. Straw was magically attracted to her hair like a magnet. "This business idea was a mistake, at least for me. I don't want to do it anymore."

"What will you do instead?"

"I don't know. Something else."

"Well that's an unusually vague plan for you." Dale held out another piece of straw between them and tossed it on the ground. "You're actually okay with that level of uncertainty?"

"I've spent most of my life worrying about doing the right thing. Having the right answer for everything. As a chef, you're always striving for perfection. But it's grueling, and I've set myself up so that no one—even me—can possibly live up to my expectations. If I'm ever going to be happy, I think I might have to give up my obsession with being right all the time."

"It might help you relax a little."

Tori ran her fingertips down the side of his neck. "I think spending so much time with you last week helped me remember what being relaxed feels like."

"It was a good feeling."

She wrapped her arms around his neck and gave him a kiss. "Very, very good."

The romantic interlude was interrupted by a goblin yelling "Eww! Gross," turning around, and running back down the passageway.

Tori laughed. "I guess Little Bo Peep kissing Robin Hood is icky."

"Characters in quaint nursery rhymes shouldn't mingle with scofflaws of dubious repute."

She looked down at her hands and placed one on his. "So have you found any new houses to look at in Alpine Grove? I have to pick up Ginny tomorrow."

"Is that an invitation?"

"It is if you want it to be."

"I do." He squeezed her hand. "But I might have to drag you out to the sticks again. All the nice places are out of my price range, which limits my options."

"I thought you sold your condo. That's how you can leave LA and move to your new pastoral estate."

"I did sell it for what seemed like an absurd amount of money, considering how the neighborhood changed. But I bought when the market was high, so the sale didn't net much money. I had a huge mortgage. I more or less only got back the money I put into it."

"I thought the real estate market was booming."

"It is, so I thought it would be a good investment. I should have made a killing. But it didn't happen. When a strip club set up down the street, the area went downhill. *Way* downhill."

"That's depressing."

"It doesn't matter because I got out of there. Now I don't have to worry about drug deals in the lobby, getting mugged, or working myself to death to pay the mortgage."

"Well, except there's that little detail that you're homeless," Tori said with a sly grin.

"I can freeload at the house for a while until my father returns." He looked into her eyes. "Okay, true confession time."

"What do you mean?"

"I didn't want to involve you in my family stuff because I'm angry with myself. The reason I could get Joel a login was because I made a deal with my father."

"About what?"

"If I can figure out what's going on with the financial anomalies at Holbrook, I get a big chunk of change. That money would help my real estate situation." He shook his head. "I vowed that I'd have nothing to do with Holbrook money, and it makes me sort of sick that I had a price. That's why I didn't tell you."

"So your father gave you access to the accounting system?"

"No, and it's not like he'll be changing his will any time soon. We still aren't exactly best buddies. I pretended to be Chip and authorized the login for Joel."

"That's kind of underhanded, isn't it?"

"Yeah, but I couldn't figure out another way. I don't know what my father thought I would do. I think he threw the incentive out there almost as a dare or a test, knowing I wouldn't be able to do anything, and I'd fail."

"That seems mean."

"It's typical of my father, and it pissed me off. It's not like I can walk up to Chip and say, 'Hey, done any embezzling lately?' But what neither of them know is that I've been able to imitate Chip for a long time, which has come in handy."

"Hope said that Chip claims you're jealous of him."

"I was for a long time. He had *everything*. When I visited, I felt like I was the defective, broken kid that had been exiled to the city."

Tori gave him a hug. "That must have been hard."

"Now you know why I didn't want you sucked into this drama. Over the years, my father, Chip, and I have all behaved badly. And now someone is stealing money from the company. If it turns out to be Chip, it's going to be a disaster on a number of levels."

"Is there anything I can do?"

"I don't know. Joel left a few messages when I was staying with you. I tried to call him, but he was out."

"Well, if you come with me tomorrow, maybe we can talk to him together."

"That would be great." He gave her another hug. "You have no idea what a relief it is to talk to someone about all this stuff."

"For me too. Deciding I want to leave the partnership is a load off my mind. Now I need to decide when and how to tell my partners."

"Are you ready to leave the land of corn now?"

"Lead the way, kind sir."

When they arrived at the table, Morgan was sitting down talking on a cell phone while Hope handed out candy. Who on earth was he talking to at ten on a Saturday night? Morgan held the phone up to his face and swore. "Why is it so hard to get a signal around here? We're in the middle of a field."

Hope said, "Where have you been?"

"I told you. I went to check out the corn maze." Tori glanced at Dale, "Fortunately, Chip found me and showed me the way out."

He winked at her. "No problemo."

Hope giggled. "That's not a surprise. One time Tori got lost in a parking lot."

Before Hope could reveal that embarrassing saga, Tori said, "I have a headache. I'd like to go home. Could you and Morgan pack everything up?"

Hope looked at Morgan, who remained fixated on his phone. "I guess so."

"Bye." Tori raised her eyebrows at Dale, giving him a silent "Let's get out of here."

He inclined his head. "I'll walk you out."

They hustled away from the table. Tori glanced at him and once they were out of earshot, she said, "You actually walk differently when you're being Chip. It's a little disconcerting."

"Like I said, I've had years of practice."

The next morning, when Tori opened her eyes, she was curled up next to Dale feeling warm and content. She could get used to waking up in his arms. You had to be seriously besotted to want to watch someone sleep, but he looked so peaceful, she didn't have the heart to wake him up.

He rolled over and flopped his arm onto her stomach. Opening his eyes, he mumbled, "What's up, Doc?"

"I'm not sure how I feel about sleeping with Bugs Bunny."

He tickled her stomach with his fingertips. "I'm not sleeping anymore."

"How many different voices can you do?"

"I don't know. I've lost count. Two hundred? Maybe more."

"How on earth do you remember them all?"

"I just do. Once I have a voice for a character, it's there in my head. Trapped forever because I brought it to life."

"That's wild. How do you come up with a new voice for a movie or TV show?"

"It depends. Sometimes I read a script and the dialogue gives me ideas. Like when I was trying out voices when you were making candy. Other times, I have no idea where the voice comes from. When it's time to play the part, the right voice just happens."

"I know you've done Harvey. Is there anything else I'd recognize?"

"You know that animated TV show *The Old School Nation?*"

"Yeah, it's funny in a sarcastic way."

"I do a few recurring roles. I'm the guy who owns the pizza place, his dog, and the three eccentric aunts."

"At one of the restaurants I worked at we'd watch reruns of that show when we were cleaning up at night. I guess I never paid attention to the credits."

"You wouldn't have recognized my name anyway. My stage name is Devon Sinclair."

"You have a secret identity! Like Bruce Wayne and Batman."

"Uh-oh." He tickled her stomach again. "I'm afraid spending so much time with me is starting to rub off."

"It's interesting. Voice acting is a whole world I never thought about before."

"The industry is changing. A lot of us do TV, but the movie biz is starting to want big names to voice the characters. Like Robin Williams doing the voice of Aladdin in the movie. Bigwigs get millions of dollars, unlike the rest of us who have been doing voiceover work for years. Now studios want a recognizable name on the credits."

"I suppose that makes sense from a marketing standpoint."

"Where they save money is when they get one of us low-budget folks to perform multiple roles. If they get me to play

the father, the brother, and the family cat, it saves time and cash-o-la."

Tori grinned. "Do the cranky old dog on *The Old School Nation.* Please?"

"Feed me. I'm hungry. I'm still hungry. What? You call that food?"

Tori laughed. "I can't believe I know a famous person."

"Not so famous. But the good news is that no one will care when I get old and decrepit. I've been performing old guys and old dogs since I was twenty-two. Your age doesn't affect the kinds of roles you can perform when no one can see you."

"That's true. I have to say that last night Rhett Butler was pretty sexy."

"Frankly, my dear, that was fun."

She ran her hand down his arm. "James Bond was even better."

"I'm afraid you're a sucker for the Brits, luv."

Tori rested her head on his chest and closed her eyes. "I'm glad you saved me from the corn maze after I was so horrible to you."

"I am too."

Tori sat up and looked down at him. "You're so easy to talk to. I'm not sure why it's different with you. Maybe it's that I feel like you listen to me."

"I don't understand why talking to you is easy for me either. To be honest, I don't have a lot of close friends."

"I know what you mean. I said something to my mom about a friend telling me something. I was talking about you, but Mom assumed I meant Hope because who else would it be? At a restaurant, your co-workers end up like your family in that you see them every day. But there's no time to talk about anything serious."

"Yeah, my friends from work are like that too. We do the job and we go home. I spent so much time working that when I wasn't working, I needed time alone to decompress."

"Not to mention sleep."

"Exactly. It feels weird not working all the time. I've only been good at one thing my entire life, and I did it to the exclusion of everything else. When my mom got sick, I had to cut back on work. I love what I do, but taking care of her helped me see how unbalanced my life was."

Tori rested her head on his chest again and closed her eyes. "Maybe that's why you can be around me. You understand my obsession."

He didn't say anything, but stroked her hair slowly. Tori let out a sigh. She was so comfortable and content. A girl could get used to this.

The phone rang and Tori and Dale both jolted awake.

Tori yelped, "Ow! You're lying on my hair." Dale rolled over and she reached to grab the phone on the nightstand.

At the sound of Kat's voice, Tori looked at the clock on her dresser. How did it get so late? Kat probably thought she'd died in a fiery car accident. She tugged her fingers through her hair, yanking at tangles. "I'm so sorry. We'll be there as soon as we can. I'm leaving right now." She hung up the phone and threw off the covers. "Get up!"

Dale untangled himself from the sheets. "Guess we overslept."

"This is terrible. What if they don't let me board Ginny there again?" Tori grabbed her clothes and ran to the bathroom. When she returned to the bedroom, Dale was dressed and looking somewhat more alert. She gave him five minutes to use the facilities, then they both brushed their teeth, she grabbed her keys, and they were out of there.

In the car, he glanced at her. "Um, I think you might want to comb your hair."

Tori looked in the rearview mirror and squeaked. "Ugh." She dug around in her purse for a comb. Why did the thing you needed most always disappear into the deepest, darkest depths of the handbag? Finally she extracted an ancient plastic comb from a long-ignored zipper pocket and dragged it through her hair.

Dale took off his glasses and scrubbed his face with his palms. "How about we get some coffee on the way?"

"I'll stop at a drive-through on the way out of town."

"Fine." He pushed his glasses onto the bridge of his nose. "Whatever works."

It was a quiet drive to Alpine Grove. Dale sipped his coffee and stared out the window while Tori fretted about being late. This was not like her. Lolling around in bed? What was wrong with her?

Dale put his hand on her leg. "You're awfully quiet. Are you okay?"

"I'm mad at myself."

"But not me?"

"Why should I be mad at you?"

"We were up late and I was asleep right there with you. I have a habit of going to your apartment and not leaving."

She flashed him a grin. "That's true. You do."

"Relax. They'll forgive you."

"I hope so."

When they arrived at the kennel, Kat was standing outside with Ginny and three other dogs on leashes. Another woman emerged from the kennel building, took the three leashes, and was dragged off toward the forest by her canine charges. The dogs were leading the way like a hyperactive sled team training for the Iditarod.

Kat walked Ginny to the car as Tori and Dale got out. Tori ran toward Ginny and scooped the little dog into her arms, apologizing profusely and introducing Kat to Dale.

Kat reached to pet the fur between Ginny's pointy ears. "It's not a big deal. Ginny got to enjoy a little extra time in my office watching me procrastinate."

"Is Joel around?" Dale asked. "I left a message returning his calls."

Kat looked toward the house. "Actually, he's out in the forest cutting firewood. He claims he's behind in his fall wood collection, so he's out there somewhere with the truck and the chain saw."

Tori handed Kat a check. "I added extra for being late. I'm so sorry."

After they said their goodbyes, Tori loaded Ginny into the car. When she got in, she grabbed Dale's hand. "She didn't banish us forever. I'm so relieved."

"I told you it wouldn't be a big deal."

"You don't know how many dog walkers and boarding kennels won't talk to me anymore."

He laughed and looked over the seat at Ginny. "Are you saying this sweet little angel has a checkered past?"

"Like a chess board. You know what she sounds like. Can you blame them?"

"Nope. Be afraid. Be very afraid."

Kat walked around the back of the house and went through the door into the daylight basement. When you were under doctor's orders to avoid stairs, having a house set into a hillside was a good thing. She was cheating a little when she went up the steps that led to the front door, but she hadn't climbed the indoor stairs in weeks. At least she was able to walk around without completely exhausting herself. Convalescing was hard work.

She settled back into her article research, although part of her mind was focused on fretting about chain-saw accidents and massive evergreens landing on Joel. It didn't matter how many times he told her not to worry, chain saws were scary and trees were big.

The sound of the phone jarred her from her thoughts. After a perfunctory greeting, Maria announced, "Horseback riding is hard!"

"Did you fall off?"

"No, but I can barely walk now. I don't understand how so many parts of my body can hurt like this when the horse does all the work."

"Perhaps cowboys are in better shape than you are."

"I beg your pardon? I'm a fine physical specimen. Although I confess that I am walking a little like John Wayne today. I hope I recover before tomorrow or everyone at work will never let me hear the end of it."

"Wear a long skirt and no one will notice you're bowlegged." Kat tried to balance a pencil on her fingertip. "How was spending time with Bob? Do you like him?"

"He was a perfect gentleman."

"That sounds nice."

"No, it's not. He's *too* nice. Bob's this really mellow guy. He's like a bartender in that you end up blabbing to him because you're just sitting there."

"You mean sitting on the horse, right?"

"Yeah. Other than trying not to fall off, there's nothing to do but talk. It's like when you're hunkered up to the bar. What are you going to do? Talk and drink. Or in this case, talk and ride."

"Why is this a problem?"

"I told him about a number of my youthful indiscretions back when I lived in Vegas. Now I'm wishing I'd kept my big mouth shut."

"You didn't tell him about the Lucifer Incident, did you?"

"Yes! And the Drunk Cow Escapade."

"Wow."

"I know! Now I've been sitting here all day thinking, jeez, this guy is never gonna call me. I'm so pissed off at myself."

"You went riding yesterday afternoon and afterward he had to deal with the Haunted Barn until late at night. I imagine on Sundays he might be busy catching up with farm stuff."

"What farm stuff? What do farmers do?"

"I'm not a farmer." Kat twirled the pencil in her fingers. "Why are you asking me? Revealing my own adventures in Las Vegas was arguably one of the low points in my relationship with Joel. It's a miracle he didn't bail out on me right then and there."

"Yeah, what is it about Vegas anyway?"

"You didn't tell Bob the Chronicles of the Missing Underpants, did you?"

Maria groaned loudly into the phone. "I did, girlfriend. The first man I've met in heaven knows how long now thinks I'm a lunatic."

"Well, if he ever calls, at least you won't have to worry about any deep, dark secrets from your past coming out later."

"Nope. He's heard it all."

After commiserating a bit more with Maria, Kat hung up and returned to her article. Linus came over and put his gigantic head on her thigh. "You'll get your walk in a little while. Be patient."

Linus didn't seem convinced, but he gave up and curled up next to her chair.

Right as Kat hit the Delete key *again*, all five dogs jumped up, launching toward the back door. She got up and followed them. Joel was standing in the hallway shooing back the canines, who were furiously sniffing at his Kevlar chaps. He waded through the fur and gave Kat a kiss. "You'd think I went to another planet."

"The forest holds great olfactory secrets."

"I'm going to take a shower and wash off the sawdust, woodchips, and dead spiders."

"Well, you *think* they're dead."

"All the more need for the shower."

Mia came to take Linus and the other dogs out for a walk, leaving Kat alone with her article. It was going nowhere, so she flopped onto the bed to ruminate on the evils of poorly designed software and stare at the ceiling for inspiration.

She opened her eyes when Joel sat on the bed next to her. "Working hard?"

"It's Sunday. The day of rest."

"This was the article that was supposed to be finished yesterday, right?"

"I begged for the weekend because unforeseen software crashes slowed me down." She sat up. "It's not my fault."

"I think I like the day of rest idea." Joel sprawled out on the bed.

Kat stretched out alongside him. "Tori finally picked up Ginny, and I met Dale. He wanted to talk to you."

"I don't want to talk to anyone. I'm wiped out."

"You're talking to me."

He smiled and closed his eyes. "You know what I mean."

"I do. You and I communicate in such a different way with each other than we do with anyone else. It's much easier to talk to you than other people."

"True."

"I was thinking that you understand me like no one else does, or ever has. I speak to you the way I think to myself, and you actually understand what I mean."

He opened his eyes again and propped himself up on his elbow. "What has prompted all this thought about thinking?"

"I talked to Maria, who told Bob all her worst secrets."

"I hope she didn't tell him about the stuff that happened in Vegas."

"She did!" Kat widened her eyes for emphasis. "Now she's worried."

"I'll bet. But maybe it's not so bad. Being comfortable enough to talk to someone like that is a good thing."

"I know. When I was alone, I'd get lost in internal dialogues with myself. I'd end up going in circles with thought patterns that led nowhere because I didn't have another perspective to break the loop. Since I have your perspective, I never get caught in that trap anymore."

He leaned to give her a kiss. "That's good to hear."

"I thought you should know." She ran her hand down his arm, and interlaced her fingers with his. "I hope Maria finds someone like you."

"Not like me. We'd kill each other."

"You know what I mean." She tickled his stomach. "Speaking of which, I was *so* right about Dale and Tori. They looked like they both rolled out of bed after an action-packed night. No wonder she was so late."

"Your nosiness is showing."

"Her hair was all over the place, and he hadn't shaved." Kat gave his hand a squeeze. "So do you know what happened to him? That's a serious scar."

"No idea."

She let go of his hand and rolled onto her back again. "If I ever wear a bikini again, people might wonder the same thing about me."

"No one makes it through life without a few scars."

"And every scar has a story."

"Spoken like a true writer."

~

Tori listened as Dale read the real estate listings from a brochure he'd picked up outside of a grocery store. He read them using different accents, which he claimed helped showcase their virtues.

He flipped the page. "Here's one. On acreage at a great price. In a recreational area renown for huge amounts of public land right out your door."

"The snooty Boston accent doesn't disguise the fact that descriptions like that mean it's in the middle of nowhere."

"You'll like this one. There's a picture of a rock pile, which is described as a rock retaining wall. I think they need to find a new mason."

"When we stop, I need to look at these pictures."

"After the places we looked at before, I've been more selective, so we don't end up stuck in the middle of nowhere looking at a broken-down shack. I'm learning the code words."

"What words?"

"It's like you said. The descriptions are misleading. Like this one. It says the home offers main-floor living with a well-designed layout that maximizes storage, use, and comfort."

"It sounds nice. What's wrong with that?"

"If you look at the photo, it looks suspiciously like a small barn. You can maximize storage because it's actually a storage shed."

Tori laughed. "I think you might be becoming a little cynical here."

"I prefer to think of it as wising up, so we avoid wasting time." He flipped another page. "This home is intended for the quiet enjoyment of the area because it is centrally located on the property."

"What's wrong with that?"

"Remember the 'private road' listing that was so bad we had to turn around? This is similar. It's code for the fact that the driveway is three miles long. In other words, you might want to include a tractor with a giant plow blade in your budget."

Tori glanced away from the road to steal a glimpse of the magazine, and pointed at a glossy photo. "Oooh, that one's pretty."

"Premiere, classic home in an exclusive area."

"Okay, even I know that's code for it costs a fortune."

"You're catching on."

"What did the listing say for the one that was falling down? Vintage?"

"I think it said 'quaint.' The ones you definitely want to avoid are the 'fixer-upper cabins' which, objectively speaking, is what I want. But if you go look at it, fixer-upper actually means falling down. Ditto for unfinished cabin."

"What about rustic cabin?"

"That's a shack that fell down a long time ago, so now it's akin to a compost heap."

"Decomposing real estate is not ideal." Tori tapped his arm. "Where are we going?"

"When we get to the highway, head north." He closed the magazine, which had a glorious log home on the cover. "Let's check out something I can't afford."

"What if you get your father's Holbrook embezzlement bonus?"

"Still can't afford it." He flipped the pages absently. "But it has a pond, which sounds nice."

Tori wound her way back into a forested area and parked in front of a driveway that led to a large house. She looked at Dale. "I don't see a pond."

"Maybe it's around back." He pulled out a piece of paper from a stack. "It says stunning custom home with mature trees and seasonal pond. Three-bedroom, two-bath home with majestic mountain and water views."

Tori looked up. "I guess the mountains are over there, but the trees are in the way."

"The way the roof is designed means that when it snows, you have to shovel your way outside. Somebody didn't think that through very well. I'll be right back." Dale got out of the car and walked down the driveway, stopped, and abruptly turned around. When he settled back into his seat, he said, "There's nothing back there. I'm thinking seasonal pond means dried up by the end of October. And perhaps swamp with bird-sized mosquitoes in April."

"Okay, cross seasonal ponds off the list."

"Let's move on. At the highway, go south. I can't afford this one either. But I want to see it anyway."

After winding along a maze of rural roads, Tori parked at the end of a long driveway. "What does the listing say?"

"Two-bedroom, two-bath, kitchen needs updating. Diamond in the rough." He set the paper aside. "It's an expensive diamond, but what the heck. I'll be right back. Hopefully, no grumpy old dude will yell at me."

"Keeping Ginny in the car will help."

Dale walked down the driveway and disappeared around a corner. Tori looked at the printout, which had the listing information, price, and a blurry photo at the top. The house was brown, but beyond that, it was difficult to tell what it looked like. Maybe it had cedar siding. It was hard to say.

Dale reappeared from behind the trees and jogged back to the car. He got in and gave her a kiss. "I have a good

feeling about this one. I'm going to see if my agent can get an appointment to see the inside."

On the way back to Gleasonville, Tori asked the question she'd been wanting to ask for a while. "I know you stole Chip's underwear, but you said there was no proof. I've been trying to figure out how you were able to hang underwear on trees at a busy ski resort without getting caught."

He laughed. "You want the nitty-gritty details, huh?"

"Every time I think about it, the logistics seem complicated because there are so many people at Snow Grove. You must have put some thought into it."

"That Christmas vacation was unusually unpleasant, probably because of how old Chip and I were at the time. Teenage boys are loathsome."

"I can't argue with that."

"So Chip was going on and on about this ski trip he was taking with his buddies at Snow Grove. What I did was actually pretty simple. I took Chip's coat while he was at lunch, borrowed his skis, went up the lift, threw underwear on the trees, and came back down. It was cold and I wore a balaclava, so no one could tell who I was. Worst case, they'd think I was Chip."

"No one on the ski lift thought what you were doing was a little odd?"

"Maybe, but what are they going to do? Jump off?"

"I guess not."

"Anyway, I skied over into the trees pretty quickly. It only took about five minutes. I got to hear people laughing on the lift all the way down, which was satisfying."

"What did Chip do when he found out?"

"He whined at my father, but as far as anyone knew, I hadn't left the house."

When they got back to Tori's apartment, she unloaded Ginny from the car and collected her things while Dale waited. She waved at him. "Aren't you coming?"

"I've got to go back to the house and call Joel and my real estate agent. Not to mention take a shower."

She walked around the car, dragging a recalcitrant Ginny behind her. "You could do that here."

"I'd like to change my clothes too." He put his arms around her. "So are you inviting me to return?"

"I am. I'd also like to invite myself on the trip to see the inside of the house you liked."

"It's a deal."

Chapter 12

Finicky Or Not

After she put away Ginny's things, Tori set to work evaluating her candy-making supplies. Even though she had made the decision to end the business partnership, she still had to live up to her obligation to provide candy for Halloween on Friday. It was only one more day, and she would see it through.

The problem was that she'd run out of a lot of ingredients, and if she wasn't going to be part of the business anymore, she shouldn't buy anything else. Normal people don't buy chocolate in bulk. Fancy chocolate was expensive, and the specter of business failure and unemployment was financially daunting. Promises were one thing, but if she kept spending money on designer food, she'd end up flat broke pretty quickly.

Doing a complete inventory of her pantry helped her avoid thinking about her recent setbacks. She pulled items off the shelves as Ginny looked on from her typical surveillance post in the entry to the kitchen.

Talking to Hope was likely to be awkward and unpleasant. She wasn't sure how she would approach it, much less avoid hurting their friendship. Bailing out on her best friend in the whole world basically made her a horrible person. She'd also managed to screw up a second business, which meant that as an entrepreneur, she was officially a two-time loser. Although her chocolates and her store had been widely adored, when a business didn't make money, it was deemed a failure. Maybe she could only be successful working as a restaurant employee. But she'd been down that road, and it was paved with stress.

Every counter surface in the kitchen was covered with candy-making supplies, and she was writing down amounts and ingredients when there was a knock at the door. Ginny went into barking overdrive, losing her canine mind with noises that should not be possible from such a small animal.

Tori tried to shush the dog as she shoved her out of the way. Dale walked in and dropped a duffel bag on the floor, which caused Ginny to stop and take a breath.

He crouched down and pulled something from his pocket. "Here. Eat this."

Ginny snarfed down the item, turned around, and went to sit in her dog bed.

He stood up and wrapped Tori in a hug. She gave him a kiss. "I missed you."

"You saw me two hours ago."

"I know." She squeezed him tight, then released him. "Doesn't matter."

He followed her to the kitchen. "What happened here?"

"Inventory. What did you give Ginny to make her stop barking?"

"One of the peanut butter things. I've been carrying them around in my pockets so I have ammunition."

"You mean the ones I made?"

"They convinced her that I wasn't evil incarnate, and you had thousands of extra naked ones that you hadn't dipped in

chocolate, so I grabbed a bunch. Whenever she gives me that look, I stuff her face full of peanut butter."

"What look?"

"The 'I'm annoyed with you, and I'm going to make your life miserable' look."

Tori nodded. "I know that look."

"Your dog could end up weighing two hundred pounds, but at least she'll be quiet." He gestured toward the kitchen. "Speaking of peanut butter, that's got to be the biggest container of PB I've ever seen."

"It was on sale at the warehouse store. I'm low on chocolate, so I think I'll make more peanut butter crisps."

"You're kidding. *You're* low on chocolate? How could that happen?"

She put her hand on her hip. "It's your fault. You wanted to play ice-cream sundae with me."

"I never knew drizzling chocolate could be so much fun."

"I only allow the finest chocolate to touch my skin."

"Tasty."

Having decided what candy to make, Tori picked up her clipboard and returned to writing down ingredients on her inventory list, setting aside what she needed for the crisps.

While she was digging around in the cabinets, Tori retrieved Ginny's dog food and poured a cup of kibble into Ginny's bowl. Normally, the dog went completely nuts for her dinner, but instead of running over to the dish as if she were starving, she turned up her nose at it and sauntered over to her dog bed.

Tori pointed at the dog. "How many peanut butter crisps did you give her?"

"Enough to keep her quiet. Maybe she got extra food at the kennel because we were late." Dale sat on the bar stool. "Is there anything I can do to help?"

"No, it's faster if I do it. I know where everything goes. This feels like the end of an era. Once I use up this bulk chocolate, I won't be buying more. I've been trying to figure out how to tell Hope that I'm a failure."

"You're not a failure."

"How come I feel like one then?" She gripped her pencil more tightly. "I don't know what I'm going to say. Every time I walk by the phone, I think, 'I should call Hope.' But I can't make myself do it. I'm going to kill her business dream because I'm a terrible person."

He took off his glasses and set them on the counter. "Leaving a business you don't want to do before you get any deeper into it doesn't make you a terrible person."

"Yes it does."

"Exiting gracefully may involve making someone feel bad for a little while, but it doesn't mean you're a bad person."

Tori pointed at Dale with her pencil. "Making someone feel bad is mean. You adore your brother so much that you threw his underwear on trees."

"I suppose that makes me mean. Do you think I'm condemned to bad personhood forever for doing that when I was fifteen?"

"Of course not."

"Then stop berating yourself. You deserve the same break you're giving me."

She set the clipboard on the counter. "I don't know how to tell her. It's all I can think about."

"What if you give yourself a deadline? Like 'On Wednesday at two in the afternoon, I will call Hope.' You can think about it until then. But on Wednesday, you do the deed. No excuses."

"What if I get her answering machine?"

"Okay, that's a good point. You can avoid that by talking to her in person. Call her today and make a lunch date or something. That makes it harder for the deadline to slip."

"I guess that might work." Tori picked up her clipboard again. "I think I can handle that. Making a lunch date is less intimidating."

"Baby steps." He walked into the kitchen and put his arms around her. "It will be okay."

She leaned her cheek on his chest. It was so nice to have someone to talk to about this mess, instead of going through another professional washout alone. Stepping back, she looked into his eyes. "I forgot to ask. What did Joel say?"

"He's tired of cutting firewood."

Tori giggled and poked him in the ribs. "I meant about Holbrook."

"Well, there's good news and bad news, I guess." He leaned back against the counter and made a face. "Or maybe it's all bad news. Joel said he's found financial anomalies, but he doesn't know who did it."

"Why not?"

"The person associated with the login ID isn't in the employee database. So he can't tell who it is, but whoever has this ID has been messing around in the system for a while. I asked Joel to determine exactly how much money is involved."

Tori picked up her clipboard again. "This is serious."

"I know. Speaking of calls no one wants to make, I don't want to have to call my father while he's in Germany. What am I supposed to say? 'Hi Dad. By the way, I have reason to believe your favorite son is ripping you off.' That's not going to go over well."

"Talking to Hope is looking easier."

"I'm also still not sure it's Chip. And I can't accuse him without evidence."

Tori fiddled with her pencil, twirling it in her fingers. "Maybe Chip didn't do it."

"We'll see. I need to figure out a way to find out. I can't ask the folks in human resources because of how I got the login."

"Hmm. That is a problem."

He picked up the Tabasco and stared at it. "I need a sneaky way to startle the cockroach from its hiding place."

"Maybe Joel can help think of a geeky way to unearth him."

"I don't know how he could do that, but it's worth asking."

~

The next morning, Tori fed Ginny and made breakfast. She set an omelet in front of Dale and sat at the table across from him. "Ginny didn't eat her breakfast, and now I'm worried about her."

"She looks perfectly happy." He got up, crouched down and handed her a crisp that she gobbled down. "Maybe these things are addictive."

"I hope you haven't turned my dog into a PB junkie."

"Hey, it's your recipe." He returned to the table and took a bite of the omelet. "Apparently, I'm not the only one who loves your cooking. This is amazing."

"Thank you." Nothing made Tori happier than compliments about her cooking. "I think the aged gouda is the key."

Dale just nodded and continued eating. When they were done, he helped her clean up, and she set to work on her peanut butter crisps.

Dale sat at the bar, flipping the pages of a script. He looked up and pulled off his glasses. "So when you're done, how would you feel about test-driving some four-wheel-drive vehicles?"

"I'd like to, but then we'd have to bring Ginny, and unfortunately she's shedding."

"I don't care."

"Fur might hurt the car's trade-in value."

"Still don't care. It will be more fun if you come with me."

"I need to finish this batch, but then we can go."

After the crisps came out of the oven, Tori set them to cool, put everything away, and leashed up Ginny. She was a little uncomfortable putting her extremely hairy dog in Dale's expensive car, but he kept saying he didn't care because he was getting rid of it anyway.

They got in and Dale asked if she'd called Hope to make her lunch date yet.

Tori knew he'd ask. She was used to being the detail person in every room, and it made her a little crazy that he never forgot anything.

266 🌺 *Susan C. Daffron*

She rearranged her seatbelt. "I was planning to do it when we get back."

"I've been thinking about your situation."

Tori gripped her seatbelt. Uh-oh. "What do you mean?"

"You seem upset about talking to her and leaving the business, but this isn't the first time you've made a big change, so I'm not sure why this time is different. In fact, from what you've told me, you've been through more than one major life upheaval. Not too long ago, you uprooted your life and moved back here."

"I know, but it's not the same."

"How come?"

"Because this involves Hope."

"I don't see what difference that makes."

Tori took a deep breath. "She convinced me to move back here. I had the health issue at the restaurant, but I planned to return to work."

"Why?"

"I was sure I could handle it. But Hope talked me out of it after I told her about Augie's prep guy, Tony."

"Who's Tony?"

"He did prep work for a chef I used to know. If you haven't worked in a busy kitchen, it's hard to describe, but the stress is intense. Many people in the industry end up with serious mental health problems."

"They do?"

"People don't talk about it, but the long hours and intense stress takes a toll. People get hooked on the adrenaline rush. Some people burn out, others take drugs, and some people have issues with depression."

"You didn't, did you?"

"Anxiety is more my style, but Tony struggled with depression and ended up committing suicide. Everyone was stunned."

"I'm sorry."

"It wasn't my kitchen, but I was involved with Augie and when I told Hope about it, she freaked out."

"I can see why."

"She knows that I can be a little anxious, so she was worried."

"A *little?*"

"Okay, more than a little. I remember her screaming into the phone something along the lines of, 'How much of a wake-up call do you need? Restaurant work is toxic. You have to get out of there.'"

"Sounds like a little tough love there."

Tori glanced at him and smiled. "Hope is good at that. Even when I'm wound tighter than a corkscrew, she's always been a wonderful friend to me. She helped me move back here, and we looked at storefronts together. I'll never forget how helpful she was."

"I'm guessing she met her husband some time after that."

"She did, and I was so busy with the store, we didn't see each other as much. The store did well, but the problem is that I'm not great with numbers, and I struggled to make a profit. Even I could tell that when they raised the rate on the lease, it couldn't work. When Hope suggested the partnership, it seemed like the perfect solution. I could work fewer hours and someone else would handle the money part."

"I can see why that would be appealing. I'm sorry it isn't working out the way you hoped."

"I think I need to accept that I'm not good at being an entrepreneur. I'm too much of a control freak."

"You were successful with many aspects of the store. There's nothing wrong with asking for help. But maybe next time pay for it. Get an accountant instead of partners."

"I'm not sure I can face starting another business." Tori pointed at a restaurant as they drove by. "Who knows? Maybe they're hiring."

"Are you kidding? Have you ever eaten there?"

"No."

"Don't. And I agree with your friend Hope. You already burned out once. Why would you go back to that life?"

"You're probably right. I don't know what I'm going to do though. Cooking is all I've ever done. All this uncertainty is tearing me up inside. I *always* know what's next."

He put his hand on her leg. "You'll figure it out. In the meantime, it's time to annoy car salespeople. How should I play this? Goofball hick? Rich snob? Surfer dude? Yosemite Sam?"

Tori laughed. "Why don't you surprise me?"

After driving a variety of different vehicles, they returned to Tori's apartment and she unloaded the dog from the car. "I think Ginny liked the Jeep best."

Dale shook his head. "George didn't. It's too squirrelly."

"I thought George was just being obnoxious, and you were saying that as part of the character. It was better than the Suburban. That thing was gigantic."

"Neil and I liked the 4Runner."

"Neil was cute."

"Thank you. When I go back to LA, I'll be Neil when I harass people at Toyota dealerships."

Tori opened the door to her apartment. "What do you mean 'go back to LA'? You're not leaving, are you?"

"Not right this second. But I'm going to have to clean out my storage unit at some point. A bunch of my mom's stuff is in storage too. But that's not today's problem. Right now, I want to make you dinner."

Tori stopped and turned around. "After all this time, you're just now telling me now that you can cook?"

"I don't cook the way you cook, so don't get your hopes up. How do you feel about grilled cheese sandwiches?"

Tori gave him a hug. "That sounds wonderful. It's been a long time since anyone has cooked me anything."

"Then it's about time we changed that. Remember, it's the thought that counts."

She laughed. "I doubt you can screw up grilled cheese."

"Famous last words."

～

After a short chat with Hope inviting her to go out to lunch on Thursday, Tori couldn't keep herself away from her kitchen. She needed some cooking therapy. Plus, grilled cheese couldn't be served alone. It simply had to be accompanied by soup. So she whipped up a fresh spinach, tomato, and garlic tortellini soup to go with the sandwiches. Although it was tricky having two people working in the one-rump kitchen, after Dale decreed it was a like a dance, they started doing the cha-cha. Tori couldn't remember the last time she'd laughed so hard. No one would ever call them good dancers, that was for sure.

Ginny seemed less amused by the cooking festivities and refused to eat anything except peanut butter crisps. Tori handed her one. "I'm afraid we've turned her into that finicky cat from the commercials."

"That's Morris, the spokes-cat for 9 Lives cat food. He's voiced by John Erwin, who did some Archies and Hanna Barbera cartoons."

"You really know your voices."

"I'm a font of obscure vocal trivia," he said in a sardonic Morris the cat voice.

The next morning, she and Dale were plotting their trip to Alpine Grove to look at the house, but Ginny didn't want to eat breakfast again so Tori called her veterinarian. Something was wrong with the little dog. Ginny was generally not even remotely picky and mealtime was pretty much her favorite part of every day. What if she had eaten something she shouldn't have when they were cooking? She and Dale had been so wrapped up in each other, it was certainly conceivable. Tori waited while the veterinary receptionist hemmed and hawed about appointments and finally suggested one the following month, which struck Tori as absurd. How many dogs could there possibly be in Gleasonville?

Tori hung up and called a few other local veterinarians, who also were booked up. No one seemed to think Ginny's lack of appetite was an emergency because the dog acted fine, didn't have any digestive issues, and was happily chowing down on peanut butter crisps.

Tori found a listing for a vet clinic in Alpine Grove, which would work since she and Dale were driving up there anyway. Maybe the animals were healthier up north. A perky receptionist said they'd had a cancellation and the vet could see Ginny at ten.

After a quickie breakfast and expedited morning routine, they hit the road. Once they were on the highway, Tori pointed at a sign listing the distances to points north. "Considering you don't live there yet, we sure spend a lot of time driving up to Alpine Grove."

"I like it there."

Tori smiled. "Actually, I do too. Now that I know you better, I understand why you want to move there. I can't imagine you enjoying life in Los Angeles."

"It was home for a long time, but I don't want to live there anymore." He gazed out the window. "There are things I'd like to forget, and I'm looking at it as a fresh start."

"You mean because of your mom?"

"She was there for me for years, and I feel like I failed her in a lot of ways. I was busy working all the time. That's all I did. I didn't pay attention when she said she was tired all the time. I didn't think about it because I was always tired too. Then when she finally did go to the doctor, the cancer was advanced."

"I know you were there for her when she was sick. You said you took her to doctors and to chemo."

He shook his head. "It wasn't enough. There are so many things I wish I'd said. Then she was gone."

"I'm sorry. That must have been terrible."

"I wanted to fall apart, but when someone dies, there are so many details you have to deal with. I had to clean out her house, negotiate with the landlord, deal with Chip, medical bills, paying off debts—it was all this horrible blur of activity.

When I finally was able to stop and look at my life again, I thought, I don't want to be here anymore."

"I'm glad you ended up here." Tori reached for his hand. "Although I can't say I've enjoyed the Haunted Barn, it's a good thing Hope made me go, so you could pick me up off the floor."

He squeezed her palm. "Any time."

By the time Tori found the vet clinic, they were five minutes late. Or maybe ten minutes because the clock in her car was notoriously inaccurate.

Dale held the door while she dragged Ginny through the door and up to the receptionist's desk. "I'm Tori Merrill. I have an appointment at ten, but I think we're a little late. We drove up from Gleasonville. I'm so sorry."

The blonde woman shook her head, the tips of her straight blonde hair brushing her chin. "No problem. Dr. C was running late, and you gave her a little time to make a couple calls. I'll tell her you're here."

Tori dragged Ginny over to a chair and hauled the dog into her lap. Dale sat next to her and bent to look at the dog. "She's not going to lose her marbles, is she?"

"I hope not. Vet trips can be tricky." She readjusted her hold on the dog and whispered, "You *have* to be good, okay?"

Ginny appeared unmoved by the entreaties but remained quiet, which Tori regarded as a win.

A tall, thin woman wearing a lab coat opened the door and gestured toward the room with a folder. "Tori. I can see Ginny now."

Dale stood up and Tori carried Ginny, figuring she didn't want to push her luck. The dog was quiet. Don't rock the furry boat.

The vet closed the door and held out her hand, "I'm Karen Cassidy. Tracy tells me that you drove all the way up here from Gleasonville. What's going on with our friend here?"

Tori handed the dog to Dale and shook hands. "This is Ginny, and she hasn't been eating, and I'm worried. She's drinking, but not eating her breakfast or dinner. And she never does that."

The vet gestured toward a stainless-steel table and Dale put Ginny down. "When was the last time she ate anything?"

"Well, you should know she *is* eating peanut butter treats," Dale said.

"They're not officially dog treats. They're little biscuits that I dip in chocolate. There were extras that weren't dipped and Dale gave them to Ginny." She paused to observe the vet gently poking at Ginny. Please don't bark. *Please.* "There's nothing bad in the treats. Organic all-natural peanut butter, flour, and a few spices. They're actually healthy, at least for people."

"It turns out Ginny really likes them," Dale added. "I mean *really* likes them."

While they were talking, the veterinarian continued leaning over Ginny, poking at the dog, who stood quietly. She straightened and looked at Tori. "Do you have any of these things?"

Dale pulled a handful from his pocket. "Don't leave home without them."

Ginny poked her nose in the air and almost fell off the table in her quest to sniff out the peanut butter. The vet grabbed the dog firmly with one hand. "You stay there." She took a crisp from Dale, held it to her nose, then handed it to Ginny, who chomped it down.

"See? She loves them. I'm afraid I've addicted my dog to peanut butter or something," Tori said. "What should I do?"

"Well, if they're healthy, I'm not too worried." Dr. Cassidy lifted Ginny off the table and put her on the floor. "I only did a cursory exam, but I'm not seeing anything obviously wrong. When was the last time you had blood work done on her?"

"A couple of months ago. Everything was normal," Tori said.

"I think she's fine, except for being considerably overweight. Feeding her treats isn't helping. Although I have to say those treats you created must be amazing."

Tori practically collapsed in relief. "I was worried because she didn't eat her dog food."

The vet smiled. "Is there a possibility that she's holding out for something better? Some dogs can be stubborn."

"Well, that would be like her, I suppose," Tori said. "She's a little bit set in her ways."

Dale chuckled. "In other words, that dog is totally playing you."

Tori fired a shut-up glare at him and turned back to the vet. "What should I do?"

"Cut back on treats, for one." Dr. Cassidy crossed her arms. "You also should give this dog more exercise, or she will end up with health issues. Do you take her for walks?"

"Sort of. I take her outside. She's not a big fan of moving around a lot," Tori said. "I know I should try harder, but she doesn't like it."

"It's important that she get more exercise. Obesity can considerably shorten the canine life span."

Tori said, "When I first got Ginny, I tried going running with her, but it didn't go well."

Dale added, "You don't want to hear what it sounds like when this dog doesn't get her way."

Dr. Cassidy bent down to pet Ginny. "What if you take her for your warm up?"

"I could give it a try. I have a friend who keeps telling me I need to get back into running."

"Well, she's probably right." The vet stood up. "Exercise is good for humans too."

~

After being chastised by the veterinarian for having a fat dog and paying the bill with a check from her ever-dwindling bank account, Tori tucked her wallet back in her purse. Soon money would be in short supply, and the thought made her stomach hurt. Taking Ginny's leash from Dale, they walked out of the vet clinic.

Dale put his arm around her shoulders. "Why do you look so upset? Ginny is fine."

"I'm relieved that she's okay." But now Tori was officially both a bad business owner and bad dog owner. Kids hated her candy. And at the same time, she was a bad dog owner for irresponsibly feeding her swinish dog overly fattening treats. She couldn't win.

"C'mon, what's wrong?" He gave her shoulders a squeeze. "You look like you're about to cry."

"I'm fine. Let's go check out your house."

"It's not *my* house. At this point, it's just *a* house."

"A house that you might buy."

"Not likely, but it is under consideration if I win the lottery."

"Or get the Holbrook windfall."

"That's not looking too promising at the moment. But since we're here in Alpine Grove, I was thinking we could find a phone. I could give Joel a call after lunch and see if he found out anything new."

After stopping by a deli to grab sandwiches, Dale called Joel, who suggested they come by the boarding kennel after they looked at the house. Dale said, "It sounds like he's created spreadsheets or something."

"Oh boy. That sounds like lots of fun."

They navigated to the house that was for sale, and this time Tori drove all the way up to the house, rather than stopping at the end of the driveway. The house was a pretty, single-story Craftsman-style home with cedar siding. A large detached garage with two doors sat off to one side.

The real estate agent said the place wasn't occupied, so they ate the sandwiches in the car while they waited for the agent to show up.

Dale crumpled up his napkin and threw it in the paper sack. "If you're done, do you want to walk around a little? I didn't have a chance to get a close look at this place when I walked up the driveway the other day."

Tori agreed and went to unload Ginny from the back seat. The listing claimed the garage had enough room for a shop, but when Tori peered in the windows, she couldn't see much of anything. It was dark and empty.

They walked to the house, and although the real estate agent had said it was vacant, it still felt like they were sneaking around, trespassing. Tori half expected a grumpy homeowner to appear from behind a shrub and start yelling at them. Tori and Ginny followed Dale around the back of the house, which sported a huge screened-in porch.

Dale cupped his hands around his eyes to peer through the screening. "I didn't see the porch before. It's so quiet here. Can you imagine sitting out here with a cup of coffee, listening to the birds?"

At the sound of a car engine, Tori picked up Ginny, and they hustled back around front. A black sedan was parked next to Tori's dirty car, and a woman jumped out waving her hands and ran to Dale. "I'm so sorry I'm late."

Dale shook her hand. "No problem. We were just looking around. It's nice to finally meet you in person."

He introduced Tori to the real estate agent, whose name was Margie Basil. "Like the spice!" she proclaimed.

Tori said, "Technically, basil is an herb."

"Never argue with her in culinary matters," Dale added. "Tori knows everything about food."

Margie was unfazed by the correction and went to the door. She was probably in her early fifties with a short mop of heavily frosted platinum hair. The woman was so perky that Tori wondered if she'd swallowed a fistful of amphetamines or guzzled three pots of coffee. No one was that chirpy without chemical assistance.

At the front door, Margie fumbled with a gigantic ring of keys. "It's in here somewhere. Aha! Here we go. Welcome, welcome!"

Tori and Dale followed her inside and were greeted with the acrid scent of burned wood and plastic.

"Yuck. What happened?" Tori asked.

Margie scuttled off through a dining room to the living room, which had a pretty stone fireplace and opened out to the screen porch. She opened the sliding glass door to let in the cool, pine-scented air. "There was a little fire."

Tori and Dale followed her path through a tiny dining room to the living room. A doorway off to the left went to the remains of a kitchen. Tori leaned in and pressed her fingertips to her nose. "It smells like the inside of a campfire ring."

Margie gestured to them to follow her through the doorway. "Let's get through this area first. This cottage is a great opportunity."

"Opportunity for what?" Dale crossed his arms. "It's a mess."

Tori rearranged Ginny in her arms and kicked a piece of a singed cabinet door out of the way, moving into the room. "Do you mean remodeling?"

Margie clapped her hands together. "*Exactly*. You have the right idea. All this house needs is someone with a bit of vision."

"And a lot of money. Why didn't the owners fix this before they put it on the market? This damage will take thousands of dollars to repair." He looked up at the ceiling, which had a few crispy black spots. "If it *can* be repaired."

Margie said, "Unfortunately, there was a small kitchen fire the day before the owners moved out."

"More like an inferno," Dale grumbled.

"Why did they move?" Tori asked.

"Job transfer. Actually, they moved overseas, and they simply didn't have the time or inclination to make the repairs. They asked me to lower the price until it sells. Which I have. Several times now. This house is now an unbelievable value thanks to the massive price reductions. With a little bit of elbow grease, this house could be amazing."

Tori walked around and looked at the charred remains of the kitchen. The appliances had been pulled out, so it was a tiny blackened cube with the crisped remains of a closet off to one side. She opened the door, which creaked ominously. "I'm not sure why there's a closet over here, but if you take out the closet rod and put in shelves, it could be turned into a walk-in pantry."

Margie came over and looked inside. "That's a wonderful idea."

"As it is, this kitchen isn't much bigger than mine." Tori walked to the wall next to the doorway. "I don't know if it's possible, but if you knocked out this wall, you could expand the area. With more room, you could put in more counters and cabinets. Maybe even commercial-grade appliances."

Margie leaped over next to Tori like a hyperactive frog. "Brilliant. That's absolutely brilliant! I love it. Can you imagine how fantastic it would be for entertaining? You could put in a huge island with bar stools looking through the living room out onto the porch. It would bring the outdoors inside."

Clearly not inspired by the extent of the fire damage, Dale uncrossed his arms and gestured toward the hallway. "We're here, so we may as well look at the rest of the house."

Margie made a shooing motion with her hands. "Please feel free to explore. I'll stay here to give you two a little privacy so you can talk it over. But do let me know if you have any questions."

Aside from the kitchen problem, the house had a nice layout with two good-sized bedrooms, big closets, and recently remodeled bathrooms. The master bedroom had a sliding glass door that led to the huge screened back porch.

Tori nudged Dale. "Check it out. All you have to do is plug in a coffeemaker, and you can roll out of bed and go visit the birds with your coffee."

"I like that idea, particularly if you were in the bed with me."

Her heart did a panicked flip-flop, almost as if she had tripped over something. He wasn't implying she'd live with him here, was he? "I, um…"

"But this house is still expensive. I can't afford it. Even with all the so-called *massive* discounts, it's too much money. Add in cleanup, tearing down walls, and a complete kitchen remodel, and it's completely out of reach." Dale looked out the sliding glass window as a squirrel scampered up a tree. "It sure is pretty here though."

Margie rushed into the room. "Isn't it lovely? This house is worth far, far more than they're asking. It needs a little TLC, that's all. The setting is picturesque, and it's a desirable area close to town, yet private and quiet."

Tori couldn't argue. She was in love with the place. If she had money, she'd buy it in a nanosecond. It killed her that her professional and financial life were at such a low ebb. Although he was cranky about the kitchen, she could tell Dale actually liked the house too. He kept running his hand across the smooth, honey-colored wood on the Craftsman-style windowsills and door frames in a way that suggested he might share more of Margie's "vision" for the house than he was letting on.

Margie seemed to realize that she wasn't in any danger of closing this deal today, so she bid them farewell and exhorted

Dale to call her if he should need even the tiniest shred of information about the house.

They got back into the car and Tori headed north toward the boarding kennel. Dale gazed out the window and Tori put her hand on his shoulder. "You'll find something eventually."

"At this rate, I'm going to end up living in a tent. Right now, most of what is on the market is either derelict hovels or palaces on the lake, built for millionaires. Talk about needing to win the lottery."

"Maybe the place we just looked at will drop in price." Tori gestured toward the trees. "I really liked it."

"I did too. It's almost perfect. So many houses are huge. I don't want or need a four-bedroom 'family' home. All I need is a cabin with maybe an extra bedroom where I can set up some recording equipment."

"With a new kitchen, that house could be amazing."

"Although I'm not a chef like you are, even I draw the line at cabinets that go crunch. That whole side of the house has to be gutted. And I have no idea how you'd get rid of that smoke smell."

"I've thought about my dream kitchen a lot. For example, most kitchens have little tiny sinks. Why is that? It's completely idiotic because you use a sink every single day. So if you remodel that kitchen, you need to promise me you'll select a sink that can accommodate larger pots—I mean the big ones you use to cook big pasta like lasagna noodles. Even if you have a dishwasher, you'll need a sink that's large enough to rinse veggies and pasta and clean your cookware. Two sinks would be even better. Then you could really spread out."

He chuckled. "I'm not buying or remodeling that place, but if I were, you'd be the first person I'd consult. You take your kitchens seriously."

"Oh, I'm just getting started. Here's what I *really* want in my dream kitchen. First, a walk-in pantry instead of the crappy shelves I have in my apartment. Second, a large island work area with cabinets and also shelves for my cookbooks. Third, places to put my appliances and a built-in microwave, so it's not hogging up a lot of counter space."

"Anything else?"

"Well yes, but you probably don't need my opinions about appliances. We'd be here all day."

"You may as well give me the run down. We're still miles from the kennel."

And without the slightest hesitation, she did.

Chapter 13

Fun with Numbers

While Tori wound her way down the now-familiar forested roads toward the kennel, she gave Dale a detailed accounting of her elaborate and outrageously well-equipped fantasy kitchen.

Finally, she took a breath. "I'm sorry. This is probably way too much information and incredibly boring to someone who doesn't cook."

He shook his head. "I enjoy listening to people who are passionate about what they do. It's like me when I talk about sound equipment. To tell the truth, audiophiles can be obnoxious snobs."

"I doubt they're worse than food snobs. Put a room full of chefs together and you'll get an earful of pretentious commentary about everything from presentation to spice combinations and ingredient sourcing."

When they arrived at the kennel, it was oddly quiet. Perhaps the dogs were asleep. They got out of the car and Tori looked up the driveway toward the house. "We're not customers boarding a dog. Do we ring the buzzer or walk up to the house like normal visitors?"

"I'm not familiar with dog-boarding etiquette, but Joel knows we're stopping by, so maybe we should just knock on the front door."

Tori carried Ginny up the long driveway, past the gate to the log house. Dale grinned at her. "What happened to the exercise-the-fat-dog program?"

"We're going to have to ease into it. I didn't want to tell the vet that my warm-up could take hours if I bring Ginny along. She'll sit and stare at me in disgust. It's like trying to walk a rock. The idea of running with her is laughable."

"What if I go running with you tomorrow? Maybe we can figure something out."

Tori agreed and knocked on the door, which resulted in a cacophony of barking from within the house. "I think they know we're here."

Joel opened the door and invited them inside. "Sorry about the noise. Come on downstairs."

Tori stole a quick glance around as she followed Joel to the stairs. The entryway led to a kitchen, which was connected to an open living and dining room area with cathedral ceilings. Log houses were so pretty. Too bad Dale couldn't find one of those to buy.

Joel opened the gate at the bottom of the stairs and shooed back the dogs. Tori set Ginny down and the canines engaged in their complicated sniffing ritual.

Most of the surfaces of Joel's office were covered with printouts and enormous books that were so geeky, Tori didn't even understand the titles. Why did computing involve so many acronyms anyway?

Joel handed Dale a printout. "This report shows you the transactions that looked off to me."

Dale scanned the text. "What's Tell Blue? I've never heard of it."

He handed the paper to Tori. She stared at it blankly. Why was he giving it to her? It looked like a lot of numbers.

"I didn't know either." Joel sat in a rolling office chair. "I called the Secretary of State to find out. It's a subsidiary of the Martell Toy company. But I haven't been able to find out what they do."

"Martell? That's odd. Why would Holbrook be paying them so much money?" Dale took the printout back from Tori. "For services? What services?"

"I wondered the same thing. The invoices say that Tell Blue is providing services, but it doesn't say what they are." Joel handed him another printout. "I think I mentioned that there are logins that don't have any records in the HR database."

"Have you figured out who the people are?" Tori asked.

"Not exactly. There was an old database that appears to have been migrated over to the new system. The person who paid the questionable invoices has one of these old IDs."

"What do you mean old?"

"Employees from the earlier system have logins that are cryptic, like Hol0012. They're sequential. Some of them are associated with people. Like Hol0001 is the president of the company."

"That would be good ole Dad," Dale said.

"Some of the data associating logins with a person has been erased. The person who has been creating the invoices is Hol0012." He handed Dale another printout. "Here are the old IDs that have users associated with them."

Dale looked at it. "This makes sense. Dad, Chip, Lenora. They've all been around Holbrook for a long time."

"So have you. But your name isn't in any databases. You don't have an ID," Joel said.

Dale rubbed at the scar on his cheek. "I know."

"I assumed that you had access to the system, but you don't." Joel leaned forward in his chair. "So how did you get me a login?"

Dale glanced at Tori before responding to Joel. "It's fairly easy for me to imitate my brother on the telephone."

Joel raised an eyebrow, but didn't say anything. Tori volunteered, "Dale doesn't work for Holbrook."

"I don't." Dale took off his glasses and folded the earpieces. "Leonora has been with the company forever though. I used to hang out with her at Christmas parties. She was the one my father directed to buy Christmas presents for me. Anyway, I called, pretending to be Chip and asked her to set up a login for you. I gave her all the address information, so you're in the system."

"Sort of illegally though," Joel said. "I'm not committing a crime here, am I?"

"No, because the investigation is indirectly authorized by my father. He asked me to look into it, and I asked you." Dale fidgeted with his glasses. "Who is Hol0012?"

"I have no idea," Joel said, but was interrupted by the back door opening and the clattering noises of dogs rushing outside. Once the noise subsided, he continued, "Whoever it is has full access to everything. Holbrook needs to reexamine their security policies. In general, different logins should have different levels of access. Users are assigned roles so a guy in the mail room can't see the payroll accounts, for example. But these old, dead IDs weren't ever purged. Whoever migrated the IDs was lazy about it and assigned the IDs the

administrator access role. That means anyone with one of these old IDs can do anything."

Tori said, "Like move money around?"

"Exactly. Whoever Hol0012 is can pay invoices without anyone noticing because that login is authorized to do so."

"Wow," Dale rubbed his eyes with his fingertips. "That's not good."

"At least it isn't Chip," Tori volunteered. "According to this printout, he's number 11."

"So my brother isn't a criminal, but someone else is ripping off the company," Dale said. "But we don't know who. Great."

"We do know that they aren't on-site. The logs show that this login has been accessing the system remotely the same way I am," Joel said.

"You mean through the Internet?" Tori asked.

"If you check the access logs, you can tell that I'm logging in remotely from Alpine Grove. Hol0012 has been logging in from Los Angeles," Joel said.

Dale stared at the papers in his hands. "How can you tell?"

"When you log onto the Internet, you're connected to a server. That server has a numerical address. The logs show what addresses have accessed the system. I can then trace that number back to its location," Joel said as he handed Dale another piece of paper. "Here's what I learned about that subsidiary of Martell. Maybe you should see if you can find out what the company actually does."

"And who's involved with it," Tori added. "Do you think it's Chip's ex-girlfriend, the toy heiress? I've forgotten her name."

"That's a definite possibility, since Sienna lives in LA and obviously is involved with Martell. But we're back in the same situation of having to confront someone and say, 'Hey, have you done any embezzling lately?' which is not my idea of a good time. If it's Sienna, that still implies Chip is involved somehow." Dale said. "But why would Chip be funneling money to Sienna's company? They broke up spectacularly and publicly. He looks for any opportunity to say how much he detests her, and I don't think he could fake that level of animosity. He's not that good of an actor."

Kat tapped on the office door jamb with two fingers because Ginny was cradled in her arms. "I think you misplaced something."

Tori got up. "Was she bothering you?"

"No, it's fine. I didn't want you to think she escaped when the other dogs went charging outside for their walk."

Joel said, "Did you pick that dog up or did she magically fly into your arms?"

"I'm fine," Kat walked to Tori and set Ginny on her lap. "I was reading on the bed and she wanted to get up there with me. How could I refuse? Look at that face."

"I know. I'm such a sucker." Tori hugged Ginny and smiled at Dale. "If you can find the embezzler, maybe you can afford that house."

"The whole crispy-fried-kitchen problem isn't a selling point." He nodded at Joel. "I know you worked on the kennels. I don't suppose you do kitchen remodels, do you? I looked at a house that suffered a significant kitchen fire. I'm not sure it's structurally sound at this point."

"Even though you'd have to start over with the kitchen, it could be amazing." Tori added. "The rest of the house is wonderful and the land is beautiful."

"Although he has experience with fire-restoration work, if Joel did any work on kitchens, ours would be first in line." Kat raised her eyebrows and widened her eyes for emphasis. "Because we *need* a dishwasher."

"The cabinets aren't set up for that. There's no space for one." Joel scooped the papers on his desk into a pile. "I've never done construction work for anyone other than myself because I'm too slow. I do know a general contractor though."

Kat said, "Luke did excavation work for us, but he's been involved in the restoration work on the local theater."

Joel handed Dale a card. "Here you go."

"If I can figure out a way to rearrange the cabinets, does that mean we can get a dishwasher?" Kat said.

"Maybe," Joel said.

"I need to find a tape measure. See you later." Kat waved and headed for the door. "Good luck finding the elusive Number 12."

～

After they got home from Alpine Grove, Tori started on dinner while Dale made a few calls. He discovered that although the suite number in the address on the Tell Blue invoices implied it was in an office building, it was in fact essentially a post office box. The company didn't appear to have a physical location at all.

After they ate, she and Dale settled in on the sofa to watch a movie. She had her bare feet in his lap and he was massaging them, which was incredibly relaxing.

Although she'd watched *When Harry Met Sally* probably a hundred times, it was significantly different watching it with no sound. Dale did the male voices and encouraged Tori to do the female ones. Or try anyway. She was no Meg Ryan, and she kept interrupting herself with fits of laughter.

Dale stopped rubbing the sole of her foot and reached for the remote to pause the movie. "I'm pretty sure that's not what she'd say."

"I can't do the fake orgasm scene. It's too embarrassing."

"Why not? You can do the real thing." He zigzagged his fingertip along her toes. "It's just us."

"It's different." She drew her knees to her chest. "I don't know why, but it is."

"Okay, I'll do Meg for this scene then." He pulled her feet back onto his lap and emphasized the dialogue with remarkably erotic caresses that ventured up to her ankles and calves and down to her toes.

Tori slumped down on the sofa, doing a credible impression of a saucer full of Jell-O. "I don't think my feet have ever been so happy."

"You have cute feet. They should be happy as often as possible."

They subsequently lost interest in the movie, opting for other forms of entertainment. Later, Tori was standing in front of the mirror brushing her teeth when Dale walked into the bathroom.

He picked up his toothbrush and pointed it at her reflection. "I just remembered something important."

"Mmmff."

"Sorry to interrupt, but I'm going to need your help. Before the gigantic flame-out between Chip and Ms. *Persona*

Non Grata, Sienna, she agreed to do an appearance on Halloween at the Haunted Barn. It was set up months ago. As far as I know, she didn't back out after the breakup because it's for charity. And it will end up being a PR thing for that cheesy reality show she announced not too long ago."

Tori rinsed the toothpaste from her mouth. "So you're saying she's going to be at the barn on Friday?"

"I think so. It's probably our only chance to find out if she's involved with those Tell Blue invoices somehow. I need you to help me think up a plan."

"You mean something other than walking up and saying, 'Hey done any embezzling lately?' I assume."

He kissed her cheek. "I'm confident we can come up with something a little more creative."

The next morning, Tori donned her running shoes for day one of the Ginny fitness program. As he promised, Dale joined her for the morning exercise excursion.

Outside they were greeted by a blast of cold air. Tori did a few stretches, and Ginny sat down hard, having apparently determined that the human activity meant this wasn't a typical do-your-business trip around the parking lot.

Tori clapped her hands together, "Okay Ginny, it's time to go!" She took off at a slow jog and Ginny followed in a waddling trot.

Dale jogged alongside her, turning his head to check on the dog. "I'm going to feel bad if we give her a heart attack."

Tori slowed to a walk. "We'll alternate walking and jogging for a short distance. Maybe just around a couple blocks. Then we can take her back inside and go for a real run."

By the time they made it back to the apartment building, Ginny had expressed her displeasure by barking, howling and shrieking at various neighbors, sitting down, rolling over on her back, and resisting being hauled back up onto her feet. To avoid another embarrassing doggie tantrum, Dale carried Ginny inside the building. "That was unpleasant. I think all of your neighbors hate us now."

Tori unlocked the door to her apartment. "I knew it would be bad, but I'm going to have to get over the embarrassment and keep doing it."

"She takes stubborn to a new and especially irritating place."

They dropped off Ginny at the apartment and she stomped off to her dog bed and collapsed in a heap with her back turned to them.

Back outside, Tori launched into a jog. "Now that we've ditched the cranky stubborn dog, this should be more fun."

"Running always sounds like more fun before you actually do it."

Tori followed her typical route that wound through the neighborhood around a park. Dale certainly wasn't going to win any speed records, that was for sure.

She slowed her pace so he could catch up. "Are you okay?"

"Great. Fantastic. Just dandy."

"Are you sure?"

"I'm pondering the meaning of life. And death. And pain. How short life is. And how much longer it seems when I'm doing this."

Tori slowed to a walk and took his hand. "I get the impression you don't typically go running."

"Not unless someone is chasing me."

"I'm sorry if I went too fast. I guess I assumed that you run regularly."

He swung his arms back and forth. "If you run with me, you should be prepared to spend a lot of time walking. Or standing and watching me gasp for air."

"You should have said something."

"Running is supposed to be good for you. The fact that I hate doing it shouldn't enter into the equation."

"Yes it should. Why did you volunteer to do something you hate?"

"Because when you love someone, sometimes you do things that you might not completely enjoy."

"What?" Tori's heart flip-flopped as if she were careening off the high dive into a pool. Did he say what she thought he said? She stopped and faced him. "What did you say?"

"You heard me. I know you did because you aren't even winded. You're definitely not desperately gulping air like I am." He put his hands on her shoulders and looked into her eyes. "And I think you love me too. Otherwise you would have told me to get lost by now."

"I do." Overwhelmed by the truth of the statement, she grabbed him around the waist, hugged him hard, and leaned back to look at his face again. "But just so you know, I'm one of those people who latches onto a friend and doesn't let go. I'm like a parasite you can't get rid of—ask Hope, she'll tell you. Although I can walk into countless restaurants and know a bunch of acquaintances because I worked with them, they aren't real friends. Yet somehow, in only a few weeks, you've turned into my best friend. I don't know how that happened, but you're right, I do love you. I hadn't even admitted that to myself, but I truly do. How did you know?"

He gave her a kiss. "Real friends just do."

~

After showering, Tori made omelets with gouda cheese again since Dale liked them. She set a plate in front of him on the table. "*Bon appétit.*"

He grabbed her hand and pulled her down into his lap. In a sing-song Julia Child voice he said, "Thank you *mon chou*, for sharing your love of food with me."

She laughed and placed her hand on his cheek, "You just called me a cabbage or a cream puff."

"Whichever you prefer. I love you either way."

"I love you too. I'm not sure why that's so hard to say."

"I confess to being more than a bit scared about those three words." He kissed her palm. "My parents' divorce was terrible for them and everyone nearby. It's not a great example."

"My parents had a polite divorce. What everyone calls *amicable*, but no matter how cordial, there's still a lot of emotional fallout. For me, the idea of falling in love has always felt too out of control. What if the other person doesn't feel the same way? I couldn't bear an awkward silence, or even worse, total rejection."

"I know what you mean. I've been rejected a lot." He pushed a long tendril of hair behind her ear. "Although I kind of blurted it out, I thought about how I feel about you a lot. And I decided that I didn't need to have a specific response from you. I wanted to say it because it's true. I feel the way I feel. I'm only responsible for that, not how you feel."

"Lucky for you, I feel the same way."

"Well, yeah, that did work out well for me. Rejection sucks."

After breakfast, Tori dipped the last of the peanut butter crisps in chocolate. She set the last ones to cool and cleaned up the kitchen while Dale read another script.

He set down his pencil and looked up. "When is your lunch with Hope?"

"I should leave in an hour or so. Now that I've finished cooking, my stomach is twisting in knots."

"Have you figured out what you're going to say?"

"Not at all. I keep thinking of how to approach it and nothing works. I keep thinking about the surprised expression on Hope's face when I say, 'I don't want to do this anymore' and I sound like a pathetic whiner."

"Just be honest about how you feel. It's better to tell her this now than later after everyone has invested a ton of money and time into it."

"I know. I'm sorry I keep going over this with you."

"No problem. I'll be here holding down the fort, reading a crummy script and watching your dog sleep. All that exercise was hard on us."

Tori's stomach didn't feel any better as she changed her clothes and got ready to go meet Hope. By the time she got to the restaurant, she had no interest in food, so she requested a ginger ale to sip while she waited for her friend. The restaurant was one that she was familiar with because one of her prep cooks had worked there a number of years ago. He'd told a lot of war stories about the dysfunctional kitchen. It looked like the systemic ills continued to plague the place.

Although waitresses smiled at the customers, the moment they turned away from a station, how they felt was obvious. Problems in the kitchen filtered out to the front of the house every time. The clues were easy to spot. The exhausted waiter, the anxious busboy, the disappearing hostess, and the overall downtrodden atmosphere.

Hope rushed to the table. "Sorry I'm late. Morgan wanted to go shopping for new shoes and I lost track of time."

Tori did not want to talk to Morgan. She looked around. "He's not here, is he?"

"No, his watch died, and he wants to buy a new one before his next trip." She picked up the menu. "Did you order?"

"Not yet. Just a ginger ale." Tori flipped open the menu and evaluated what items were least likely to offend her palate. They probably couldn't screw up a sandwich too badly.

"There are so many yummy-looking things. I don't know what to choose."

Tori wasn't going to say anything about the food, no matter how much she might want to. "So, I invited you to lunch because I wanted to talk to you."

"I know. That's why we're here, isn't it? Are you getting excited for tomorrow? I can't believe it's the last day of the Haunted Barn. It has been so much fun. And they got Sienna Martell to be a guest. I heard she's going to dress up as a vampire. Or vampiress. Is that what you call a female vampire?"

"I'm not sure. And yes, I heard about Sienna the other day." Tori took a deep breath and folded her hands on the menu, willing them not to shake. "But that's not what I need to talk to you about."

Hope stopped perusing the menu and set it aside. "You sound upset. You have that quaver in your voice. What's wrong?"

"I don't know how to tell you this, but I want to leave the partnership. I know I'm not an investor, but I don't want to be involved. There's probably something I need to sign."

"*What?* What are you talking about? We need you. Where is this coming from? You're the whole key to this—you're the chef with all the ideas and recipes."

"I'm sorry. It's not your fault. I...well, I changed my mind."

"Why?" Hope spread her arms wide. "What happened? I thought we were testing. Figuring stuff out."

Tori set her hands in her lap and gripped her napkin. "We were and you still can. I made candy for this weekend. And there are a few leftovers that the dragon didn't hit when he barfed. You'll have plenty to hand out tomorrow. I'm sure of it."

"But what's changed?"

"Me, I guess. Dealing with kids and testing and complicated manufacturing issues. It's all too much. I started thinking about what I want, and this isn't it."

"Why not? Taking this national means we could make a lot of money. We've talked about this so many times."

Tori wrung the napkin in her lap like a dishrag. "I know. But what I realized is that I was only involved for the money. That's the wrong reason to go into a partnership."

"Making money is what business is all about."

"Yes, but you also have to care. Or I do anyway. I loved restaurant work. Even when it was stressful and awful, it was still wonderful in many ways. I felt like I was making people happy on their special nights out. I made a difference in people's lives, even if it was for only one meal."

Hope picked up her menu and set it back down again. "Well, candy makes kids happy."

"Apparently, not the kind I make. Maybe it's selfish, but I want to feel appreciated and have a passion for what I'm doing. Money can't be a goal by itself. No matter how hard I work, I could fail to create anything that seven-year-olds deem cool. I could try dozens of candies and fail at them all."

"That's true in any business." Hope took a drink of water, glaring over the rim of the glass. "It's called testing. That's what we were doing."

"I know." Tori pulled her hands from her lap and folded them on the menu again. This wasn't going well. "I need to find a way to build something myself that's based on something real, not the cool thing of the moment for random elementary school children. I need to be passionate about my work. If I don't love what I'm doing, it's not worth it. And I don't love this. I sorry, but I just don't."

Hope gestured toward the windows. "Well what are Morgan and I supposed to do now?"

"Write up something for me to sign. You can have my recipe for the Choco-critters if you want it. That's the candy you're most enthusiastic about, isn't it?"

"Yes, but it's not going to be fun without you."

Tori tried to smile. "Sure it will. You have Morgan."

"I guess." Hope laid her palms flat on the menu. "Will you still be at the Haunted Barn tomorrow?"

"I'm going to attend, but it would be great if you and Morgan could be at the table. I need to help Dale with some stuff."

"I thought you broke up." Hope picked up the menu and tilted it toward Tori. "Why do I feel like you're not giving me the whole story here?"

"It's not my story to tell."

The next morning, Tori and Dale drove out to Alpine Grove yet again to drop off Ginny. The temperature had dropped considerably in the last twenty-four hours, emphasizing the fact that the seasons were changing and it was now late fall, whether anyone liked it or not. Tori was thankful she wouldn't have to wear a costume when the temperature dropped below freezing. In the children's picture books, you never saw Little Bo Peep clad in a ski parka, after all.

When they were leaving the kennel, Kat thanked them for helping her finally convince Joel to put in a dishwasher. As they got back into the car Tori said, "You sure were quiet during all that kitchen talk."

Dale leaned over and gave her a kiss. "I'm thinking about the crispy house, that's all."

"That house feels right to you, doesn't it? Ha! I *knew* it."

"It does, and I'm considering making an almost insultingly low offer, on the off chance they might take it. I'm told that in this area, real estate sales drop considerably in the winter. Prospective buyers don't like tramping through the snow, I guess."

"And some places might be impossible to access, if our experience is any indication."

"Although it might take the rest of my life to fix the kitchen myself, I could set up a hot plate and make a lot of grilled cheese sandwiches. It would still be better than my place was in LA."

"Wouldn't it be great if they accepted your offer?" Tori turned to flash him a grin. "When you get sick of grilled cheese, you can come over to my place for dinner."

"I wish I'd paid more attention in shop class when I was in high school. My only accomplishment was an ugly, lopsided lamp base, and that worries me."

"I have no experience, but I can provide moral support. And food."

"You're all about the food." He chuckled. "I must be nuts to consider extensive kitchen repairs. I can barely change a lightbulb."

"Even if buying the house doesn't happen, it's still fun to dream about."

When they arrived back at Tori's apartment, Dale gave her a kiss before heading to his car. "Happy Halloween. See you at the barn."

Tori went over their plan in her mind as she put candy into boxes and assembled her costume for the last time. She held up the Little Bo Peep dress in front of her. She wasn't going to miss this uncomfortable pink outfit one bit. She tossed it onto the bed in disgust. Tonight, she didn't have to be a vendor or appeal to children, so maybe she could wear something else. Almost anything would be better.

She went to her closet and flipped through the hangers, which were dominated by chef coats. If she wanted to go as a chef, she was all set, but the concept wasn't inspiring.

She tossed her favorite little black dress on the bed. Maybe it would work as part of a costume. The glimmer of an idea struck, and with a giggle, she began rummaging through her drawers and found a string of fake pearls, long gloves, and a pair of cheapie oversized dark sunglasses. If she put her hair up into a French twist and wore a whole lot of eyeliner, mascara, and ruby-red lipstick, she'd make a halfway decent Audrey Hepburn playing Holly Golightly in *Breakfast at Tiffany's*.

Although little kids wouldn't understand the costume, Dale would. She grinned at the reaction he was likely to have to this getup. Considering his encyclopedic knowledge of everything Hollywood, if she did it right, he might swoon. Was that the right word? Did men swoon? Maybe she'd get to find out.

The plan they'd devised was simple. Tori would distract Chip while Dale talked to Sienna. The unanswered question was how. After the disastrous non-date with Chip, it wasn't like Tori could lure him with her feminine wiles. Not that she had adorable flirty moves to speak of anyway. Even dressed as Audrey Hepburn, no one would confuse her with Audrey. There wasn't enough eye makeup in the world to make that happen.

For the big Halloween finale at the barn, the event organizers were going to go all out. Dale said that in addition to the scare actors, scare zones, corn maze, and other attractions, they planned to put on a show for the final night. That was where Sienna came into the picture. In theory, she would arrive, do a bit of glad-handing and photos with the ghoulish crowd, and make her big speech up on the stage that was set up for the show. In addition to Sienna, Dale reported that there was supposed to be a magic show and various scary theatrics. Dale had been a little hazy on the details, but the bottom line was that he wouldn't have much time to question Sienna.

Tori got into her dress, donned her nylons, and applied an extraordinary amount of eyeliner. Using a brush, she created the distinctive winged tip at the outer edge of her eye for the classic Hepburn cat-eye look. She applied a set of garish fake eyelashes and leaned toward the mirror to examine them. How did people stand doing this every day in the sixties?

In the harsh light of her bathroom, she looked distressingly like a streetwalker, but maybe the fog and weird lighting in the barn would help transform congealed and plastic into playful and captivating. She used approximately three hundred and twenty-three bobby pins to secure the French twist, and for the final touch doused her head with hair spray to immobilize every strand of hair into a helmet that would last the evening.

Achieving the Audrey look required wearing stilt-like killer heels, which wouldn't work for hauling boxes of candy into the barn, so Tori put on a pair of socks and her running shoes over the nylons. She could be tall and slinky after the candy was safely ensconced.

Tori said a small thanks to whatever weather deity had convinced the rain to hold off until the weekend. Audrey probably never had to worry about her makeup running down her face during a deluge. That was a zombie effect the world could do without. After one last appraisal in the mirror, she grabbed her keys, put on her coat, and hauled the candy down to her car. It took a few trips, but driving to the Barn was a lot more pleasant without a long skirt getting in the way.

When she arrived, attendees were already lining up outside. If there were this many people now, it would be

utterly mobbed by the time the doors opened. She grabbed a banker's box of candy and headed for the vendor entrance.

As usual Hope wasn't at the table yet, so Tori got to haul all the candy inside by herself one final time. When you work alone, you don't have any expectations. That was an advantage of being partner-free Tori hadn't considered before. As the sole operator of her store, no one helped, but she didn't expect anyone to either. Everything was so much simpler that way.

Although it had been an awkward and sad conversation with Hope, it was like a great weight had been lifted from Tori's shoulders. Like the old song said, freedom basically meant you had nothing left to lose. She was trying not to dwell too long on the loss side because whenever she considered the reality of being jobless, her thoughts spiraled into a vortex of anxiety.

Tori still couldn't say she liked Halloween overly much, but she found herself getting into the holiday spirit. The radio was playing through the speakers instead of the usual groaning zombie noises and screams. People were doing little jigs, dancing to tunes as they set up their tables. Everyone seemed to be in such a good mood, Tori couldn't help but feel festive too.

Better late than never.

Chapter 14

Monster Mash

Tori waited for Hope at the table, listening to Halloween classics ranging from Warren Zevon's "Werewolves of London" to "Thriller" by Michael Jackson. She closed her eyes for a moment as the tune infiltrated her brain. It would be stuck in her head for the next few hours. Or maybe days. Ugh. It was amusing watching the people going by doing Michael's trademark zombie stomp from the video though.

Hope and Morgan walked up to the table carrying boxes with the decorations. She was in her Red Riding Hood outfit, and rather than dressing like a business owner in a suit, Morgan had outfitted himself as a pirate.

"Nice costume," Tori said, bending to reach below the skirting and grab the banker's boxes out from under the table.

"He's Captain Morgan," Hope said. "You know—like the rum. I love it."

"I'll be celebrating with the real thing when this is over," Morgan added.

Tori secretly thought Dale had been a better pirate, but she kept the sentiment to herself and patted the boxes. "Here you go. Have fun."

"Wait! What happened to Little Bo Peep?" Hope leaned over to examine Tori more closely. "That's a lot of serious eye makeup."

"Haven't you ever seen *Breakfast at Tiffany's*?" At Hope's blank stare, Tori added, "Like on late-night TV? It's an old movie with Audrey Hepburn."

"No, but you look great," Hope said. "I love the dress."

"Thanks. Gotta run." Tori grabbed her coat, put on the sunglasses, and peered over the huge frames. "Have fun, you two!"

She turned and walked down the long aisle toward the door. Time to find Dale before the hoards of kids barreled inside. The dimming of the lights and the change from the radio to ghoulish moaning meant it was almost the witching hour.

The huge doors squealed as they were shoved open and the red beams and purple lights came on, along with a cloud of fake fog. Screaming children ran by to get to their favorite scare areas and attractions at the back of the mammoth building.

A tiny Superman head-butted her, lurching Tori to one side and tipping her off her heels into a stall filled with hay. She ended up sprawled across a hay bale in a decidedly unladylike position. Grabbing her coat and sitting up, she made an effort to collect herself.

A pair of leather boots came into her field of vision and she looked up.

Robin Hood held out his hand. "Greetings m'lady. You seem to have taken a bit of a tumble."

Tori laughed and let him pull her onto her feet. "I'm looking for a place that makes me feel like I do at Tiffany's."

"Methinks this isn't it, fair maiden. We need to stop meeting like this." Dale leaned to her ear and whispered, "This is so much sexier than Little Bo Peep. I shall be

anxiously counting the minutes until this event is over and I can ever so slowly peel all that clingy fabric from your lovely body."

It was a good thing it was so dark because under all the pancake makeup, Tori was blushing. "I shall look forward to that, kind sir."

He stepped back from her and said in Chip's voice. "I need to find Sienna."

Mildly shaken by the sudden vocal change, Tori stammered, "Right...I'll find, um, someone else." Obviously, he hadn't been kidding about his years of practice. He was way too good at that particular impression. The first time he'd done it, she'd been too angry to notice, but now the insta-switch from the person she loved to—yuck—*Chip* was more unsettling.

On the other hand, he was doing it for the greater good. Embezzlement was wrong, and Sienna needed to stop. Tori took a deep breath and said in a clear voice, in case anyone was listening, "Thank you for your assistance. Perhaps I'll see you later."

"Indubitably, m'lady." With a final bow, he set off down the aisle and disappeared into the fog.

Tori scanned the area. Dale had mentioned that Chip tended to move around a lot during the event. He'd stop by the office to shoot the breeze with the people working there, gabbed with people operating the rides, and loitered with scare actors taking a break. Because she'd been trapped behind a table at the Candy Land Stand, Tori had never seen any of these places. So she would have to wander aimlessly and see if she ran across Chip anywhere. Fortunately, unlike the corn maze, there were lots of signs, so she was less likely to repeat that disorienting debacle.

Although Dale had been appreciative, stilettos might not have been the greatest footwear choice for chasing down a potential embezzler at a large, crowded event. She walked by a nun who was not acting particularly pious with the farm owner, Bob Jensen. Wow. Could you be excommunicated for feeling up a farmer? Nuns did get to wear comfortable shoes though. Tori's feet would be sporting painful blisters by the time this event was over.

She walked through various crowded scare areas with dizzying lights and effects. The Demented Circus zone featured lots of creepy clowns, many of whom she now recognized. The scare actors seemed disappointed that she wasn't screaming and yelling like everyone else. Being a multi-week veteran did have a few advantages. At this point, even the most revolting clown zombie makeup didn't freak her out.

She moved into a zone called the Crypt of Demons that had multiple beams of purple and green lights spinning across a graveyard scene. Hope had told her that the scary chain-saw guy tended to hang out here, so Tori was prepared when the machine fired up. Brushing a few fake spiderwebs that had gotten trapped in her hairspray, she moved on. Finding Chip could take a while.

Wandering through the Scarecrow Haunt, she dodged a few fake scarecrows along with a couple real ones, who leaped out from behind hay bales brandishing rakes, pitchforks, and other farm implements, trying to startle the kids. Having been knocked over before, Tori kept her focus on dodging the runners.

She made another pass down both of the vendor aisles and still didn't find Chip, so she ventured outside. Given all the hay in the barn, it was hard not to think of Chip as a needle. With the crowds, it could take all night to find the guy.

The night air was cool and Tori put her black wool coat on. If she'd been smart, she would have grabbed her sneakers when she went by the table. They were sitting under the table skirt, which didn't do her any good while she was tromping across fields.

A movement off to the left caught her eye. Near the Tilt-a-Whirl ride, one Robin Hood was facing another Robin, as if he were arguing with himself in a mirror.

Tori sidled up behind a tree to eavesdrop. Although they were the same height because she was now so intimately acquainted with Dale's body, she could tell that he was the Robin on the right.

The Robin on the left had broader shoulders and when he spoke, it was obviously Chip. He waved his arms wildly, and for a moment Tori thought he might throw a punch at Dale. Instead, he poked Dale in the chest. "It's about time you showed up. Where have you been? I haven't seen you at the house for weeks. Dad said you were supposed to help out here."

Dale crossed his arms. "I've *been* here."

"Yeah, sure you were. I saw you once. Okay, maybe twice. I bet you went back home, didn't you?"

"I found another place to stay." Dale glanced away from Chip, scanning the people around them. "But I've been here every single night as promised. Ask Bob, he'll tell you."

"Okay, whatever. But Dad and I are gonna have a chat about you." Chip pointed at the office. "Isn't Sienna supposed to be here by now?"

"I don't know." Dale turned to face the office. "I'm surprised she didn't back out."

"That witch is sorta psycho. And always whining about money. She probably wants the dough."

Dale turned back to Chip. "We're actually *paying* her?"

"Yeah, I asked Dad." Chip gestured toward the line of people waiting for the ride. "He thought she might bring in more people. Turns out he was right. Bob said it's the biggest crowd, ever."

"Well, that's what we're here for." Dale cast his gaze at Tori in a way that indicated he knew she was listening. He inclined his head slightly toward Chip. "Given your troubled history, it might be a good idea if you stay away from Sienna, so she doesn't make a scene."

"I know she's going to want to yell at me."

Dale waved his arms in exasperation. "So do something else. Look busy."

"Fine. Whatever."

∼

Dale turned away from Chip and while Chip wasn't looking, he pointed at Tori and waved at her.

She got the hint and scuttled over next to Chip, who was walking toward a spinning ride called the Scrambler. "Hi Chip!" The environment was incredibly noisy, but she sounded absurdly squeaky and overly cheerful, even to herself. She pulled her shades down her nose and peered over the top. "It's me-Tori."

His expression was blank and uncomprehending. Tori wanted to throttle him, but gamely continued, "You had dinner at my house. With Hope. You know, the candy business? Remember?"

"Oh right. Wow, that was some dinner. And the candy was good too."

Tori reached for his hand. "There's lots more. We have a number of new varieties. Why don't you come with me and try them?"

He pulled his hand away. "I can't right now. I need to keep my eye out for, um, someone. Or there could be a big scene."

"We have zombie clowns and guys with chain saws here and you're worried about making a scene?"

"It's different. I need to find out where this person is, well, before she finds me."

Tori kept looking around her as she continued to chat up Chip. Presumably Sienna would have an entourage, so it would be obvious when she showed up for her big show. Tori hadn't thought to wear a watch because it didn't work with her slinky gloves, so she had no idea how close they were to show time.

He turned suddenly. "Nice seeing you. I gotta go to the office and talk to Bob."

Tori stopped. That didn't go too well. She followed slowly and once Chip was inside, she peeked in the windows to see if there was a clock. Chip was sitting in a chair with his feet up on the desk, eating a donut by himself. What on earth was he doing?

She loitered near the office for a while. This was absurd. No one had to worry about distracting Chip if he was going to spend all night snarfing down donuts. She turned around and went to find Dale.

Back near the Tilt-a-Whirl, she stopped. Dale was talking to a woman in a sparkly witch costume. How come they didn't have costumes like that when Tori got stuck with Little Bo Peep? As she got closer, she recognized Sienna from the magazine photos Dale had shown her.

Sienna Martell in black pumps was almost as tall as either Dale or Chip, with legs that went on forever. But her real claim to fame was her gorgeous thick, wavy reddish-blonde hair. Tori would kill for hair like that, and it was no wonder that Sienna was a favorite of paparazzi. Being a rich heiress was one thing, but looking like a slinky hair model didn't hurt either.

Tori couldn't tell what they were saying, but she was close enough to hear the audible smack of Sienna's palm slapping Dale across the face. Good thing he was wearing the mask. She put some real momentum into that whack.

He stepped back and looked around quickly. Tori just stood there, waiting to see what might happen next. Sienna stalked off toward the office and Tori hurried over to Dale.

She grabbed his hand. "What did you say?"

"Nothing. I barely got out a hello, and she hit me." He rubbed his cheek. "Ow. Have you seen Chip?"

"He's in the office eating donuts."

"Is Bob there? She wants to talk to him."

"I didn't see him there."

Dale grabbed her hand. "Let's go this way. You need to see if you can get Chip out of there before she finds out I'm not him."

Tori followed Dale around a bunch of rides, which turned out to be a shortcut. He stayed outside, and she opened the door to the office and found Chip exactly where she'd left him, leaning back in the office chair eating another donut.

"Hi." She took off her sunglasses. "Me again."

He sat up and thumped his feet on the floor. "I don't think vendors are supposed to be in here."

"That's fine. I'm not a vendor anymore."

"You said you sell candy."

"Nope. I quit that." Tori glanced around, desperate for something to tear him away from sugary confections. "So, I heard there's a show soon. Maybe you could show me where it is."

"Over by the maze."

"Could you take me there? If there's music, maybe we could dance." Tori wiggled her butt a little. "Wouldn't that be fun?"

Chip paused and put his palms together. Maybe he was considering his possibilities for getting some action this evening. Ick. Tori smiled sweetly. "This farm is huge. I don't want to get lost."

Finally he stood up. "Okay, I'll show you."

They went outside and Tori furtively looked for Dale. Fortunately, neither he nor Sienna seemed to be around. Tori struggled to keep up with Chip, who was swiftly motoring toward somewhere. What had possessed her to wear heels? They crossed the gravel driveway, which made matters worse.

She tripped on a rock and let out a shriek. Because her skirt was so tight around her knees, she landed mostly on her palms in a downward-facing dog yoga position.

Chip was focused on his destination and kept walking. She yelled at the top of her lungs. "Hey, a little help here!"

He turned and had the decency to look sheepish as he ran back to her. He took her hand and held it as she righted herself "Sorry! I didn't see you fall down."

"I'm fine. Perhaps we could walk a bit more slowly." She glanced behind her, where Dale had confronted Sienna again. Crap.

Chip pointed ahead of them. "The stage is over there. Those donuts kinda got to me and the restrooms are that way. If you don't mind, I'll meet you at the stage in a couple minutes."

"Are you okay?"

"Yeah, I'll be right back."

He vanished into the crowd and Tori looked back at Dale, who was following Sienna toward her.

Tori raised her eyebrows, and he mimed a shrug. They were getting nowhere. But she had an idea.

As if possessed, she yelped and ran past Sienna toward Dale. "Chip, I can't believe it's you! Gimme some sugar, right now!" She threw herself into Dale's arms and gave him a long, sloppy kiss, and an overt display of extremely public affection. Initially startled, he quickly got over it and played along enthusiastically.

When they came up for air, Sienna was standing in front of them with her hands fisted on her hips. Even her witch hat was perched at an angry angle. "You've got a lot of nerve."

"Me?" Dale said in his best Chip voice. "Maybe I wanted someone who wasn't going to whine about money every single day."

Sienna pulled an arm back, and Tori was sure she would smack Dale again, so she clapped her hands together to interrupt. "Well, you know I'm an entrepreneur, and I know that new businesses can be really hard."

Sienna turned to look at her. "Who in the world are you?"

Tori placed her palm on her chest. "I'm Chip's girlfriend. Have you heard of Omelet Hotels? We've been written up in all the major business magazines."

"What? Give me a break." Sienna turned back to Dale. "You slime."

He said, "She's right about new businesses. Are your finances better these days?"

"That's none of your business," Sienna said with an indignant snort.

Dale made his move. "I heard about your new company. Blue something or other, right?"

"How do you know about Tell Blue?" Sienna fisted her hand again.

Dale said, "It's your company, isn't it?"

"Yes, but how do you know about it?" Sienna stepped closer, so she was two inches from Dale's nose. "Did you find something on your computer? You are the absolutely lowest form of pond scum."

"My computer has super-cool tech." Dale said. "You know, like tracking. Kind of like spying. The trackers are there so you can tell stuff."

"You can tell I used the computer?" Sienna said, taking a step back.

"Sure."

Tori kept her mouth firmly shut while Sienna dug the hole deeper. "I only borrowed it once."

"Yeah, I know," Dale said. "I found a bunch of other stuff in the system too."

"You mean you know about the invoices?" Sienna moved closer and put her hands on his shoulders. "It's no big deal. I was going to give all the money back once you and I got married. It was just for a little while."

"Too bad I dumped you." He smiled as he pulled her hands off him. "You're kinda in trouble, you know."

"But you won't tell, will you? When we were in Tahiti, you said you'd do anything for me. Remember that night? I promise I'll put everything back. Really." Sienna jerked her head toward Tori. "Oh, and you'd better not tell either."

"I don't think my Dad's gonna be too excited when he hears about this," Dale said.

"Wait! You can't tell him. He'll tell my parents. And they'll kill me. We had so many plans. You know I still love you. Remember Tahiti? How magical it was? We just had a little misunderstanding, that's all. Let's start over. We could still get married. Wouldn't that be great?"

Dale said in his normal voice, "I'm afraid that ship has sailed."

Sienna leaned closer. "Waitaminute. You're not Chip. Who *are* you?"

"Dale Holbrook. Pleased to meet you."

Sienna's face fell as realization set in. "How did you find out about Tell Blue?"

"I'm smarter than my brother is." He put his arm around Tori. "And my friends are even smarter."

"You mean this Omelet person?"

"My name is Tori Merrill. I lied about the hotels."

"She's the woman I love," Dale added. "And she's also the person who just witnessed your confession to embezzling from my family's business."

Tori couldn't help but smile as Sienna mumbled, "Oh crap."

~

The next morning, Tori slept late, curled up with Dale. She'd known that it would be a late night at the barn and although she could have picked up Ginny that day, she wasn't going to risk being late again. Instead, she'd opted to pay for Ginny to spend an extra day at doggie camp while Tori enjoyed a lethargic morning.

It was a good thing she'd planned ahead. While Sienna was performing, Dale had called his father and local law enforcement, who quietly appeared on the scene and advised Sienna not to leave the Haunted Barn until they talked to her. After the crowds dissipated and the doors closed for the last time, Bob cranked up the music and all the vendors and scare actors danced around doing the Time Warp and the Monster Mash while they cleaned up. By the time Tori and Dale got back to her apartment, they were physically and mentally exhausted.

She lay on her side with her arm around Dale's waist and her cheek pressed to his back, listening to him breathe. He rolled over and smiled at her. "Good morning. You look awfully thoughtful for someone who hasn't had her coffee yet."

"I've been lying here wondering what kind of heiress has money problems."

Dale chuckled. "I don't know. A greedy one?"

"I suppose. I'm glad you found a way to verbally corner Sienna into saying something. And thanks for helping me carry boxes of candy back up here."

"Too bad Hope isn't a fan of peanut butter."

"I know it's candy, but peanut butter is healthy. I was thinking I could donate the extras to the food bank."

"Your dog is going to be disappointed that you're never making those crisps again."

"I should make a few to help cajole her into running with us."

"By *us*, I hope you don't mean me. And as the vet pointed out, stuffing Ginny full of treats pretty much counteracts the running."

She poked him in the ribs. "I'm going to be a little more sparing in my treating than you were."

"Hey, they kept her quiet. Maybe you could develop a low-calorie version."

Tori sat up and looked down at him. "You know what? I *could*. I could talk to the vet in Alpine Grove and get her thoughts on how that might work. She might have ideas about ingredients that would be healthy for a dog."

"Ginny will be pleased."

"Not just Ginny. Lots of dogs. I'm not the only person with a stubborn, piggy, hard-to-train dog, you know."

"You want to make dog treats?"

"Why not? I could make irresistible, veterinarian-approved, homemade dog treats that are healthy and

handcrafted with love." Tori jumped out of bed. "Talk about a marketing tag line."

"Even better, your customers aren't focused on coolness. Dogs don't do cool."

"I know!" She clapped her hands together. "I need to call Dr. Cassidy."

That afternoon they went to talk to Dale's real estate agent, Margie, about making an offer on the crispy kitchen house. He filled out lots of forms that Margie then faxed up to Alpine Grove. When they left the office, Tori gave his hand a squeeze. "Are you excited?"

"I'm not letting myself think about it yet. How about if we go out to lunch to celebrate my impulsive dive into the land of fixer-uppers? Is there a place you're willing to eat anywhere near here?"

Tori pointed at a sign across the street. "Well, that Mexican place has failed multiple health department inspections. And the cafe over there on the corner recently changed hands. The guy who bought it used to own a bed-and-breakfast, but he and his wife got divorced. I know one of the people who worked at the B and B, and she said that he was a nightmare boss, so I'm not optimistic about the cafe. Bad management can kill a little deli like that one. There's a Chinese restaurant on the next block, but they use so much MSG, you'll end up preserving yourself for posterity."

He swung their hands between them. "We're never going to eat out, are we?"

"Well, you do realize that my favorite overpriced gourmet grocery store is right around the corner." She grinned. "If you're buying, I could come up with something fantastic. This time, I promise there won't be any wine pairings."

"It's a deal."

After lunch Tori was reviewing her peanut butter crisp recipe with the idea of making it for dogs instead of dipping the crisps in chocolate. The phone rang, and it was Dr. Cassidy.

Tori waved her recipe at Dale, who was sitting on the sofa. "Thank you for calling me back."

"I'm not sure Tracy wrote down your message correctly. She said you wanted to talk about dog treats. Is your dog okay?"

"Ginny is fine. I want to see if I could meet with you about developing healthy dog treats. I was looking at my recipe and calculating calories and nutritional information. But I don't know what's healthy for a dog. I was wondering if I could meet with you to go over it."

"You want to make treats yourself?"

"Yes, as a business. If other dogs like them half as much as Ginny does, it could be great. I've written up tons of notes. I could make little tiny training treats, low-calorie treats, shaped treats—anyway, I know you're busy, but I was hoping to get your input."

"Sure. I'd be happy to look over what you have and tell you what I know. Also, I have a friend I went to veterinary school with who specializes in veterinary nutrition. I'll give her a call and see if she'd be willing to review your recipes."

Tori made an appointment to talk to the vet at her office in Alpine Grove and hung up the phone. She ran over to the sofa, thumped down next to Dale, and gave him a hug. "This is going to work, I just know it."

"I have no doubt that once you believe in something, you will make it work."

The phone rang, and she gave him a quick kiss before getting up to answer it. "Thanks for the vote of confidence."

A vaguely familiar voice asked to speak to Dale, and Tori waggled the receiver at Dale. As she handed it to him, she whispered, "I think it's Margie."

He took the phone and made a face at Tori, who was standing in front of him, trying to read his expression. He stuck out his tongue at her and said, "Okay, let's do that. Thanks."

He hung up the phone and Tori spread her arms wide. "Well, don't just stand there! What did she say?"

"They accepted the offer. Margie says the sellers want a thirty-day closing. I said okay."

Tori threw herself into his arms. "I'm so thrilled for you!"

"I know. It feels right. By the time it closes, my father will have approved what he calls my finder's fee for snagging Sierra, so I can pay someone else to fix the kitchen." He hugged her hard. "Want to go to the cavernous hardware store and drool over shiny new kitchen appliances?"

"Are you kidding? Of course I do!"

Chapter 15

Epilogue

A week before Thanksgiving Tori loaded Ginny into Dale's new SUV for the trip to the boarding kennel. She and Dale had been spending a lot of time in Alpine Grove lately, between trips to talk to Dr. Cassidy about Tori's new business, dubbed Ginny's Barkery, and Dale's discussions with various contractors. Fortunately, Ginny was amenable to all the time in the car driving back and forth from Gleasonville to Alpine Grove.

Little did the dog know that this time, she was getting to visit doggie camp again while Dale and Tori went on a road trip to Los Angeles to empty out his storage units. Although he hadn't said much, she could tell he was anxious about returning to the city and going through his mother's things after avoiding the task for so long. Tori's parents had invited her to Thanksgiving, and it made sense to get everything moved well before the holiday and the inevitable arrival of wintery weather.

As they wound down the long driveway, Tori gazed at the huge cedar trees. "It looks like they got snow up here last weekend. Coming out here in the winter must be interesting."

"And by interesting you mean scary because you might not make it to the kennel. I'm glad I didn't end up buying a place this far out of town."

"Hey, you've got a four-wheel-drive vehicle now."

"But I've lived in LA most of my life. I'm a winter-driving wimp. I may avoid going anywhere for the next six months." He smiled. "I'm going to have a home recording studio now. It's possible I may never leave the house again."

"I'll be happy to give you a few other reasons."

"That sounds promising."

When they drove up Kat was standing in front of the kennel talking to her dog walker, who turned and went off toward the forest with a gang of four dogs on leashes. How that woman didn't get tangled into a knot was one of those canine-related mysteries that Tori would never be able to solve. She had enough trouble managing just one recalcitrant dog.

Tori unloaded Ginny, and Kat crouched in front of her. "How's my favorite office mate?"

Joel emerged from the kennel with a fluffy white dog and a fat black Labrador. "Meet Swoosie and Rosa. Swoosie, *sit.*"

Ginny wagged her tail and Kat said, "Ginny already knows them. You said that Ginny will go on walks now, so maybe we can all go together."

Dale observed Joel trying to contain the white dog's enthusiasm and added, "The word *walk* might mean something different to Ginny than it does to a sled dog."

"Swoosie is a Samoyed," Joel said as he stroked the fur between the dog's pointy ears.

"Who needs lots and lots of exercise, so she gets multiple walks. Pretty much as many as we can stand," Kat said. "How's the new house? Did you talk to Luke?"

"He looked at it before I made the offer, and the fire damage is fixable. As soon as the house closes, he's signed up

to begin destruction," Dale said. "Then reconstruction. He's pleased to have an indoor job in case it snows."

"We went over plans with him, and the kitchen is going to be amazing." Tori pressed her palms together. "I can see it in my mind so clearly, and it's been hard waiting for it all to finally happen."

"I'm glad you're not having to wait for your new kitchen. And I'm eternally grateful that you've inspired my husband to agree to put in a dishwasher," Kat said.

"It's more or less a new kitchen," Joel said. "Thanks for the finder's-fee bonus."

Dale smiled. "You're welcome. You did the work, so you should enjoy some of the spoils."

"Can you say new appliances?" Kat grinned. "Your house isn't the only one that had kitchen fires. My aunt was a terrible cook, and the stove is scary. I can't wait for it to go away. She also didn't necessarily construct the house in the most conventional ways."

Joel said, "What she means is that none of the cabinets are standard sizes. Or the same size. The whole kitchen has to be torn out and redone. I'm going to do it in two phases, since we still have to eat."

Dale said, "It sounds like kitchen remodels are going around."

"Joel was looking for something to do other than programming," Kat said. "I was more than willing to help him find something to do."

Joel put his arm around Kat. "After I finished work on the kennels, I guess I missed the variety. I enjoy programming, but I realized it's not enough."

"I know what you mean," Dale said. "That's part of why I decided to move here. I'm looking forward to doing new things."

"Well you're not alone. To continue to live in a small town, a lot of people around here have more than one job," Kat said. "I run the kennel and do freelance writing. Rosa's owner, Jan is a librarian, but also does research for the ad agency. And you know Tracy, the vet tech for Dr. Cassidy. She also is a digital artist who works on web sites. And the person who runs the local dog rescue also works as a legal secretary."

"Then there's Luke's girlfriend, Tess," Joel said. "She sells printing and runs the theater company."

The kennel door opened and they all turned and stared at Maria, who was wearing a t-shirt, jeans, and tennis shoes. "Hey, I didn't know anyone else was here. No one is *ever* supposed to see me looking like this."

Kat said, "You're fine. You remember Tori, right? This is her friend, Dale."

Maria greeted them and rubbed her hands together. "Thanks for letting me use the dog tub, girlfriend. Those clothes aren't ever going to be the same. Farm life is disgusting. No one tells you about all those animals taking big dumps everywhere. While I was squishing clothes around, I had a brainstorm. I'm telling you, this is a million-dollar idea that could change farming. I'm talking about livestock toilets. I mean, come on, people. Why isn't this a thing?"

Tori squinted. "Were you dressed as a nun at the Haunted Barn?"

"Yes, I was. My new beau owns the place. And the aforementioned stinky livestock. Horses and cows smell.

Good thing he's a hunk of the highest order. That man is built."

Dale said, "Bob is a nice guy."

"Yeah, he is, but he hasn't bought into my vision for stink-free farming, although I know he'll come around eventually." Maria rubbed her hands again. "Ugh. I think I'm contaminated. Everything smells like poo. I need to go to the house and disinfect myself. Do you have any rubbing alcohol? Or maybe peroxide. Maybe bleach would work. I could mix it with a couple gallons of perfume."

Kat's eyes widened, and she handed Ginny's leash to Joel. "I'll help you find something."

Tori and Dale said their goodbyes, got back into the SUV, and slowly wound down the driveway.

Tori reached over and put her hands on his thigh. "I still can't quite believe you're moving here and I'm starting a new business. Massive changes usually feel out of control to me. But for once, I'm okay with it. Like you say, it feels right."

"Quite so, m'lady. Quite so."

Thanks for Reading

Thank you for dedicating some of your reading time to *Who's Afraid of Virginia's Woof?*. I hope you enjoyed the adventures with Tori and Dale. I'll be writing more books that will feature Kat, Joel and various other residents of Alpine Grove who bring dogs to the boarding kennel, so keep your eye out for the next book in the series.

If you would like to be notified by e-mail when I release a new book, you can sign up for my New Releases e-mail list at SusanDaffron.com.

I know that not everyone likes to write book reviews, but if you are willing to write a sentence or two about what you thought of *Who's Afraid of Virginia's Woof?*, I encourage you to post a review at your favorite book vendor site or share a message with your social networking friends.

If you would like to share your thoughts about the book with me privately, you can reach me through the contact page on the SusanDaffron.com web site.

I look forward to hearing from you!

~ Susan C. Daffron

Acknowledgements

Writing a novel is never easy and I'd like to thank my husband James Byrd for his support and encouragement throughout the publishing process.

I'd also like to thank my alpha and beta readers for their eagle-eyed reading and great feedback.

About the Author

Susan Daffron is the author of the Jennings & O'Shea mystery series and the Alpine Grove romantic comedies, a series of novels that feature residents of the small town of Alpine Grove and their various quirky dogs and cats. She is also an award-winning author of many nonfiction books, including several about pets and animal rescue. She lives in a small town in northern Idaho and shares her life with her husband and three really cute dogs.